FAKING FOREVER

VM RHEAULT

To my cousin Velma.
Your support and belief in my talent is very much appreciated.
Thank you.

ABOUT THE BOOK

"Kiss me like one day you'll be my wife."

Fox

Posey is my best friend, and when my sister tries to make good on a bet, I ask her to pretend to be my fiancée to win. All we have to do is spend the weekend together at my uncle's ski chalet. I already give her all my free time and sharing a room—with that king-sized bed—will be easy.

I didn't think our fake kisses would get under my skin, but they do, and I fall hard. I want our engagement to be real, but when I propose, she says no. I'm not still in love with my ex like she thinks I am, but I can't tell her the real reason I'm stuck in the past. She'll hate me forever, and I'll lose more than our engagement.

I'll lose my best friend.

Posey

Fox isn't one of those arrogant, playboy billionaires. He's happy spending quiet evenings at my apartment, and we listen to jazz and drink wine while I cook. We've been friends for years, and there's no one I'd rather be with.

When he asks me to pretend to be his fiancée for the weekend to win a bet, I agree. What's a little kissing between best friends? Sharing a bed won't matter . . . we've fallen asleep on my couch more times than I can count.

I'll just have to be careful I don't let my heart get too carried away. Our engagement can never be real for reasons I can't let him know, and I'd rather keep his friendship than end up with nothing at all.

CHAPTER ONE

Fox

"Plans tonight?"

My business partner and second-place best friend leans against the doorjamb of my office, his hands shoved into his pockets.

He's asked me the same question every Friday afternoon for the past year, and every time my answer is the same. "Nope."

I don't go out, and I don't date. I might be Fox Caldwell, half of WellStone Interactive, one of the biggest gaming companies in the world, but I do not live up to the public's perception of how I should be living my life. Playboy. Partier. Fucking anything that moves. I'm too old for that shit, and I lost my taste for it a long time ago.

"Come on, Fox. It's been a year. She wasn't the one for you, and you know it."

"I need more time, and there's no reason to rush. I'm happy—"

Paul raises his eyebrows.

"—as happy as I'm going to be for the foreseeable future. I don't need to party it up. I'm fine."

"Just worried about you, that's all."

"Don't be."

"All right, all right." He holds his hands up, palms facing me. "Seeing Posey later?"

"Not sure. She wasn't at her desk the last time I walked by."

"Okay, well, I'm out of here. Remember that thing tomorrow night."

I scowl and lean back in my chair, my foot tapping under my desk in sudden agitation. "I thought you were going to handle that."

"We both own this company, and you have to keep up your side of it, you know. It's not the end of the world. We go, accept the award, say a few words, and then I'll let you leave." For the first time since my breakup, Paul's angry. "I'm tired of doing this shit alone."

"Fine, I'll be there." Chagrined, I study his weary face. I didn't think I've been skating that much, but maybe I have.

"Ask Posey to go with you if it will buff your edges, but I need you to start stepping up. I hate to force you, but it's time."

"Yeah, I get it. I appreciate you understanding."

"Good boy. I'll see you tomorrow night at eight. Don't be late."

He slaps the doorjamb and ambles away before I can change my mind. I owe him for the leeway he's given me the past few months while I've mourned, and he's right. I need to get my life back on track.

I'm about to call it a day and head out to Posey's desk when my cell rings and my sister's name glows on the screen. She's calling to bitch at me about something and I want to ignore her call, but that has never led to anything I haven't regretted.

"Hey, Darcy, what's up?" I answer, ramming so much cheer into my tone that my voice almost cracks. Like Paul, her annoyance is only meant to express concern and worry, but all it does is put me on the defensive.

"Do you remember what next weekend is?" she asks, forgoing a polite greeting as usual. All business with my sister.

I purse my lips and glance at my blotter's calendar. February in Minnesota can't get any bleaker, besides the dreaded Valentine's Day. Last year I hid in my penthouse and drank alone. Posey had been invited to a "Galantine's Day" party and I'd shooed her off. Later that evening she stopped by and we drank champagne and swore off love and marriage. I didn't know her reasons for it—and still don't—and I've managed to keep the most devastating thing that has ever happened to me to myself.

"Should I?"

"It's Uncle Rodney's sixty-fifth birthday. You're coming to Chaska to celebrate, remember?"

"Darcy . . ." A birthday party is the last thing I'm in the mood for, even if it is for Uncle Rodney.

"Nope. Apparently you forgot, and I need you to write me out my check."

Fuck.

I did, indeed, forget all about it, but like hell I'll let my sister win. "Whoa, now who said I'd be writing any checks?"

She snorts, very unlady-like, into the phone. "You remember what that bet was for, right? I don't see you've made any progress in that area, quite the opposite, in fact, from what little you've told me about your love life. Though, you know I'd be thrilled if you met someone and at least started dating for fuck's sake."

"I'll have you know I have some very important news, and

I'm announcing it tomorrow night at the Starlight Awards. It's live streaming if you want to watch."

"The Starlight Awards? What's that?"

"I guess our development department did something," I say nonchalantly. "I need to ask Paul."

"God, Fox, you're accepting an award and you don't even know what it's for? No wonder he's pissed at you."

Straightening, I ask, "Did he call you and say something?"

"No, but it's not a secret you've been phoning it in. So, are you flying out or am I going to be looking for some stocks to invest in?"

"I don't know why this has to be about money. You have plenty and you know I wouldn't miss ten mil."

"Yeah, but it's the principle of the thing. I rarely win against you, big brother, and I'll enjoy cashing that check."

"We'll see about that."

She laughs. "You know I'm going to need more proof than a bogus announcement online. I want to meet her. Invite her to the party."

"What? No."

"Yeah, it's hard to bring a woman who doesn't exist to a party. Pay up."

The line beeps and I toss my phone onto my desk. Shit.

Because of what happened, I forgot all about the bet I made with Darcy two years ago. I should just pay her and accept defeat. I'm not in the mood to play, even if it will save me ten million dollars and my beach house on one of the Florida Keys.

Next weekend. That buys me some time, but there's no one I can drag into this charade, no matter how much I want to win. I should call her back right now and admit I haven't met anyone, let alone proposed to the woman of my dreams.

I have a few days before I'll need to come clean, and instead of calling and listening to her gloat, I push away from my desk. The floor's quiet. Not many people work past five on a Friday. It's not unheard of for the geeks in research and development to order pizza and beer and test out our products, noting and fixing glitches before we announce that the hottest game of the year is coming soon, but things are calm right now, our newest limited-edition console and exclusive game, *Fool's Gold*, winning the Starlight Award for best plot and graphics. Last year the game brought in millions in pre-order sales alone, and Hollywood's already producing a movie tie-in.

We're sitting pretty, and I shouldn't dread celebrating it. We put a lot of blood, sweat, and tears into that console and game, and the research and development team deserves that award.

My own assistant is already gone for the day, escaping while Paul raked me over the coals. It's what it felt like he did, even if the coals are cooling. If you've never experienced what I have, it's difficult to find empathy and I've used up all his sympathy.

Talking about sitting pretty, Posey's at her desk that's in front of Paul's office speaking into her headset, letting someone know he isn't still here. "I can take a message or you can call him back on Monday. You can also email him. He does check it over the weekend," she says, her fingers clicking at her keyboard.

She's been Paul's assistant for several years now, and I love watching her work. There's a quiet efficiency to her movements, a sophisticated air to the way she handles herself. It isn't her ash blonde hair or her aquamarine blue eyes, or even her high and sculpted cheekbones. There's something almost, I want to say melancholy, about her, though I've never seen her cry and she's never been anything but cheerful whenever we've hung out.

It was the happiest day of my life when I discovered we lived in the same building.

I said Paul is my second-place best friend. Posey's my first.

"Hey, are you ready to go?"

She points to the headset and does the "blah-blah-blah" motion with her hand. "No, Mr. Tisdale. You can call him on his cell." Pause. "No, I'm not at liberty to give out his cell phone number."

I reach over and pick up the handset. "Bob, is there a reason why you're giving Paul's assistant a hard time on a Friday afternoon? Late, at that, and Posey doesn't keep booze in her desk to deal with this kind of shit."

Posey quirks her mouth in amused disbelief that I would talk to a client that way, takes her headset off, and while I listen to Bob do more blah-blah-blahing, she shuts her computer down and takes her purse out of the bottom drawer of her desk.

"Yes, he's aware, and if you'll be at the Starlight Awards tomorrow night, you can talk to him, us, about it then."

Posey looks at me and widens her eyes. I'm known in social circles to be somewhat of a recluse, and news I'm at the awards dinner tomorrow night will have traveled all over the city by the time the appetizers are served.

"Yes, I'll be there. Goodnight to you too."

I hang up.

"You're really going?" Posey asks, lifting her wool jacket off a hook on the coat tree behind her desk.

I tug it out of her grasp and help her slip into the thick, knee-length coat. The color is a brilliant blue that highlights her eyes, and on dreary winter days, it's always a welcome bright spot.

"Yes. Paul guilt-tripped me into it, but I was hoping to talk to you about it later tonight. Are you coming up, or am I going down?"

I don't mean it in a crude way, and Posey doesn't interpret it that way, not even playfully hitting me on the arm. We spend almost every evening together. Sometimes she comes up to my penthouse, but usually I change out of my suit, grab wine, and it's not ten minutes later I'm at her door. I like spending time in her little place. Her apartment feels like home.

Mine . . . does not.

Tying a scarf around her neck, she says, "I have ingredients for beef stroganoff. It's up to you if I carry it up or you come down."

That's another reason why I like spending time with Posey. She's a fabulous cook. If she didn't invite me for dinner, I'd never have a home-cooked meal.

"I'll change and come down."

The elevator carries us to the lobby and my car's waiting when we reach the curb. My driver, Rusty, loves Posey just as much as I do—not love in a romantic way, just so you know—and she leans over, rests her arms on the back of the seat, and chats with him about weekend plans. Rusty's wife just had a baby, and I try to block out their conversation by looking through my emails while he navigates the Friday evening traffic to my building.

She smacks a kiss to his cheek and tells him to have a good weekend. He laughs as he turns to climb out of the car, but I wave him back and help Posey onto the sidewalk myself with a strong grip to her arm.

The February wind whips at us, and I try to shield her from it as much as I can until we reach the door. She smiles gratefully at the doorman, and despite the chill, asks him how his family's doing. They only talk for a second before the cold hustles us all inside.

I look around the lobby noting the old paintings and the marble floor. The furnishings should be updated, and I write a mental reminder to approve the renovation. I bought this building not long after I moved into the penthouse, one of several I've picked up in Avondale over the years.

Posey leans into me in the elevator, her cheek pressed against my coat as the frantic week seeps out of her and we drift into the weekend. I wrap my arm around her and rest my chin on the top of her head.

"I need wine," she says, her purse dangling from one hand, the other grazing my thigh.

"If you can wait, I have a red that will go well with the Stroganoff. Deep, a raspberry, I think, with earthy notes."

"Hmmm. Sounds lovely. Don't be too long."

"I won't."

On high heels that accentuate the graceful line of her calves, she shuffles out of the elevator. The doors close before I can watch her walk down the carpeted corridor to her apartment.

People who know us are waiting for one of us to fall in love with the other and ruin our friendship. Even though Paul encourages me to spend time with her because she loosens me up, he's told me in no uncertain terms that if our relationship ever goes sideways, she will remain his PA for as long as she wants to be. I know she's a good worker and I've been tempted a time or two to lure her away from him, but in the end, I never do. I don't want our friendship to change with a new dynamic and I think her working for me would negatively affect what we have.

I shower to wash the week off me and change into jeans and a t-shirt. With my hair still wet, I snag the bottle of wine out of my cooling cabinet and barefoot, head downstairs. If I know Posey, and I think I do by now, she'll have changed into yoga pants and a tank top, leaving her socks off, like me. Last year we dropped any formalities we had left when I fell asleep on her couch and drooled all over a throw pillow. I woke up with a paper towel tucked under my cheek. It was the first night after Michelle said she couldn't see me anymore and I hadn't wanted to be alone. I'd slept hard, her cat snuggled into the curve of my belly.

If anything has kept me going this past year, it's Posey. Even if she doesn't know it.

I can hear Adele singing hello before I reach her door, and without knocking, I let myself in. The apartment isn't large by any means, but the foyer's spacious, containing a wide coat closet that serves as additional storage. The walls are painted a greyish blue and cream and her furniture matches, creating an elegant aesthetic. Most units have an electric fireplace, and hers is no exception. The flames flicker, the orange glow fighting off the winter dark. A breakfast bar separates the living room from the kitchen, and a corkscrew and two wine glasses are already sitting there waiting for me to fill them up.

Posey's standing in front of the stove browning beef for the stroganoff dressed how I knew she would be. Her hair's pulled away from her face in a long ponytail that sways between her shoulder blades as she sings along to the music.

She looks over her shoulder at me. "Do you need something?"

Caught staring, I mutter, "No," and look away.

It hit me that one day she's going to meet someone and I won't get to do this anymore. We'll still be best friends, but friends have boundaries. Boundaries that don't include eating dinner and watching a movie on a Friday night when those activities belong to another person.

While I was dating Michelle, my evenings with Posey stopped. I didn't hide Michelle from her, only the reason she left me, and very few people, even a year later, know the truth. Posey understood that as my girlfriend Michelle was entitled to more of my time, and she would expect the same courtesy if she ever met someone. I can say I didn't miss Posey, but it wouldn't be true. She was the one I ran to after Michelle and I broke up. She didn't ask for any explanations, only opened her door and her arms and let me heal on my own terms.

She still is, letting me heal, I mean, without asking why I'm so raw, and I'm beyond grateful she's in my life.

I pour a glass of wine and pass it to her while she stirs the beef, onion, and mushrooms. She sips and closes her eyes. The steam turns her cheeks a delicate shade of pink and little tendrils of her hair curl around her face. I brush a piece away from her eyes.

"So, Starlight?" she asks, holding the wineglass in one hand and a wooden spoon in the other while her hips sway.

I lean against the counter with my wine and lift a shoulder. "Paul's been pretty understanding, but that's about to run out. If I don't get my shit together, he's going to be seriously pissed, and with good reason. I've been doing my share of the work, but barely. I think if I wouldn't have agreed to go tomorrow night he would have snuck into my penthouse and slit my throat."

"Oh, I don't know. He has more patience than that. He's excited you guys won and wants to share it with you, that's all." She sets her wineglass near the stove and rests her hand on my forearm. Her touch is warm, strong, and steady, exactly like the friendship I've come to depend on. "I'm sorry you're still dealing with your breakup. You must have loved her a lot. Do you ever think of calling her, maybe trying to work things out?"

I haven't spoken to Michelle since the day she told me she couldn't look at my face ever again. "No. She had her reasons, very good reasons, for leaving me. We don't have it in us to try a second time."

She tries to smile. "I'm sorry."

"That's life. You better stir that."

"Crap. I'm burning our dinner and it's your fault."

I help her throw the meal together, putting water on to boil and slicing dinner rolls in half. It's nice to dance around her in the small kitchen, our bodies brushing as she finds broth in her cabinet and I look for egg noodles.

As I'm setting her table, I ask, "You'll come with me, won't you?"

"To where?" She dumps the steaming noodles into a colander sitting in the sink.

"The awards dinner tomorrow night."

"Really? Don't you want to bring someone—"

Better, she's going to say better, and I stop her.

"No. The only person I want to go with is you, and if you can't be my plus one, I'll go alone. Unless, do you have a date?" My tongue has a difficult time spitting the word out of my mouth.

She wrinkles her nose. "No, I don't have a date. Why would you think that?"

I block her against the sink, the bowl of noodles between us. "I don't want our friendship to be in the way of you meeting someone someday." I cup her face between my hands and ask her to meet my eyes. I could drown a million times, die a million times, and I would still never tire of looking into the blue.

Searching my face, she lets out a sigh, and after a moment, it turns into a shaky laugh. "I don't think that's anything you need to worry about, but thanks for letting me know. Let's eat, and I need more wine."

I frown but do as I'm told and pour her another glass. I want to ask why she thinks she'll never meet someone, never fall in love, but I don't dare. I don't want to push, especially since I'm not in a place emotionally to follow my own advice.

The meal passes pleasantly, talking about the awards dinner and her musing she might go shopping for a new gown.

"Send me the bill if you do," I say, clearing my plate from the table.

"I can afford a dress."

"Yes, but you wouldn't need it if I hadn't asked you to go, so send me the bill."

"Okay, whatever you say. Ice cream and a movie?"

I should go up to the penthouse and go to bed. I don't sleep well, and if I turn in at a decent hour, sometimes I can get five or six hours. On bad nights I get less, regardless of when I go to bed. In the past year, the only time I can get any real rest is when fall asleep on Posey's couch, waking to the scent of coffee when she starts her day. After a year of doing it, it's a dangerous habit, and knowing I'm dealing with a dependency I should break myself of, I still say, "Sure, but only if it's chocolate."

It's a silly request. She always keeps chocolate in her freezer for me.

On her TV, I bring up the home screen for the WellStone streaming service. Posey's part of our beta team and she tests our products with a handful of others before anyone else.

She steps into the living room with two bowls of ice cream and coffee dripping for an after-dessert drink. "What are we watching?"

"You choose. I don't care."

"*Hope Floats.* I'm in the mood for a little Harry Connick, Jr."

If I was worried I was going to have trouble falling asleep, I'm not now, but I find the movie without arguing and we settle on the couch as the opening credits roll.

About halfway through we lie on our sides and spoon, her cat, Peaches, loafing on the armrest by our feet. I wrap my arm around her stomach and bury my nose in her hair, not even pretending I'm watching the movie. I'm too content, too . . . I don't know how to describe it. Michelle and that loss will always be in the back of my mind, but when I'm with Posey, the pain fades. Not completely, but at this point, I'll gladly accept any relief I can find.

I'm dozing, Sandra Bullock's—and Posey's—warm laughter heating my skin when I remember Darcy's request. I need a fake fiancée to win that bet, and I need her before next weekend. Teasing my sister with a big announcement tomorrow night wasn't a good idea, but the solution lies in my arms, her fingers linked with mine.

"Posey?" I mumble, and the delicious pressure of her ass against my cock, the way her body fits mine so perfectly, I don't know if it's my brain or my heart that's asking.

"Yeah?" she whispers, her lips brushing my arm.

"Will you marry me?"

CHAPTER TWO

Posey

I freeze, and when I finally find the nerve to roll over and ask what he means, he's sleeping. I push on his shoulder, and his eyes flutter open. "Hmmm?"

"What do you mean, will I marry you? Are you joking?"

His eyes are a dark green in the fire's light, shooting sparks.

Fox and I have been friends for a long time, have seen each other through a lot of life's ups and downs. It hurt, more than I'd like to admit, when he dated Michelle. I thought they were going to get married, and then one night he stumbles to my door, drunker than I have ever seen him before, and just like that we were back to how our friendship used to be.

He'd changed, though. More quiet, more reflective. Hurt and hollowed out. He never told me what went wrong. I met her a few times, and to me, she seemed too hard for him, but that could have been my personal bias.

"No, I'm not joking. Well, kind of. A couple years ago Darcy bet me I wouldn't be engaged or married by Uncle

Rodney's sixty-fifth birthday party. That's next weekend. She knows what happened between me and Michelle, but she's not giving in. A bet's a bet. I need you to pretend you're in love with me for the weekend. I figure that should be easy enough. Then I can tell her we didn't work out and that will be the end of it."

"How much did she bet you?"

"Ten million plus my beach house."

Ten million dollars.

Carefully, so I don't fall on the floor, I turn onto my back, and Fox's eyes drift shut again in exhaustion. He thinks I don't know he has trouble sleeping, borderline insomniac after Michelle broke up with him, and I always feel better when he falls asleep on my couch. I like watching over him.

Staring at the ceiling, I think of what that kind of money could do.

Fox's hand is splayed on my belly, gently rising and falling with my breathing. If he knew what I wanted, he'd probably give me the money—that's the kind of guy he is—but I would never ask and take advantage of our friendship that way. If I can help him and feel like I've earned it, that's something different.

He can afford to pay me, but how much can I afford to give him in return? I skim my fingers over his stubbly jaw. Fox Caldwell is sexy, kind, and rich, and we've been platonic friends for years. I've never let myself become too attached, and I was thankful for that when he started dating Michelle.

Fox's uncle lives in Colorado. If Darcy's throwing him a party at the ski chalet he owns, we'd be spending the weekend there. Engaged couples share a bed, and they kiss a lot. I'd have to keep my eye on the prize and remind myself almost to the minute that I'm damaged goods and he would never want me for a real lifetime commitment.

Of course, I'm getting ahead of myself. He doesn't feel that way about me. He's never once made a move, drunk or sober. This is the closest we've been, his arm wrapped around me while he snores, fatigue dragging him under as it always seems to on my couch. Or maybe that's my choice in movies.

If this worked, I could stop scrimping and saving every penny. People won't be surprised, and we'll be Avondale's hottest gossip topic. Fox landed the city's most eligible bachelor tag last year after word got out he and Michelle were no longer seeing each other, and every tabloid site had their own bets going on whether Fox and I would finally tie the knot.

It seems men and women can't be friends, and friends without benefits, no less.

The publicity won't help me, but after we break our engagement and things die down, all I can hope is that my stability won't be called into question. I'd get further if I was married, but I've given up thinking a man would want me and what little I have to offer. Anything I want in life I'm going to have to reach out and grab, and grab by myself.

I don't wake Fox to answer him. He needs sleep. Instead, I focus on his breathing, his chest rubbing against my shoulder with every inhale and exhale. Our bodies align almost perfectly —I'm just short enough I can tuck my head under his chin. His arm is strong across my stomach, and I trail my fingers over the corded muscle.

The movie ends and the credits fade. The homepage for the streaming app flickers and then dies when the TV's energy saver kicks in and the screen goes black. Set on a timer, the fire cools, and yet I still lie here not wanting to move. There isn't room on the couch for both of us to sleep comfortably, and usually, I get up and sleep in my own bed, but tonight I don't want to leave Fox alone.

I wish it had been someone other than Fox who needed this

favor. Paul, maybe, or one of the guys in research and development. I'm going to tell Fox yes, if he agrees to my terms, and I don't know why he wouldn't. This isn't about saving money, it's about getting the best over his sister, but out of anyone who could have asked me, Fox has the potential to hurt me the most because pretending to have what will never be mine will only break my heart in the long run.

He nuzzles his lips against my cheek, his whiskers scraping my skin, a lonely soul searching for solace. Reluctantly, I roll off the couch and cover him with a blanket. I'm not strong enough to say no if he wants more, even in his sleep. He sighs, and with the extra room he has without me, he wiggles flat onto his back.

Kissing his forehead, I whisper sweet dreams.

After a restless night's sleep, I walk groggily into the kitchen. Peaches is chowing down on breakfast and Fox is sitting at the table sipping a cup of coffee. He regards me cautiously, like a drunk who can't remember what he said the night before but knows it's bad.

"Did I ask you what I think I did?" He gets up and pours me a cup of coffee, adding the exact amount of milk I like.

"Yes, you did, and I'm going to say yes, too, but I have some conditions."

He blinks. "Really? You're going to go along with it?"

"Yes, but like I said, I'm not going to do it for free."

His gaze sharpens. "I'm willing to negotiate."

"I thought you would."

He picks up his phone and opens the Notes app. "Hit me."

Last night while I was tossing and turning, I gave this a lot of thought. I need the money or I wouldn't risk doing this at all. I don't want to be greedy, but if I'm going to ask, then I should go big, and with any luck, he'll agree because he can afford it.

"First, I want to keep the engagement ring you'll buy me."

That had been a maybe, but I decided to go along with it. He'll need to buy me one, and I can keep it as a pleasant memento to think back on or I can sell it and invest the cash.

"I never thought otherwise," he says, his thumbs flying across the screen.

"Second, if I'm going to save you ten million dollars, I think I should be entitled to some of that. I want twenty-five percent."

He looks up, his eyebrows raised. "You think a weekend getaway in a Colorado ski town is worth two and a half million dollars?"

"I think you'll pay whatever you need to if it will put Darcy in her place." I don't know a lot about Fox's family, but I do know that he would never let his sister win anything if he had the power to come out ahead.

He nods. "Touché. What else?"

"We should sign a contract and NDAs. I don't know how long we'll have to keep up the lie for Darcy to believe it, but eventually we'll 'break up.'" I do the finger quotes in the air. "I don't want it to get messy and I want to try to keep our friend-ship intact after this is over."

"Try?" Fox smooths his fingers over my cheek. "Posey, you're my best friend. Nothing will ever change that."

It would be petty to point out that his relationship with Michelle almost *did* change that, but we're only friends and we both have the freedom to fall in love with whoever we want. I never said one bad thing about Michelle or about the time he suddenly didn't have for me. Had he and Michelle stayed together, I doubt we'd even be talking anymore. She hated and resented me and she would have succeeded in completely cutting me off.

Appealing to the business side of him, I say, "Then there's no harm in us signing one, is there?"

"No, I guess not, but I don't see how pretending to be engaged will hurt our friendship. We've been friends for a long time and we'll be able to pull this off without a problem. We already enjoy being together. Darcy will see that and leave us alone."

My jaw drops open. "Are you crazy? You have no idea how an engaged couple is supposed to act."

Fox frowns. "I've never been engaged, so I guess, no, I don't. I didn't realize you were an expert on the subject." He narrows his eyes. "Have you been engaged before? Is there something you're not telling me?"

I shake my head. "If you don't know, I'm not telling you."

He huffs. "That's mature. Is there anything else you want? The ring, twenty-five percent, a contract and an NDA? That's it?"

Biting my lip, I pause. I want to add that we're not going to have sex, but he doesn't think we'll be acting any differently than we are now, so mentioning it might be more trouble than it's worth. "No, I think that covers it."

"Okay. I have one condition of my own, and I apologize in advance."

"What?"

"I told Darcy that I'd announce our engagement tonight at the awards dinner."

I groan.

"I know, and I'm sorry. I was trying to poke at her, not turn the whole thing into a fiasco. I didn't realize I was shooting myself, and you, in the foot, but think of what the announcement will do for you. All the attention you'll get. I'll give you access to all my credit cards. You can have Rusty at your disposal—that will be easy with us living in the same building—and we'll spend our evenings together until we leave for Colorado."

Crossing my arms over my chest, I say, "Besides the money, how is that any different from what we have now?" Fox is more than generous with Rusty and his car, especially in the winter, and we already spend most of our free time together. I might need the money he'll pay me for doing this, but even if he did put my name on his credit cards, the last thing I would do is use them.

Fox rubs the back of his neck, and he looks like an adorable little kid caught with his hand in a cookie jar. I'm not mad. Annoyed that his announcement tonight will turn something that could have been private into a public display, creating a situation we'll have to deal with longer than necessary, but what he's paying me will more than make up for it. I'm more concerned with how we're going to have to behave in front of Uncle Rodney, Darcy, and whoever else is at the party. If Fox wants to win the bet, we need to be believable, and that's doing things in front of people we don't do in private. Because we're only friends.

"Well, it's not, but you've always been a good sport."

Yeah, because I don't have the right to complain about anything. Again, because we're only friends. It would be interesting to see how he'd act if I was the one to have a steady boyfriend and didn't have time for him. If he'd be hurt. Maybe after this bet, I should date. Not to make Fox jealous, but even if I don't think I'm marriage material, I could find a man who didn't want that.

Fox wants that, and occupying myself elsewhere will give him space to find someone. Someone who can heal his broken heart and make him forget about the pain Michelle caused.

"It's fine. You better text Paul. He's not going to like this, and you should warn him. I need to shower and go shopping."

"I'll go with you. I don't happen to have any engagement rings laying around the penthouse."

"You're going to let me pick out my own ring?"

He lifts a shoulder. "Why not? You said you wanted to keep it. After we break up, you can have the setting redone and wear it on your right hand if you want."

His answer lets me down, but I don't know why. There's no reason for him to properly propose if we're not going to have a real engagement, a real wedding, or a real marriage. It's not his fault this will be as close to marriage as I'll ever get, and it's not his responsibility to feed my fairytale.

I force a smile. "Yeah, sure. Sounds great."

Fox sets his phone on the counter and cuddles me in his arms. His t-shirt is soft against my cheek, his heartbeat steady under my ear. I've never wanted more with Fox, but this fake engagement is going to shove all kinds of inappropriate thoughts into my head and visions of a life that aren't meant for us.

"We'll always be friends, Posey. I promise."

His words don't comfort me.

I know how easily promises are broken.

CHAPTER THREE

Fox

I meet Paul at a wine bar not far from the office after shopping with Posey and dropping her off at our building. Before I started going to her place in the evenings, Paul and I would unwind over a drink or two. He never said anything when I stopped, and I realize as we sit at a high-top near the window and watch people hurry by in the cold, I've missed it. Working in the same office isn't the same as bitching about employees and clients in a bar full of yuppies still thinking they can change the world.

We've been friends for a long time. Not, we-built-gaming-consoles-in-his-mom's-basement long time, but we've known each other since university and stayed in touch after we graduated. It was a couple of years later we found ourselves at the same sports bar complaining about our respective company's lack of vision and courage in the industry. We decided to say "Fuck it," go all in, and create our own.

After fifteen years, we're listed in the top half of the Forbes

Fortune 500 list. All the risks we took paid off, and we struck it rich doing what we love.

Paul's radiating excitement and success. Winning the Starlight is a big deal, and he vibrates with victory. "Getting the party started early?" he asks, knocking back a lowball of whiskey. I'm treading lighter, sipping a glass of the red Posey and I drank last night. Not because it reminds me of snuggling with her on the couch while we watched *Hope Floats*. I like the notes and the flavors that burst on my tongue with every sip. I don't think of Posey's beautiful blue eyes or her smile, or the way I held her in my arms this morning trying to assure her things would be okay.

I wasn't prepared for her apprehension or the wormy feeling it caused in my stomach.

"Actually, I wanted to talk to you about something. She said I should let you know, and I suppose she's right, so it doesn't come as a shock tonight."

Paul leans forward and lowers his voice. "Is this about Michelle? Are you bringing her to dinner?"

I swallow around a lump in my throat that always seems to form there whenever someone mentions her name. "No. A couple of years ago, before Michelle, Darcy bet me I wouldn't be engaged or married by the time our uncle Rodney's sixty-fifth birthday rolled around. She called me yesterday and reminded me that his birthday's next weekend and she's throwing him a huge bash. I don't want to lose the bet, so I asked Posey to pretend to be my fiancée. We hammered out the details this morning."

Silently, he traces his finger around the rim of his empty glass. "Don't hurt her, Fox. I know you and Posey have been friends for a long time, and to tell you the truth, I don't know how you've been able to do that, but playing at being engaged is something different."

"Don't worry about it. We're on the same page. She's treating it like a business deal and I'm compensating her."

"If you're sure."

"I am. I don't want her hurt any more than you do. Next to you, she's my best friend, and I don't want to ruin that. I told you because I mentioned to Darcy I'd announce it tonight at the awards dinner and she's going to watch it online. Posey and I went shopping earlier and I bought her a ring—a ring she negotiated into keeping, by the way. It'll be fine."

I finish my wine and raise my hand to order another glass, Posey's liquid blue eyes as I slipped the ring on her finger haunting me with the sadness of it all. It wasn't romantic, it wasn't real, and I'd turned her first proposal into nothing more than a heartless transaction.

"This is going to turn into a shitshow, and you're going to deserve everything you get," Paul whispers furiously, his eyes hard with anger. "I know Michelle messed you up and what happened was a horrible thing. I've never been one for being trite, but sometimes things happen for the best. Michelle wasn't the one for you, and instead of wallowing in the unfairness of it all, maybe you should be thanking your lucky stars things turned out the way they did. Posey shouldn't have to pay for that. She's a good girl and she's always been there for you. What have you given her, huh? Friendship goes both ways and all I've seen you do since Michelle dumped you is use Posey for whatever the fuck you can get. I've kept my mouth shut because we're friends too, but this is going to go down in a bad way and if I have to choose between you and her, I'm going to choose her. Just so we're clear."

The truth is written all over his face, and I say, my voice rough, "You're in love with her."

His throat works as he jams his arms into his jacket. "Me and half of Avondale. Get your head out of your ass, you selfish prick." He jerks his briefcase off the floor and pushes violently out of the bar as the waitress sets my second glass of wine in front of me.

I lift it to my lips, my hand trembling.

Jesus Christ.

I didn't know. He never threw me envious glances whenever I'd help Posey put her jacket on. He never looked as I'd help her step into the elevator. He never came down to the lobby with us and never saw the way I'd escort her to the curb so we could get into my car. He never saw me do any those things because he always left the office first.

So he wouldn't have to watch.

I'm so stupid.

He suggested I invite Posey out tonight. He knew going would be difficult for me and her presence would help . . . or he suggested I bring her because he didn't have the balls to ask her himself and he wanted to see her outside of work.

Fuck.

Darcy's bet has screwed up the two most important relationships I have. I can't do anything about Paul, not right now. He'll have to see that Posey and I will be okay after the fact, and what he does with her romantically won't be any of my business.

Posey and I *will* be okay. No matter what happens during Uncle Rodney's birthday party, when we come back from Chaska, we'll be exactly the same as we are now.

I finish my wine and sit and stew and picture Posey and Paul as a couple. Even their names sound good together. He's a good looking guy, single, not having found the woman he wants to spend the rest of his life with. I scowl and throw some cash on the table. Maybe he has and didn't know how to ask her out. It's always a gamble and playing right into the hands of the biggest cliché on earth: dating your PA and fucking her over your desk. Paul has too much class for that, and so does Posey. She deserves a bed and a fire, chocolate and champagne.

Rusty's waiting for me when I step out of the bar. The drive to my penthouse is short, despite the Saturday afternoon traffic and the snow falling in a thick sheet of white that lowers the visibility in the street. I don't want to go to this dinner, and after what I discovered about Paul, don't want to announce my engagement, either. I should call Darcy and tell her she won. I can afford to lose and I can buy another beach house. Then I can tell Paul Posey is all his and get of the way.

He lets me out in front of my building and I remind him I need the limo at 7 PM. He salutes me, but his antics don't lift my spirits. In the elevator, my finger hovers over the button for the fifteenth floor, but I skip stopping at Posey's apartment. She'll be napping or maybe soaking in the tub. I've already made enough of a mess and spending extra time with her won't smooth things over.

I try to nap, but sleep hasn't been my friend for a while now and I lie in the dark, memories of Michelle and what we could have had flickering behind my eyelids.

I must doze, and I rouse confused, surly, and needing a drink. I shower, and while I dress, sip on a scotch. This will be nothing. The announcement, a few days at the office with Paul glaring at me, and then the weekend in Chaska. A week from Monday everything will be back to normal. Casual dinners with Posey, falling asleep on her couch, and simply enjoying our friendship.

The dry cleaning chemicals embedded in my tux turn my stomach and I spray on too much cologne to cover the smell. I take my jacket off the hanger but I don't put it on yet. Posey may not be ready to go and I don't want to sweat while I wait. I pat my pants pockets but Posey's wearing her ring and besides my wallet, there isn't anything else I need. Maybe some sanity, but there's nothing I can do about that now. Darcy's going to go crazy when she finds out Posey's my fiancée. She's always liked Posey, and I expect she'll call me before dessert is served to congratulate me and ask why it took me this long to find some sense.

The fifteenth floor is quiet, and tonight there isn't any music drifting from Posey's apartment. I knock, and the door swings open a second later. I need a lot longer than that to find my tongue. "You look great." She looks more than great, but that's all my brain could puzzle out, my synapses frying as my gaze sweeps her figure.

Posey pinned her hair into a sophisticated updo, exposing her graceful neck. She isn't wearing any jewelry except for the ring I pushed on her finger earlier today. She lets the dress speak for itself, and holy shit does it. A column of silver, the bodice shows a hint of décolletage, and in the back, ropes of Swarovski crystals barely hold the material together, revealing sculpted shoulder blades and an elegant spine. A slit up her thigh exposes her long, lean leg, and silver sandals are strapped to her feet.

"Too much?" she asks, biting her bottom lip that shines with just a hint of gloss.

I clear my throat. "No, not at all."

"Okay, good. I was worried I'm overdressed."

"You look perfect. A lot of press will be there tonight. I couldn't have picked a better place to announce our engagement. Everyone is going to tell me I'm one lucky son of a bitch."

"I suppose you are—I'm saving you ten million dollars. Why did Darcy think she could bet you so much money? And why did you go along with it?" She takes her winter jacket out of her closet, and after I put mine on, help her with hers.

I shrug and hold her purse while she locks her apartment door. "That was a long time ago, and she thought she was going to lose when I was seeing Michelle. She knows I haven't been dating since we broke up, and she decided to call me on it, thinking I didn't stand a chance of winning. I would have lost too, if we weren't friends. Not just anybody can fake what we have. Darcy would've been able to see right through me if I would have tried this with anyone else."

Posey laughs, and with my hand to her lower back, we walk down the hallway to the elevator. "You mean my couch is the only one you fall asleep on and I'm the only one you barge in on when I'm in the bathroom and you need something?"

"It was once, and the shower was running. I thought you were already in there." I press the Down button and the doors slide open.

Shooting me a dirty look, she says, "You saw me sitting there, and *you didn't leave*. You asked me what kind of takeout I wanted while I was *peeing*."

I grin. "What are friends for?"

She scoffs, and amused, I nudge her into the lift.

It's true that I'm more comfortable with Posey than I am with any other woman in my life. Michelle's moods were volatile, and most days dating her was like walking on eggshells. When she was steady, everything was wonderful, but when she was low, everyone suffered, and I never knew when she would flip. Darcy has the patience of a hungry toddler at nap time, and your guess is as good as mine what will set her off. Posey's the only woman I can be completely myself around, without fear of repercussion. After a long day at work or a business deal that goes south, spending time with her is like playing slow jazz on a rainy afternoon while sipping cognac and puffing on one of my favorite cigars.

She relaxes me and sets my upside-down world right again.

I remember what Paul said this afternoon. "Posey, can I ask you a question?"

The elevator stops at the lobby and the doors glide open.

She steps out. "Yeah, sure."

"What do you get out of our friendship?"

"Why do you ask?"

"Just curious."

She squeezes my hand and brushes a kiss over my cheek. "A friend."

CHAPTER FOUR

Posey

Fox is oddly quiet in the limo, rubbing my ring between his finger and his thumb, as if dumbfounded he's the one who put it there.

I'm not worried about tonight. I don't have anyone who will be shocked or otherwise when he announces our engagement. It did feel strange getting so dressed up, though. I haven't been to something like this with him in a couple of years. While he was seeing Michelle, she was always his date, and after they broke up, he never attended social events and Paul had enough brains not to ask. Paul would have been furious, but Fox probably wouldn't have gone tonight, either, if he hadn't decided to use the dinner as a tool to help win the bet against Darcy.

I don't mind. If I wouldn't have agreed, I'd be sitting at home with Peaches, reading or watching TV. My life wouldn't be very exciting if Fox wasn't a part of it. In fact, I was pretty lonely the year he dated Michelle, and my therapist heard a lot about my fear of him getting married and what I'd do if I never saw him again.

Rusty stops in front of the Avondale Hotel, one of the first hotels built in the city. Sitting off the street, it gleams with old world sophistication, and I feel like a princess when Fox helps me out of the limo and shields me from the bitter wind. He cuddles me close to his side and we walk up the short set of wide, concrete steps. One of my heels slips on some ice and I lose my balance, my heart in my throat.

"Easy," he murmurs and tightens his hold. "I've got you."

"Thanks."

The paparazzi shouts at us, asking to take our picture, and Fox turns me toward the wall of cameras. We smile, letting the photographers grab a decent shot while they call out questions we're too cold to stand outside and answer.

I forget about my frozen toes as we walk into the grand lobby of the hotel. All cream and gold with a huge crystal chandelier hanging from the ceiling, I stare in awe at the opulence.

I'm not poor by any means, but I've never had a reason to visit the hotel. If I go out to lunch with a friend, we choose something a little more more down to earth, where a carafe of coffee isn't twenty dollars and a sliver of cheesecake double that. The ladies who lunch in the Avondale Hotel tearoom are married to men who make millions of dollars a year. If my engagement to Fox was real, I'd be invited into those social circles to drink mimosas at brunch while I pretended to diet and a nanny watched our children.

At least, that's the kind of life I imagine those women having.

I'll never know.

Fox walks confidently through the hotel, and I follow him and the light strains of an orchestra down a brightly lit corridor full of people dressed similarly to me—thank God—sipping champagne.

We get more than a few surprised looks. I hope because Fox is here and not because he's with me.

An attendant hangs our coats and Fox pockets the tickets she trades him in exchange.

"What do you think?" he asks.

"I see a lot of our clients." I'm surprised there are so many familiar faces in the crowd.

"Lots of competition, too. There was a runner up and an honorable mention." Fox snags two champagne glasses from a passing waiter. "It's a big deal. Thanks for coming with me. You know I hate this bullshit."

"Since Michelle," I say, knowing full well he'd go to these kinds of events with her without complaint.

"She enjoyed them." He tightens his jaw.

Someone pulls Fox into a conversation about updating game consoles and if the older models can handle the new 5G wireless connection, and I stand close to his side, watching people gawk at each other and gossip behind their hands.

The tables are stylishly set, and the guests' names are written in beautiful calligraphy. I squeeze Fox's hand before I step away, curious to find where we're sitting. I'm halfway across the ballroom when Paul strides to me, his eyes twinkling. "There you are. Fox said he was bringing you. Jesus Christ, Posey, you look fabulous."

"Thanks. We went shopping this afternoon." My left hand twitches, and I drop my arm to my side.

Paul notices. "He told me. Seems a bit extreme, don't you think?"

I blush. "What do you mean?"

"All this to win a bet? It's childish, really."

We walk the edge of the ballroom, skirting people

mingling and the large tables covered in pristine white table-cloths. A dais with a podium is set up at the front of the room waiting for the guest speakers and winners to claim their awards.

"I'm an only child, so I guess I wouldn't know," I murmur. "And it *is* a lot of money."

Paul scoffs. "Not to Fox. I have four brothers and we're the epitome of sibling rivalry, but something like this is completely ridiculous. What are you getting out of it, Posey?"

"Besides a trip to Chaska, Colorado?" I smile, trying to diffuse his temper.

Paul and Fox are good friends and I've never heard them have a disagreement about anything. They've always been on the same page regarding business decisions. It was only after Fox and Michelle broke up that things started to grow tense at the office. I was hoping Fox attending tonight's event would dispel some of that animosity.

"Yes, besides a trip you could go on alone."

"But that wouldn't be any fun." I'm not getting anywhere calming him down and his quiet fury is radiating around us.

He grabs my hand, and I try unsuccessfully to pull away. How is this going to look when Fox announces our engagement later?

"I can bring you anywhere you want to go, and there won't be any strings attached."

None too gently, I tug my hand out of his grasp. "My friendship with Fox isn't a string."

"Is that all you are?"

"You've worked with us for years. You know that's all we are."

Paul stares over the crowd, but I don't think I see what he sees when I do the same. The expensively dressed guests, the stoic waiters circulating the floor carrying trays of champagne, the candles flickering on the tables, the lush bouquets of flowers.

"You've *never* fucked him? Not once in all the months, maybe years, he's fallen asleep in your apartment? He's never held you in bed, or on your couch, spread your legs, and pushed his cock inside you? He's never touched that one delicate spot and made you come?"

My face heats and my nostrils flare. I step to the side putting much-needed distance between me and my boss. "Not that it's any of your business, but we've never been intimate."

"Then he's a goddamned fool. When you're back from Chaska, go out with me. We'll see a play, have a quiet dinner, and we'll talk, get to know each other. I won't waste your time like he does."

"We've never— He's never—" How do I explain we've never wanted more from each other because friendship has always been enough? "We're only friends."

"Good. Then it should be easy for you to say yes."

"After he publicly announces our breakup, then I will, but it might be a while."

"I'll wait."

"Paul, I'm not who you think I am. I can't give you what you want."

He turns to me, his expression grim. "Let me decide that for myself."

Slowly, I nod. "All right."

He leaves me standing here, holding my champagne glass too tightly, hoping we were far enough away no one heard what he said. I don't want Darcy to win before we even tried. The unexpected money Fox is going to pay me will speed up the things I want to do.

I've never thought of Fox as more than a friend. Even while he was dating Michelle, I wasn't envious of her, at least, not in a romantic way. The times he's spent the night, all the weekends we've spent together, they were for me just as much as they were for him. He took his breakup hard, and I stopped looking for a relationship that day in my doctor's office when my dreams turned to ash. Maybe we've been wasting each other's time, maybe we've been running from different things, I don't know. All I know is for me, I'm not emotionally available and I'll never fall in love. Paul will find that out the minute he tries to kiss me. It won't be the first time I've been called a cold fish.

"Hey, are you too warm? You don't look very good." Fox appears by my side and rubs his thumb over the curve of my cheek. I lean in, his touch anchoring me.

"Hungry," I lie. "I didn't eat today. I wanted to look good for tonight."

"You always look amazing. Dinner will be served soon. Let's find our seats."

He wraps his arm around me, and Paul glares at us, his eyes narrowed into angry slits. In the years I've been his PA, I never would have guessed he had feelings for me and I didn't have one thought about dating him.

I lift my chin. I won't let him turn my friendship with Fox, or our fake engagement, into something dirty. We're friends helping each other, that's all.

The guests hush as the waitresses and waiters begin to serve the salads. Fox holds my hand under the table forcing me to eat left-handed. I don't want him to let me go, and I awkwardly spear lettuce with my fork.

The main entrée looks delicious, and I do have to pull my hand away to cut my filet. He doesn't seem keen to eat and drapes his arm across the back of my chair instead, skimming his fingertips along the side of my neck while he talks to the gentleman sitting next to him. If he's intentionally acting this way to convince everyone we're a real couple, it's working. I don't think a man has touched me as often as Fox has tonight, and we're barely an hour into the evening.

Our table seats ten, and Paul's distracted by cheerful conversation. My nerves smooth out as the evening goes on and he doesn't look my way. Dessert is served, and the founder of the Starlight Awards, Greg Simpkins, approaches the podium and begins the program by thanking everyone for attending.

I lean back and Fox's hand drops to my shoulder.

"It wasn't difficult to choose this year's winner," Greg says. "The numbers don't lie, and *Fool's Gold*, an apocalyptic treasure hunt and WellStone Interactive's hottest new release, blew away the competition. This isn't the first time WellStone has earned top accolades, and it won't be the last. Fox, Paul, will you come up here and say a few words?" Greg holds up a trophy shaped like a star mounted on a pedestal.

Fox kisses my cheek before he stands up, and several pairs of curious eyes scrutinize us. Paul adjusts his tux's tie and winks at me. In the past, when they've won an award, he's thanked me for being a wonderful assistant, saying he couldn't do his job half as well without me, and when the game was in the marketing stages, I did put in long hours with him, eating takeout in one of the conference rooms with Fox and Lydia, his assistant.

Their camaraderie shines through as they shake Greg's hand and slap each other's backs. I don't want the bet to ruin their friendship. I want to go through with it for purely selfish reasons, but I would back out if it caused problems between them.

Paul speaks first. "When Fox and I started WellStone, we had visions, we had dreams. We said they didn't understand what we wanted to do, and we didn't have any regrets when we walked away. See? You should have listened." He points into the crowd where his and Fox's previous employers are sitting, their fingers still in the gaming pie.

Everyone laughs.

"We didn't play it safe," Paul continues, tilting the trophy toward Fox. "We wanted to push the envelope, then push it some more. *Fool's Gold* is doing exactly that. The graphics, the story, we go where no game has gone before. People warned us. They said, 'Don't do it. It will cost you money and you'll be a laughingstock in the gaming industry.' But where do you go if you're afraid? What kind of progress can you make? Fox understands that kind of risk. We hold each other up, and because of that, we've never fallen." He pauses. "The saying, behind every great man is a greater woman, has never been truer. While Fox's assistant couldn't be here tonight, Posey Palmer, my personal assistant, is here with us, and without her intelligence, skill, and work ethic, I wouldn't be standing here. Fox?"

He hands Fox the trophy to hold while he speaks, and his strong hands grip the award. He surveys the crowd for a moment and then says, "Playing it safe has never been my forte, and I'm fortunate I have a friend and business partner who plays by the same rules I do. Meaning, none."

The crowd murmurs appreciatively.

"We'll always push harder, always climb higher. If you want to keep up, you're going to have to give better than what you have. Throw caution to the wind, take a chance. Paul and I gamble in business and in pleasure." He sucks in a deep breath. "Not many people know I went through a rough patch last year, and like a lot of things that don't go as planned, it left a mark. It's time to put that behind me, and tonight, I'm celebrating more than WellStone Interactive winning the Starlight Award. Paul thanked Posey for all she's done for the company, but I'm thanking her for what she's done for my heart. Sweetheart, can you come up here for a moment?"

We didn't discuss what his announcement would entail, and I don't want to go up on the dais, not in front of all these people and certainly not in front of Paul who looks like he could commit murder at any second.

I shake my head, and the people sitting at our table smile indulgently.

"Go, dear. I want to hear what he has to say," says the wife of one of the businessmen. Her cheeks are rosy and her eyes sparkle with curiosity and champagne.

Great.

Fox gestures for me to join him, and I slide my chair away from the table and straighten, everyone's eyes on me. If this doesn't convince Darcy, nothing will. This would be terribly romantic if it was true, but it's almost humiliating, Fox declaring his love for me when it's a lie. I'm getting something out of it—I can't ever forget that—and doing my part, I smile so brightly I think my face is going to crack in half.

Greg helps me up the stairs and we meet Fox and Paul at the podium. I'm a couple of inches shorter than Fox, but I can easily see over the microphone and look at the dinner guests. When Fox begins to speak, I freeze, and he passes Paul the trophy to hold again.

"I've worked with Posey for years, and we've been friends for a long time. Maybe some of you have seen us, going to the opera or the symphony, or out to dinner and enjoying each other's company. Men in our position," he says, lifting a hand to include every male in the room, "need to be careful. It's rare to find a woman who wants us for who we are when we live how our resources allow us to live. Posey was never impressed, and if she was, it was because she knew how much work it took to get to where we are. She has a rare understanding, and as our friendship grew, that understanding turned into something I couldn't live without. One evening while we hiked through the state park not far from here, the moonlight glittering in her hair and stars literally shining in her eyes, I knew I couldn't let her get away."

Fox is looking at me like I'm the rarest treasure on earth, and I'm swept up in it, his words fizzing in my blood.

"I asked her to marry me, and I'm the luckiest son of a bitch on earth because she said yes."

Applause ring in my ears, and Fox lowers his head. He's kissed my cheek before, brushed kisses across my forehead, but he's never kissed my lips, in passion or in fun or anything else.

"Is this okay?" he murmurs. No one can hear him over the exclamations and bated breath as they wait for him to kiss me.

"Yeah." What am I going to say? No? My heart wouldn't let me even if my brain wanted him to keep his distance. I've resigned myself to living alone for the rest of my life. Sometimes Fate deals us cards and we have no choice but to finish the game. Fox's kiss will be the closest thing I have to love, and as he seals his lips over mine, I know I will cherish it. Always.

He cradles the side of my face in his hand, and I wrap my arms around his neck. He nudges the seam of my lips with his tongue and I open slightly, letting him lick at me, just a little bit. He needs the kiss to look genuine and I don't want to ruin it.

A light mist covers my skin, and it's not because the lights hanging over the dais are too hot.

Fox pulls away and I blink.

"Breathe," he whispers and presses a familiar kiss to my forehead. I've always taken them as friendship kisses, comfortable and casual. Now it feels protective, and for reasons I can't explain, I feel safe.

I turn to the crowd, a hand to my heart. "Whew. Ladies, I think he's a keeper," I say into the microphone.

People laugh, and one tipsy gentleman whistles.

"Thanks again for the honor," Paul says, holding up the

trophy, and Greg steps behind the podium to announce the first runner up and to acknowledge the honorable mention.

With an arm wrapped around my waist, Fox helps me off the dais. Too caught up with Fox's announcement, no one is paying any attention to Greg and the other award winners, and they stare at us. The women with envy, and the men, their gazes raking up and down my figure and the possessive way Fox pushes his body into mine. They've thought of me as nothing but a secretary and now they search for what Fox sees when he looks at me. I try to act like this happens every day, but at our table, I guzzle my water and Fox's too, what's left of the the ice clinking against my teeth.

We sit through the rest of the program, and my heart calms and my mind wanders. What would the rest of my evening look like if this was real? Would we be living together by now? Would we go up to his penthouse, undress, and make love? Maybe he'd draw us a bath and we'd soak off the evening, sharing a lowball of scotch. Then we'd go to bed and make plans for tomorrow. Sunday brunch. Maybe a movie. Not so much different from how we spend our Sundays now.

With some of the money Fox is going to pay me, I'm moving out of our building. It's probably for the best—I'll need the distance after this is done—though that had always been part of my plan before he asked me to do this favor. A house that has a yard and fence in a quiet neighborhood near the outskirts of Avondale.

Will he invite me up for a drink?

I can't ask him to stay.

Loneliness has always been with me. Time with Fox helped it fade, similar to depending on ibuprofen for a wound that won't heal, and I can't let myself use our fake engagement as a bandage. All we need to do is convince Darcy and Rodney our engagement is real, and once we're back in the city, things can return to normal. As normal, and as lonely, as my life is supposed to be.

After the last award is announced, no one stays to socialize. Paul disappears, and I'm glad. It won't be pleasant seeing him this week, not if he acts the way he did when Fox and I first got here.

Fox calls Rusty and we retrieve our coats from the attendant. Always the gentleman, he holds it for me and I push my arms through the sleeves.

With the late hour, the wind has died down, and it's pleasant when we step outside. Now that we're clear of the hotel and the etiquette that's required inside, several people yell out congratulations, and Fox grins and waves, accepting the well wishes.

"How big would our wedding ceremony be if this was real?" I ask because I'm a fool and can't stop myself.

He looks at me, his green eyes glowing in the gold lights attached to the hotel. "You and me, my parents, your parents. Darcy. Uncle Rodney. That's it unless you wanted someone else there. I would marry you in private. Our love wouldn't be up for inspection."

Surprised, I let my mouth drop open. What an extremely romantic thing to say.

Fox stands aside and waits for me to slide into the limo.

"Then the reception," I press.

He settles next to me as Rusty closes the door with a firm thud. He slides behind the wheel and we glide away from the curb.

Fox shrugs. "I wouldn't care."

"You and Michelle talked about getting married," I say, but I don't know that for sure. My only reason for thinking it's true is because I witnessed firsthand how much he loved her.

He turns away and stares out the window. He doesn't touch

me and I huddle in my coat, missing the warmth of his arm around me.

Avondale is a large city, and Saturday night traffic clogs the streets, lengthening an already long drive from the hotel to our building. Silence around Fox is usually never uncomfortable, but the last words I said still hang in the air, shoving an invisible wall between us. I want to go home, hide in my apartment, and pretend I didn't bring up Michelle on a night that should have been special.

Rusty lets us out in front of our building, and the doorman opens the lobby door.

Fox stands stiff and quiet in the elevator, his hands tucked into the deep pockets of his coat. We stop on my floor, and I pause before stepping out. He stares over my shoulder, and in disappointment, I turn away. It's late, and he's tired. On Monday we'll go back to the way we used to be and I'll never bring up Michelle again. It would be a lot easier if I understood what happened, but as far as I know, he didn't tell anyone. Paul might know, but it would be crass to ask and it would cause more problems than it would solve.

I step into the hallway and before the doors close, he says, "Posey."

Hopefully, I turn toward him and say, "Yeah?"

"Thanks for tonight. You're a good actress."

The way he says it, it sounds like an insult.

I prefer to take it as a compliment. I've hidden a lot of heartache behind my smile. Lifting my chin, I say, "Thank you. Sometimes I have to be."

The doors close, cutting Fox off from meeting my eyes and searching for the reasons why I would need to pretend to be happy. It's none of his business what's happened to me, what I've lived through, or the strength it took to fight to get to where I am, and I won't let him steal my pride.

Michelle broke his heart, and I won't pay her price to glue the shattered pieces back together.

I'm not sure if I can.

The elevator carries him up to his penthouse, and I unlock my door and lean against it, sliding in the deadbolt in place. Fox has a key if he wants in, and I never use the chain. Tonight, I do.

I don't want to see him until he sulks off what I said. I feel guilty I pushed when I shouldn't have.

I change into lounging pants and a tank top and sip on a cup of decaf coffee in bed while I try to read. I don't feel good, but I don't mean physically. It doesn't dawn on me what it is until I give up on my book and turn out the light.

In the dark, I pad back to the foyer and unchain the door.

I fall into a broken sleep, and the next morning when I get up to make coffee, my couch is empty.

It didn't matter I unchained the door.

Fox never came down.

CHAPTER FIVE

Fox

"You didn't tell me it was Posey," my sister accuses me on the phone the next morning.

I'm barely awake and her voice rakes over my skin. I spent most of the night wondering if I should go downstairs and apologize. I don't know what I'd be apologizing for, but it felt like the right thing to do and the fact that I didn't grates just as much as Darcy's voice.

"You didn't ask."

"I wouldn't have believed you. You two have been friends for years. When did it happen?"

"When did what happen?"

"When you knew you loved her?"

If I smoked, now would be the perfect time to light up, but I don't, and instead, I trap my phone between my shoulder and my ear and tug on a pair of sweats.

Coffee is the next best thing.

"My, aren't we the little romantic this morning."

"I just want you to be happy, but I want to hear about it, too."

That earns her a chuckle. I usually get along with Darcy—especially since we live in different states and she has a harder time meddling in my business. She cares about me and thinks I'm too old to be alone. That might be true, but it isn't like I haven't tried. Michelle may have been the wrong woman for me, but I would have followed it through to see where our relationship ended up. I loved her. Well, that's not exactly fair. I loved the idea of us. Isn't that the same thing?

"The same way I asked her to marry me. We were at the state park one evening last winter. The stars were out and the temperature wasn't threatening to kill us. We were the only ones out there and we were walking along the river on a trail that hadn't been completely covered in snow. She tripped over a branch and I helped her up. Our eyes met, and that's when I knew. That's why I asked her to marry me out there. That trail has sentimental value."

Her sigh puffs over the line and I wince. I didn't think this through properly. I didn't understand how many lies I would have to tell to convince everyone this is real. It didn't feel like a lie last night, not when I don't care about any of those people, but this is my sister and all she wants is what's best for me, even if I am nine years older than she is.

"What did she do?" Darcy's voice is barely a whisper.

Fuck it. I'm on a roll now.

"She didn't want to at first. She didn't want to ruin our friendship." At least that part's true.

"You've been seeing her for a whole year and didn't tell me? That's got to be the world's best kept secret."

"We didn't tell anyone because of work."

"Hmmm. I suppose that's true. Anyway, I'm excited for you

to come out. It's been a while, and we're planning a huge party."

"Great."

The coffee starts to drip and I watch it, willing it to brew faster. I can't handle much more of this conversation without caffeine.

"Hey, Fox?"

In anticipation, I slide a coffee mug out of the cabinet. "Yeah?"

"I'm really happy for you, even if I'm losing the bet. After Michelle, I didn't think you'd want to try again. But you said last year you brought Posey out to the park? Weren't you still seeing Michelle then?"

Timeline, timeline, timeline. *Fuck.*

"No. We broke up in December, remember? It was a few weeks after that." It could have been. If it had really happened. Michelle broke up with me a year ago last Christmas and that leaves three months of winter when a trail, any trail, could have still been covered with snow. Posey and I need to get our stories straight.

"Then you didn't love Michelle as much as you think you did," Darcy says, "if you could fall in love with Posey so quickly."

"You're right," I say, filling my mug with what's in the carafe so far. "Michelle breaking up with me was the best thing that could have happened. It opened my eyes to the woman I was meant to be with. She was right in front of me the whole time."

Darcy sighs again. "That's sweet. Tell Posey to call me, will you? I don't think Uncle Rodney would mind sharing the attention if we wanted to throw you guys an engagement party. What do you think?"

I almost spit out a mouthful of coffee. "That's a great idea."

"Okay, well, I need to get going. There's a huge ski group checking in and staying for the week. What time are you flying in on Friday?"

"I'll ask Paul if he can spare Posey for the afternoon and I'll try to get us to Chaska before dinner."

"Sounds good. We're going to have a great time! Bye."

"See ya, Darce."

She disconnects, and I chug the rest of my coffee and pour more.

On the weekends, I hang out with Posey doing odds and ends, shopping, cooking meals at her place, whatever. I prefer spending time there, and after Michelle and I broke up, Posey gave me her spare key. She said I could hang out whenever I didn't want to be alone, which, back then, was a lot, and I never stopped.

But this morning I'm reluctant to head downstairs and ask what her plans are. The way she looked at me last night before the elevator doors closed . . . a mix of pride and pain on her face. I don't know what I said that hurt her feelings. She was a real trooper, letting me kiss her, my paws all over her in a creepy attempt to convince everyone we're together.

I touch her all the time, but last night it felt wrong.

It *was* wrong.

Those caresses were nothing but a big fat lie, and she played along with grace. She's going to earn her fee.

And that kiss.

Sweet.

Soft.

It unsettled me, and in the limo, I couldn't stop thinking about it. It hadn't meant anything, but it sure felt like it had. Like it could have gone further if we'd been alone, but along with a fake proposal, we have fake feelings. She's never hinted she felt anything more for me than friends, and all the nights

I've fallen asleep holding her on the couch, I've never wanted to carry her to bed.

The mornings I've woken up hard, my cock pressed against her ass, that's natural. Any man would have that reaction with any woman. Especially a man who hasn't gotten any for as long as I have.

Posey's gorgeous, but I'm not attracted to her.

I just want to win this damned bet so Darcy will stop thinking I'm a lost cause and get off my back. I appreciate her concern, but I can live my own life without her interference.

I shower and try to plan the day without Posey in it. It's damned near impossible. She's as much a part of my life as coffee and work. Cutting her out would be like cutting off my own hand, and just as painful. I might as well admit that.

I refuse to let this fake engagement fuck us up.

I need her.

What are you doing tonight? I text her.

I don't know. What am I doing? I can picture her quirking her lips in that way she has when she's amused but doesn't want to let it show.

Let's go out.

Where?

It's a surprise. Wear something warm and your boots.

????

I ignore her question marks and reply with a, *I'll be downstairs at 6.*

That leaves me a whole Sunday I don't normally have to myself. I'd rather go downstairs and flop on Posey's couch and watch football while she cooks and her cat sleeps by my feet, but that seems a little too . . . husband and wife. Instead, I spend some much-needed time with my personal trainer and after he beats the shit out of me for three hours, I take shower, lie down, and try to fall asleep without the sounds of Posey puttering around in the background.

I don't succeed.

Promptly at six, I'm at her door, and she opens it dressed in jeans, a long-sleeved shirt, and a down vest.

"That's not going to be warm enough."

I checked the temperature before I came down, and it's what you'd expect in Minnesota in February. Fucking cold.

"Not with my jacket?" She blinks.

"No. Put a sweater on over your shirt and wear that coat I bought you for your birthday, if you still have it. I'll find your hat and I hope you have mittens."

"Where are we going? Antarctica?"

"No, but it will feel like it." This is the stupidest idea I've ever had. Well, no. Scratch that. Thinking I could lie to half the world and get away with it is the dumbest thing that's rattled around inside my head, and that includes the day my buddies and I tried to bike down the steepest set of public stairs we could find. It wasn't pretty.

Posey goes back to her bedroom and comes out wearing a thick fuzzy sweater that adds twenty pounds to her frame. The jacket I bought her is hanging in her closet and I pull it off the hanger. That winter had been particularly cold, and I'd had an inexplicable fear she'd freeze to death and I wouldn't be there to help her.

"Can't I put it on in the car? I'm already sweating."

"Fine. But I'm driving. Rusty has the night off."

"You're driving? Should I be worried, Fox?"

"I have it all under control," I say, but I don't sound like I have anything under control.

"If you say so." She pushes on a pair of leather boots.

"Don't you have something warmer than those?"

"These are the only winter boots I have. Where in the hell are we going?"

"Never mind." Her boots will have to work, and we don't have to be out there that long. At least they don't have heels. She'd never make it half a mile down the trail.

My vehicles are parked in the underground parking garage, and I unlock my Range Rover and help Posey into the passenger seat. I haven't been this close to her all day, and I woozily breathe in her light vanilla scent.

She rests her forehead against mine. "Have you eaten today?"

"What? Why are you asking me that?"

"Because you didn't spend the day at my place like you usually do, and I'm wondering if you remembered to eat something."

"Of course I did." *No, I didn't.* I completely forgot after working out and that piss-poor nap.

She turns away to buckle her seatbelt, her jacket in her lap. "Good."

I want to say something nasty, ask her if she thinks I can't take care of myself, but she was only asking out of concern. Besides, she was right. All I've had today is coffee with a side of bad attitude.

Before I drive out of the garage, I plug the Avondale River State Park's address into my GPS. I've never been out there before, and I have no fucking clue where the idea came from to say I proposed at the park. Darcy doesn't know me as well as she thinks she does or she'd know that I would never ask Posey to go hiking. Downhill skiing at Uncle Rodney's chateau is the closest thing I've ever gotten to being an outdoorsy type and even that's stretching it.

Posey doesn't comment as she watches me choose our destination.

I toss my phone on top of her jacket, drive out the parking garage, and turn onto the street. A light snow is falling and it melts against my windshield.

"What did you do today?" I ask, heading east and feeling a little bitter I don't know how she spent her time. The GPS estimates the park is forty-five minutes from here.

She doesn't say anything, and after I clear a stoplight, I look at her. "Posey?"

"Are you mad at me? Did I do something wrong last night?"

I hold her hand in mine. "No. You were great."

"Okay. If you're sure."

"I am."

She stares out the window as we leave the city limits, the skyscrapers giving way to smaller buildings, and those fade into farms and farmland until there's nothing but trees on both sides of the highway. The city's lights glow in my rearview mirror, a bright pink haze in the sky.

I slow when my headlights light up the sign indicating the park is just ahead, but the turn is sharp and slippery and my tires skid on the ice.

Posey squeaks and grabs the door handle.

"Sorry," I mutter. "I'm not used to driving out here."

I drive down the narrow road that's hugged by snow piles on each side, the absolute darkness swallowing us. We have to pay before we can enter the park, and I stop at a building that looks like a log cabin. At almost seven on a Sunday night there's no one here, but there's a wooden box attached to the side near the door, and I get out and fill out a registration envelope using a stubby pencil tied to the box with a string. I don't have a five dollar bill to pay for a day pass and I donate a twenty, scrawling

"Keep it" at the bottom in case an honest soul has the bright idea to mail me the change.

I climb back in the truck, Posey eyeing me like I've lost my mind, and slowly, I follow a sign's directions to a parking lot. No one has been out here tonight, the snow undisturbed. A beat-up truck that has several inches of snow on its hood is parked near an evergreen tree, its branches white and shimmering in the moonlight.

"Come on." I unbuckle my seatbelt and get out.

There isn't any wind, but I still put my hat on. My breath leaves my mouth in white puffs.

Posey zips her jacket up and adjusts her hat and mittens. She looks around curiously, the milky blue glow of the parking lot light glinting off her hair and highlighting her already rosy cheeks. "What are we doing out here?"

"Darcy called me this morning. She said she watched the live stream of the awards dinner and asked me when I knew I had fallen in love with you. I told her at the park, and that's why I asked you to marry me out here. Then I realized I've never been here before and I thought this would be a good time to get our stories straight. Darcy's got a memory like an elephant. She'll remember if we don't tell her the same thing."

"Why did you say you proposed at the park?" Posey asks, following me to a map protected by a sheet of glass. I need to find a trail near the river. I trace my finger along a potential path.

"This way. Because I thought it would be romantic?"

"I guess it could be if I didn't feel like a serial killer was about to jump out from behind the bushes and hack me to pieces."

"I'll protect you."

"Was *that* supposed to be romantic?"

My mouth dries. "No."

"Good, because it wasn't."

"You have high standards."

"Standards that include heat."

"If you remember, I asked you to marry me on your couch. You were warm then."

"Hmmph."

Twigs snap under my boots, and the air bites at my skin. It's not as cold as it could be, and I admit, there's a certain beauty in the evergreens covered in snow, the frigid temperatures sharpening everything. Almost otherworldly, but not in a kind or gentle way. The bare branches of the birch trees look like gnarled fingers, and the path disappears in the dark as if leading us to a frozen hell.

Perhaps in the fall this could be romantic, but the harsh winter freezes out any softness.

We step off the path and onto a wider one, the trees sparser near the river, the inky black carving a wide gash in the earth. An owl hoots, and I imagine him warning us to leave.

No, this isn't romantic at all.

"What else did she say?" she asks, picking up the thread of conversation I forgot.

"She wants you to call her to talk about an engagement party."

"It sounds like she believed you."

I look over my shoulder. Posey's lagging behind, her steps smaller and more cautious over the debris.

"She did, but she also asked *when* I knew I fell in love with you and I said last year around this time. Michelle had broken up with me not long before that and Darcy did the math. I hadn't, so now she thinks Michelle didn't mean that much to me. That's fine. I don't owe her any explanations."

"We were all worried about you."

"There's no reason to be."

Maybe back then there had been, but over a year's passed and the ache has turned into a dull, almost imperceptible, throb. I don't feel it most days but this fake engagement will open old wounds. Everyone wants me to move on, but can anyone truly move on after a tragedy? All you can hope is that time erases as much of the pain as possible, but I'm not ready to let things go.

I stop near the bank, ice chunks floating on the river's surface. The moon's light illuminates more than I thought it would out here, the snow glowing a strange silver, kind of how white turns purple under a blacklight.

Posey stops near me, and the fabric of our jackets brush.

Eerily quiet, only a train's low whistle echoes over the park.

"I told Darcy you tripped on a branch and when I helped you up, that's when I knew I was in love with you. I said I told you, but you were hesitant to admit you felt the same because you didn't want to ruin our friendship."

"Okay."

"Then I said I asked you to marry me out here because the trail had sentimental value. If you add any more details when you talk to her, let me know so we're on the same page. We don't have to keep this up for long and I'll try to think of a reason why we break our engagement. You want kids and I don't, something like that."

She shifts, and the snow crunches under her boots. "You don't?"

"Michelle and I talked about it. That's all I want to say."

I feel like shit shutting her down, shutting her out, but me and babies don't mix. We'll never mix. There is nothing I want less in my life after what happened than babies.

"Then if she asks if I'm pregnant I should say no."

"If you're pregnant, it's not mine, and that will be your problem to deal with." I gnash my teeth together.

She turns away and starts walking farther up the trail. "You don't have to worry about that."

Relief floods through me, along with a tsunami of guilt for already hating the faceless bastard who will give her everything I never will. "Why?"

"You know I'm not seeing anyone at the moment, and if I was, do you think I could help you? I'm as far away from having a family as you are. Where does this trail go?"

"I don't know."

"Then let's look."

"I told you everything I had to say. Don't you want to head back?"

She keeps walking, her white parka gleaming. "I like it out here. There's a hopelessness, I think, in the cold. The animals waiting for it to warm up, for some warmth to come back. This is a different kind of desolation, not the kind we live with in the city."

"It's worse."

I don't know where the words came from, but Posey smiles sadly in response. "Maybe. Come on. You've been acting strange since the announcement but things will work out."

My long strides catch me up with her in an instant. "What do you get out of this?"

"Besides all the attention being your fiancée is going to give me?" she asks, teasing me. "The money will help a lot, Fox. I have plans that I've had to put on hold while I saved. What you're paying me will speed things up."

"What do you want to do? Buy a country house in England? Go on a cruise around the world?"

She grins cheekily, the Posey I know coming back, the moonlight catching her eyes, and I swallow around a lump lodged in my throat.

"Nothing you'd be interested in."

"Why haven't we talked about this before?"

"I don't tell you everything, just like you don't tell me everything. There's more to your breakup than Michelle deciding she didn't want to see you anymore. We all have our secrets, our hopes and dreams, nightmares too, and I'm not sharing mine."

"What if I want to hear them?"

She looks at me, the twinkle gone. "That will never happen."

I frown and scramble for something to say. Suddenly, the toe of her boot catches on a partially covered branch, and she stumbles, landing on her hands and knees in the snow.

"Ugh," she says, kneeling and brushing snow off her mittens. "Now my jeans are going to be all wet."

"Careful." I reach out to help her up, and our eyes meet. Just like what I told Darcy.

And just like what I told Darcy, something stirs, an emotion I don't want to name, and I smooth out my face as she clasps her hand in mine and I pull her to her feet.

We explore until neither of us can feel our noses and we drive back to the city, sleepy and loopy on fresh air. This time when the elevator stops on her floor, I step out with her, and we warm up drinking hot chocolate spiked with peppermint schnapps and nibble on chocolate chip cookies she baked while I was being a stubborn ass.

Later, we lie on the couch like we always have, streaming a movie I couldn't care less about, her body tucked against mine.

It's the same, but different, and after our weekend in Chaska, things will have changed too much for me to go back to the simple friendship we had. Things are already changing, hesitation in our relationship that never used to be there before. The thought rivals the day Michelle told me she couldn't keep pretending, that everything that happened would be a part of our history that could never be repaired.

I'm falling for my fake fiancée, and damned if I can tell my heart to stop.

I think I'm in the clear with Paul until he proves me wrong Wednesday afternoon. Quietly, he steps into my office and closes the door behind him. It's near quitting time, and I'm piling papers into my briefcase to work on at Posey's while she cooks spaghetti and Peaches purrs at my feet.

"Hey, what's up?" I sift through another stack and add a few more sheets. Chances are good I won't get much work done —talking to Posey and watching her putter around the kitchen while she sips wine is always more enjoyable—but I was hoping to get ahead before the weekend.

"You and Posey leaving Friday?" He shoves his hands into the pockets of his slacks. It's a gesture I know well. He's trying to keep his cool.

"Yeah. We'll be back Sunday afternoon and then we'll lay low for a bit. I already told Posey I'll think of a reason, and I'll break the news to Darcy and call a contact at the newspaper. She can print it in her gossip column. There's nothing to worry about."

He helps himself to a drink from my little bar, pouring a couple fingers of my best scotch into a lowball that's part of a set Posey bought me for my birthday. For a good six months after Michelle said she couldn't handle seeing me anymore, I had to keep alcohol out of my office or I'd spend the day drunk at my desk. My half year of abstinence stuck, and I don't drink much at all anymore. Unless I'm sharing a bottle of wine with Posey and I know I can fall asleep on her couch.

Alcohol is a depressant, and it sure as hell depresses me.

"I asked her out, after your little charade is over. She said yes." He studies me over the rim of his glass.

My hands tremble, and I latch my briefcase closed. Paul's a good guy. Out of anyone in the world I'd trust to look after Posey, he's one of few. "Is there something you want me to say to that?"

"No. I'm letting you know what my intentions are."

"Understood."

His shoulders drop as he lets down his guard. "Fox, we've been friends for decades. Built this company from scratch. I don't want a woman to come between us. We're better than that, but I have to be honest. After what happened between you and Michelle, you're not a good match for Posey. Her history and yours are like oil and water. After this weekend is done and you've won your bet, let it go. Please."

I still. "Her history?"

Her hopes, her dreams, her *nightmares*. For as good of friends as we are, we don't know everything about each other, and that was a decision I made.

"She's been through a lot, and you know the worse it is, the harder it is to shake off. Hell, I bet you still can't get through a day without thinking about Michelle or where you would have been right now. Married, yeah? Maybe she would have moved into your penthouse or you would have built a house in the suburbs. You wouldn't be giving Posey rides home—Michelle would have forbidden it. I still say what happened was for the best, but that doesn't change the fact that you wanted her when she didn't want you enough to get help."

I lift my briefcase off my desk and round the corner. "I've already decided to pull back after this weekend. In fact, I've been meaning to ask, how do you feel about expanding? Maybe opening a branch in Seattle. I *do* think about Michelle, every day, and a change of scenery would do me a lot of good." Sweat starts to drip down my back. "I need to get out of here."

Paul stares at me and his eyes turn hard.

I wonder if we were ever friends at all.

"I think the idea has a lot of potential. We'll talk more about it when you get back. We haven't been to Sergio's in a long time. I'll buy you a meal."

"Sounds good. Have a good night."

"You too, Fox. You, too."

Posey isn't at her desk, but I park my ass against the edge and take my phone out of my pocket to wait. Paul might be a jealous ass, but I'm not going to let him bully me out of my friendship with her. Seattle flew out of my mouth with no thought to it actually happening, but if Paul goes through with his threat and he and Posey start seeing each other, I don't want to watch that. It's too easy to picture them walking down the aisle, a matching cake topper waiting for them at the reception.

Starting fresh could help in more ways than one.

Fuck, I don't have to work. I could let Paul buy me out and I could retire.

Somewhere warm. Somewhere where my only job would be to lie on the beach and get baked. Literally and figuratively.

I hear Posey's heels clicking before I see her, and I forget every idea I had about leaving her behind as she comes into view. It would kill me. It would absolutely kill me if I moved to Washington and she stayed here.

I'm in too deep.

Paul watches us from the doorway of his office, and I want wrap my arms around her and bury my face in the sweet curve of her neck. She'd let me too. Not because we're playing at being engaged, but because we're friends and if she thought I'm having a bad day and needed the comfort, she'd give it to me. No matter the cost.

"Are you ready to go?" I ask, pushing my phone back into my pocket.

"Yeah, just let me log off." She slides into her chair and begins the routine of shutting her computer down, engaging her voicemail, and stacking anything she's completed in the outbox on her desk. She's efficient and lovely, competent and elegant, and it's no wonder Paul fell so hard staring at her through his office window every day for the past seven years.

I have her jacket waiting and she slips her arms through the sleeves. I help her pull her hair out of her coat, just like I always do, while she buttons her jacket and ties her scarf. We have a system, and anyone watching would know we've been doing this for a long time.

Anger is heating Paul's cheeks when I nod goodnight, and to add insult to his injury, I place my hand on the nape of Posey's neck as we walk to the elevator.

Paul can go to hell.

In the elevator, Posey leans against me the way she always does after a long day. It stops on her floor, and she straightens, sighing. "Are you coming back down?"

I hesitate. I should say no, that I'll grab a quick bite at my own place and work as much as I can, but I'm already starting to miss our routine, the Sunday without her like a hole I can't fill with anything else. "Yeah. If it's still okay."

She smiles. "You're always welcome."

Before she steps out of the elevator, I grab her arm and caress her cheek. Her blue eyes flare with something, but it's gone before I can figure out what it is. "You know how much I value our friendship, don't you?"

"If it's as much as I value it, then yeah, I do. See you in a couple of minutes."

The doors close and the elevator carries me up to the penthouse.

I shower quickly, change into jeans and a t-shirt, and grab a bottle of red and my briefcase. Posey's standing in front of her stove wearing yoga pants and a matching tank top, Amy Winehouse crooning from her smart home device. A wave of déjà vu hits me, and it grows stronger as she smiles over browning hamburger, wineglasses and a corkscrew sitting on the breakfast bar.

It's more than pleasant. It's necessary.

I'm forty years old, and routine is what I crave. A predictability that's soothing rather than monotonous. I need it to be okay.

"How was your day, dear?" she asks playfully.

I step closer to her. "Fine. How was yours?"

"Better now." She tilts her head.

"What are you doing?"

"I thought we should practice. Don't you think?"

It makes sense. "Sure." I lower my head and gently place my lips on hers. Those songs that say kissing or making love with the right person feels like the first time, I always thought they were stupid. You can never have a first time like that again, but those songs aren't about that. They're about how it feels to share intimacy with someone who matters.

Posey matters to me. More than I ever thought possible.

Without breaking our kiss, I drop my briefcase and set the bottle of wine on the counter near the stove. I can't stop myself from pulling her to me, and she abandons the hamburger and wraps her arms around my neck. She opens her mouth and I waste no time invading her with my tongue. Her taste is intoxicating, and I feel drunk.

My cock stiffens, and that's my sign to let her go before she can feel it press against her belly. I'm paying her to pretend to be my fiancée, not sex.

She wipes her mouth with the side of her thumb and laughs. "Wow. I don't think we'll have a problem convincing anyone this is real."

I brush a kiss to her cheek to lighten the mood even more. "It'll be easy."

I uncork the wine, pour two glasses, and settle at her table. In the quiet, the day falls off my shoulders. I open my laptop, eager to get as much work as I can out of the way before the weekend. To pull this off, I need to focus all my attention on Posey and convincing Darcy I'm in love.

"What would you think if we opened a branch in Seattle?"

She adds noodles to a boiling pot of water, the steam turning her cheeks a faint pink. "Really? Paul wants to relocate?"

"He wouldn't be the one moving."

I watch her carefully, my heart slamming. I don't know the kind of reaction I was looking for, but what she gives me disappoints me on a level I don't want to admit to.

"Fox, I think that would be great. After what happened with, well, you know, I never thought you felt comfortable here. A new city, building another office from nothing, I think that's the kind of challenge you need. A place to focus your energy. The office in Avondale is established and you don't have to do much to keep it going. You and Paul just won the most prestigious gaming award in the country. You need something new. I think it could help you find your happy again."

Nothing she said is wrong, in fact, as she speaks, my excitement grows. And let's face it. When Paul and Posey start dating, relocating would be a blessing in disguise, even if it hurts like hell.

"You wouldn't miss me?"

She stirs the noodles, taps the wooden spoon on the edge of the pot, and sips her wine. "Of course I would, but we're friends, and friends move on. I'm sure you have things you'd like to do that don't include me. I have things I want to do, too, and I made those plans knowing you wouldn't be in them. It'll be fine."

"Dating Paul, you mean."

She blinks, then looks away. "Paul doesn't have anything to do with this."

"Right."

I don't know why I'm so bitter. Yeah, I do. I want Posey to have feelings for me, and she doesn't. I'm drifting lazily in love with her, like a leaf floating on a calm river, slowly, steadily, my feelings as deep as the water, hoping Posey will return them. Only she won't because we've been friends for years and she's never given even one tiny indication she feels anything for me other than friendship.

"What do you want from me?" she whispers.

Tell me you love me, tell me you need me. Tell me you want the ring on your finger to be real.

"Keep being my friend." I turn on my chair, and she sits on my thigh.

"We'll always be friends."

The scent of tomato sauce clings to her tank top, the light vanilla of her body lotion mingling with the tangy aroma. To me, she represents hearth and home, grounding me when life tries to carry me away. Michelle swirled my emotions like a blender switched to its highest setting and often I felt the same way, broken and chopped up, whipped beyond recognition.

I move her closer, my hands at her waist. "Kiss me like one day you'll be my wife."

To my heart's regret and delight, she does.

CHAPTER SIX

Posey

I *don't want him to go.*
    I don't want him to go.
I don't want him to go.

It's all I've been able to write in my journal as we fly over North Dakota's pastures. The snow-covered patches of farmland look like a brown and white quilt held together by dark brown thread.

Paul was reluctant to let me go, but he knew I had enough vacation time to leave early. Fox and I were at the Avondale airport a little after lunchtime, and his jet was waiting for us on the tarmac, only the ground crew present, braving the cold to stow our luggage and help us board.

I dressed in yoga pants and a long-sleeved shirt, and I draped a cardigan over my shoulders to ward off the natural chill of the plane. When we settled in, I stretched out on a loveseat near a window, and now I'm daydreaming while I watch the clouds though I'm supposed to be journaling.

Fox is sitting across the aisle, working, it looks like, if I can correctly interpret the scowl on his face. I wonder if he's starting to set up the new office in Seattle. I'm trying to be happy for him—everything I told him at dinner was true. I think it would do him a lot of good to shake off Avondale, meet new people, and move forward in the personal aspects of his life as well as the professional. Maybe he'll meet someone he could love as much as he loved Michelle.

I turn back to my journal. My therapist encourages me to write, but it's difficult to put my feelings on paper. What is there to say that hasn't been said? And do I want to immortalize those words, those feelings? Turn them into something tangible? Something to go back to again and again, when, if I keep them in my heart, I can pretend they don't exist.

I don't want him to go.

What would he say if I sank into the seat next to him and told him those words, right to his face? Would he laugh? Would he pity me? *Oh, Posey, I'm sorry. Did you think this meant more than it does?*

Of course he would say that. When he told me to kiss him like I'd be his wife one day, I did. The request was cruel, but I did it and I tried to get him to feel it, tried to make him understand I'm starting to feel things for him that friends don't feel for each other. He started it with that stupid question. *"Will you marry me?"*

The only time I'll hear the words, and they were a joke.

Yesterday at my session, Audra wasn't happy when I told her what Fox asked me to do, and that I said yes.

"He's paying me," I said, a little defensively, if you want to know the truth. I'm too old to be scolded like a little kid sneaking an extra cookie after dinner.

"And how will you feel when you finally get what you

want? How will you look at that achievement, tainted by Fox Caldwell's money?"

She meant it as a jab, but I didn't take it that way. Fox helping me accomplish the one thing I want most in the world . . . he would be part of my family. In a way that's not healthy, which is probably what Audra had been getting at, but without his help, I'd need years to save up the fees and expenses. I don't want to wait that long.

"Hey, what are you working on?"

I was cloud-gazing, and Fox snuck up on me. I quickly flip the cover of my journal closed, hoping he didn't see what I wrote. "Nothing much."

He sits next to me on the cushion. "We'll be landing soon."

I'm not nervous about seeing Darcy or Rodney again. I've met them a few times, the most recent when they flew to Avondale for Christmas last year to surprise Fox. Rodney's a free-spirit and nothing gets him down. The ski resort is the perfect way for him to make a living and still have fun. He's a natural host, and he spends most of his evenings in the bar drinking with the wealthy guests who put his chalet on the map as a luxury getaway that only offers the best of the best.

Darcy's a sweetheart and looks after Fox as much as she can. I wouldn't exactly call us friends, but sometimes she calls and asks after him, particularly if he's not answering his phone. She'll be absolutely thrilled we're engaged.

"What did your family say when they heard the announcement?" Fox asks.

I lean into him. Might as well start practicing. I'm familiar with his body, with the way he moves. What I'm not familiar with is the way mine responds to his now, the way my blood fizzes when he kisses me, like I gulped a glass of champagne, or the way my breasts grow heavy and my belly quivers, yearning to connect with his in that primal dance I'll never be able to fully participate in.

He molds his chest to my back and rests his chin on my shoulder. Natural. Like we've been doing it for years.

We have, but as friends.

Can friendship turn to love? Sure. If you let it, encourage it, nurture it as a gardener would a little sprout, but I can't do that. I need to keep the physical aspects of my relationship with Fox out of the emotional.

The way his breath whispers across my skin. That's physical. The way his arms hold me. That's physical. But the way I feel safe in his embrace, knowing nothing could ever hurt me because no matter what, he'd protect me, that's where I need to keep my distance.

"I don't know if my mother knows, but I'm not going to offer the information since it's not real. Our breakup would only hurt her. Claudia probably heard—she loves all that online gossip—but she'd never go out of her way to call me, about that, or anything else."

My mother remarried after my father passed away, and when I was eight, they had Claudia. Nine years later, they divorced, and Claudia chose to stay with her father. My mother took me with her. I lost half my family the day the judge signed their papers. I don't consider Walter my stepfather any longer, and we were never close enough that I called him Dad. I know it hurt him when I cut him off after Mom left him, but it was easier on me that way.

"How about your mom and dad?" I ask.

"Darcy probably told them. My mom would love you."

I'm getting too comfortable. One small turn of my head and our lips would meet. It's too tempting, and I sit up, breaking the contact. I feel cold now, without his body heat, and alone, too, always alone.

Audra says my choice isn't necessary, but how the hell does she know anything with the bright pictures of her family on her desk? When has she gone through anything traumatic that she can give me advice? I shove my journal into my carry-on I kept with me in case I needed anything on the plane.

"They aren't coming to the chalet?" I ask, hoping against hope the answer is no. I've never met his mom and dad, and I don't want to spend time with them or get to know them. I'll only miss Fox more when our engagement is over.

"Nope. They're somewhere in Australia and didn't plan to come back for the party."

"Rodney will be disappointed." Fox's dad is Rodney's brother, and close, from what I know. They're different as night and day, but they've never let it come between them.

"It won't get him down for long. I'm going to hit the head. Can I get you anything while I'm up?"

"No, thanks. I'll do the same before we land."

He gets up and I turn to look out the window.

"Posey?"

"Yeah?"

"Thank you for doing this. I know it's inconvenient, but I appreciate it. I should let Darcy win, but she'll be happy I found someone, and even after we break up, she'll think I'm open to sharing my life with someone again."

I force a smile. "I'm glad I can help."

"You are."

He stares at me for another long moment then walks to the rear of the plane.

I follow suit when he's finished and brush my hair and touch up my makeup. I don't know what's in store for us tonight, a family dinner, maybe, but if I can get past the close proximity to Fox that will be expected, this might be a pleasant weekend. I don't travel much because I don't enjoy traveling by myself. I'd rather stay home with Peaches.

The jet lands at a private airstrip used by Chaska tourists who don't fly commercial, and a Diamond Peaks Chateau luxury van is waiting for us. I step onto the plane's stairs, the beauty of the Colorado horizon stealing my breath. "The mountains are gorgeous."

"And you'll be up in them. Come on."

Fox carries my bag and grips my hand, but my boots have enough traction that I reach the ground without slipping.

We're the only passengers in the vehicle, and we have to wait only a moment for the crew to transfer our luggage from the plane to the van. The driver navigates out of the airport's parking lot and turns onto the highway, the scenery a green and white a blur out the window.

"You have our story down, right?"

Fox's question throws cold water over my happy flame, and my excitement flickers out.

"Yeah. I thought you were crazy for dragging me out to the park, but it was a good idea."

"If you add any spur-of-the-moment details when I'm not around, try to remember to tell me. With any luck, Darcy will want to hear the story only once and we'll be free and clear for the rest of the weekend."

Except for the kissing. And hugging. And whatever else we're going to have to do to sell Fox's lie.

The courtesy van winds its way up the mountainside, and I distract myself with the view. *Get what you can out of this*, I tell myself. Think of it as a job with a paycheck at the end of the weekend. Remember he doesn't have feelings for you, that no man in his right mind would if he knew the truth, and leave it at that.

One afternoon during a session, Audra asked me, "Posey,

you've locked your heart away so tightly, for so long, do you think you could let yourself fall in love?"

I meet Fox's eyes. They crinkle in the corners when he smiles at me, and he lifts my hand and kisses my knuckles in a way that suggests he's done it for years.

Yes, I think I can fall in love, but God help my heart if I ever do.

Darcy and Rodney are waiting outside the ski resort, chatting with a young man who might be a valet. She's wearing heavy winter boots, and excitedly, she clomps up and down when she sees us. The van glides to a stop in front of the glass doors, and Rodney grins. It's nice to see them again and I press a hand to the window. The lodge is built into the side of the mountain, and with the afternoon sun glinting off the building, it's a perfect backdrop for a weekend full of fun and romance.

Fox is barely out of the vehicle when Darcy shoots into his arms and hugs him tightly, unbothered, it seems, by the loss of ten million dollars.

Rodney sweeps me off my feet, literally, whooping like a little kid while he swings me around, his scruffy chin grazing my cheek. "Posey, you're looking mighty fine. Throw off that asshole and run away with me instead." He sets me to my feet, and woozy, I stumble for a second before I find my bearings.

"Still the charmer," I gasp, laughing.

"Damn straight. Fox, how are you, you son of a bitch?" Rodney grips his nephew in a tight hug.

Darcy grabs my hand. "Let me see your rock."

Is it sad to say I'm already used to wearing it? The weight is familiar, comforting, and I hold out my hand and show it off, like a new fiancée would.

"It's gorgeous. Did he pick it out?"

"All by himself," I say honestly. I might have been at the jewelry store with him, but I had no opinion and wasn't interested. My only request was that I be allowed to keep it after he breaks our engagement, not what it looked like.

"He did a great job." She launches herself at me, giving me a fierce hug. Her display of affection takes me aback, and I stiffen. "Fox is an awesome brother, but I always wanted a sister. Now I'll have one. How cool is that?"

I swallow past a burn in my throat. If she knew this was a hoax to win a bet, she wouldn't be so happy I'm here.

Darcy doesn't wait for me to answer. "Come on, let's show the lovebirds to their room. It's early enough if you want to hit the slopes, or do you want to give Posey a tour of the resort?" she asks Fox.

"I can walk her around, after we unpack and change. We dressed for the plane," he says, wrapping his arm around my shoulders. I lean into him the way I'm expected to, completely in love with her fiancé.

"We happened to have the Honeymoon Suite open, and Darcy blocked that off for you to get things started," Rodney says, leading us out of the cold and into the elegant foyer.

I flick a glance up at Fox, but he only grins and kisses the tip of my nose. "That's perfect."

Rodney chortles and slaps him on the shoulder. "Like you need practice. These two haven't waited for their wedding night. I can tell just by the way Fox can't keep his hands off her."

"Uncle Rodney, I'm sure Posey doesn't want her sex life to be a topic of conversation," Darcy says, rolling her eyes at me.

"If she's going to be part of the family, there's no special treatment, Darce. I give you shit all the time."

"You're having sex?" Fox asks, throwing her a sideways big-brother look.

"I'm thirty-one years old. I think if I want some sexy times, I'm allowed to have some."

"I want to meet him."

Darcy laughs. "Yeah, no."

"She has a regular guy?" Fox asks Rodney, and selfishly, I'm glad I won't be the center of attention this weekend.

Rodney grins. "You betcha. He's the beginner's ski instructor. Nice fella. You won't find anything wrong with him."

"We'll see about that," Fox says, his voice low but teasing.

We follow Darcy and Rodney down a wide corridor, cream walls and blonde hardwood floors. The chalet is beautiful, light, and airy.

Darcy uses a keycard to open our suite's door, and I'm dazzled by the spectacular view of the mountains and the luxurious hot tub sitting outside the sliding glass doors. A huge bed is positioned in the center of one wall, and a loveseat and end tables take up space under the enormous window. A large fireplace sets a cozy scene, a furry rug in front of the hearth and a basket of wood near a stand of pokers.

It's a gorgeous room, and one designed with sex in mind. Lacking the customary TV, the interior decorator didn't mean for anyone to spend much time here—unless it was in bed.

"We'll let you two get settled. The dining room's open twenty-four/seven, and room service is available too. There's a menu in the drawer next to the bed. Didja wanna meet for dinner around seven?" Rodney asks, grinning hopefully and hooking his thumbs in the front pockets of his jeans. It's evident he wants to spend as much time with us as possible while we're here.

Fox pauses.

"That sounds great, Rodney, thank you," I say to fill the

silence. I don't know why Fox wouldn't want to spend time with Darcy and his uncle. It's what we came here for.

"Great! Enjoy looking around, and if you need anything, call Darcy or let the front desk know. I'm going to schmooze a couple of my regulars, but I'll be around. See ya later."

Darcy lingers by the suite's door, but she leaves with Rodney, flashing a quick smile over her shoulder.

The valet delivered our suitcases, and Fox drops my carry-on bag near the bed.

I wiggle out of my jacket and hang it in the closet.

Fox clears his throat. "I can sleep on the floor."

I try not to let disappointment wash over me. He's only trying to be polite. "Why? We've shared my couch plenty of times and the bed is a king. I'm not worried about it."

"Are you sure?" He presses his lips into a firm line.

"It will be okay. It always has been before. I don't think the floor would be very comfortable, even for two nights, and the loveseat is too small to sleep on."

"Thanks." He heaves a sigh. "I'm going to shower and try to nap. I've been worried about this weekend and I'm wiped. Did you want to nap too, or look around? I'm not going to be much fun unless I can grab an hour."

"Go ahead. I was thinking on the plane that if we can do things separately this weekend, it will be easier to pretend our relationship is real. Not so much pressure, you know?"

"Yeah," he says slowly, "that's true. We won't have to touch each other then, huh?"

He turns toward the bathroom, grabbing his satchel off the bed as he stomps past.

I don't know why what I said made him angry, and I don't get a chance to ask. He firmly shuts and locks the door, blocking me out. It *will* be easier to keep up pretenses if we don't spend every second together this weekend. I'm not used to him kissing or touching me, and I don't want to get used to it.

I change out of my boots and into a pair of ballet flats that match my yoga pants and cardigan and grab a keycard in the welcome folder that's on the little table near the door. I step into the hallway, letting the door latch behind me. The folder also included a map, but it's more fun to wander around, and I go in the direction we came. I want to see the dining room, the café, and the bar. There's a swimming pool, somewhere, a salon and spa, and a workout room.

Fox has never brought me out here, but then, why would he? He doesn't go on vacations, and when he was dating Michelle, I rarely saw him. I should do more things on my own, meet more people, but I've never wanted to venture far from my happy little bubble.

I can hear Audra now. "Posey, it's not that happy." Maybe she has a point, but what I'm looking for I can't find, not even on an exotic vacation.

I poke my head into the dining room, and though it's early, there are people wearing everything from yoga pants like me to cocktail dresses. I'll fit in tonight no matter what I wear, though I did pack a couple of dresses just in case I needed to slip into a little black something and a pair of heels.

In the café, I order a to-go cup of coffee and charge it to our room, and I wander the chalet some more, stopping in the lobby that looks over the slopes, watching the skiers zigzag their way down. The sun is sinking in the sky, but Fox and I left Minnesota early enough that even with the time change, it's far from dusk. I wonder what we'll do tonight, after dinner. There are midnight ski runs, or we could go for a walk on one of the trails. I'll go by myself, if Fox is still mad at me, or if he'd rather visit with Rodney and Darcy while I do my own thing.

That's fine, too. I'm used to being alone.

I suppose we were silly thinking our friendship would be okay after this. There's a point of no return in a question like "Will you marry me?" and my heart crossed it when I said yes.

Sighing, I turn, and Darcy's standing there, watching me.

"You and Fox have a fight already?" she asks.

I force a smile. My mother always said my eyes gave everything away, and if I'm feeling melancholy, people know.

"Why would you think that? No. He's napping. He worked hard this week clearing his schedule, but I wasn't tired." Quickly, I change the subject. "I can't get over how beautiful it is here. How do you not stand at the window all day?"

She shrugs. "I got used to it. Sounds like I take it for granted and I try not to, but I guess the novelty has worn off. Did you have a chance to look around?"

"I think I saw most of it." I raise my disposable cup. "I grabbed coffee from the café and found the dining room. I'd love to walk around town but I don't think we'll have time."

"You should ask Fox to bring you out more often. It's beautiful in the summer too, lots of hiking and camping." She steps closer to me, her heels clicking on the wooden floor. Touching my shoulder, she says, "I'm glad he has you, Posey. I don't know what he was looking for, but I've never seen him more relaxed than when you two first got here."

I blink, confused. "He found it with Michelle. We're together because they aren't."

"Is that what you think?"

"It's what I know. If you ask him if he still loves her and he tells you the truth, he'll say yes. You know it as well as I do."

"If you believe that, then why did you say yes when he asked you to marry him?"

For two and a half million dollars.

"Why does any woman say yes? We've been friends for years and not being together hurts more than him looking at me and knowing he wishes Michelle was in my place. I missed him, Darcy. I didn't know what else to do."

She tilts her head in concern. "Posey, have you talked to him about this?"

That she doesn't deny it twists my heart in a way I can't afford, and if she tells him about our conversation, I'm sure there will be hell to pay. We don't talk about Michelle, and he definitely didn't give me permission to talk about her to Darcy or Rodney.

"No, and I wish you wouldn't, either, even if you think you're doing me a favor. I know what I'm getting into." I pat myself on the back. When Darcy hears we broke off our engagement, she'll know why, or, at least, she'll think she does.

What she'll say to Fox afterward will be his problem.

"I won't say anything, but I hope you're wrong. You've been friends for a long time—"

"He dumped me easily enough when he started dating her." I let the bitterness come through, for authenticity, not because that year cut me to the bone. "He rarely had time for me."

"Yeah, but he told me when he knew he loved you. It wasn't that long after he and Michelle broke up."

Darcy's a little younger than I am, but she should know better. "Then I'm the rebound girl, right? Darcy, I don't want to hurt you, or your brother, but I know where things stand. That's better than being disillusioned, don't you think?"

She purses her lips, the same way Fox does when he's heard something he doesn't like. "I think you're wrong. He wouldn't have asked you to marry him if he wasn't in love with you."

"I hope you're right."

"What are you doing now? Do you want me to show you around, or do you want to grab your jacket and boots and go outside? There are snowmobile tours, and one starts in twenty minutes. You can ride with someone if you don't feel comfortable on a machine by yourself."

"Thanks, but I think I'll check on Fox. He was a little worried about this weekend."

Again, not a lie, but probably something he didn't want me to share.

"Okay. I'll see you at dinner then. Maybe I'll ask Austin to come by if you can make Fox promise not to give him the third degree."

"I'll do my best. I'd like to meet him too. See you later."

She hugs me and says, "Things will work out. I know my brother, and Fox never looked at Michelle the way he looks at you."

How would you know? I want to ask, but instead I say, "Thanks."

I don't let Darcy's words plant a seed of hope. There's no point in it. The things I'm starting to feel for Fox, he doesn't feel for me. We're only friends, and this is only a favor.

I can't even call what I'm feeling love, and I hope it doesn't go that far. All I know is when I see him, I want, and when he touches me, I want, and when I dare to peek into the future, I want.

As I walk back to our room, I finish my coffee and throw the cup into an elegantly disguised trash receptacle. The keycard works, the tiny dot above the pad turning green, and when I step inside, Fox is lying on the bed, a pillow folded under his head, staring at the door.

"Where did you go?"

He's still angry.

I drop the card onto the little table and toe off my ballet flats. "I took a look around, that's all. You seemed mad and I didn't want to crowd you."

"I was worried."

"Well, I'm fine. If you're done in the bathroom, I'd like to clean up."

"Posey, will you come here?"

He shifts on the bed and flattens out the pillow. I lie next to him, and he wraps his arms around me. "I wasn't mad. Maybe hurt, but after I thought about it, I realized it's a good idea. We'll try to do a lot of activities, and that will help. They'll expect us to have our hands all over each other, and I can understand how that would make you uncomfortable."

I turn my head to look at him. There are shadows in his eyes and tension tugs at the corners of his mouth. I doubt he got any sleep while I was gone. "I'm not used to being part of a couple, that's all. They'll know if they watch us long enough."

"That's fair. We'll get through dinner tonight, tomorrow we can spend the day on the slopes, and at the party, we'll mingle. Sunday afternoon we'll fly home. It will be painless, I promise."

His eyelids start to droop, and he falls asleep, his hand resting on my stomach.

Unable to resist, I snuggle into his chest and his breathing lulls me to sleep.

When I wake up, he is too, and he's staring at me, frowning, his fingers digging into my side.

I'm too much of a coward to ask what he's thinking.

I don't want to know.

We dress for dinner, not speaking. When Fox gets like this, subdued, forlorn, I know he's thinking about Michelle. Sometimes, if he's at my place, he'll go upstairs to brood. I appreciate it because I can be prone to my own bouts of, I don't want to call it depression, but I get sad too, and his would make mine worse. If he's at work, he'll shut his office door, and I know to leave him alone. They say time heals all wounds, but this past year hasn't been long enough and Fox's are barely scabbed over.

I decided to wear a black skirt and a black and silver blouse. It's just the right amount of elegance for a dinner like this, especially when I twist my hair up and add little sparkling earrings to my ears. My engagement ring shines, and I appear as a woman engaged to a billionaire should appear: happy, put together, excited for her future. Limitless possibilities. When anything you want is at your disposal, how can you not be happy? No one bothers to dig under the façade. They're too busy being envious of the things they think you have.

"You look nice," Fox says, coming up behind me and resting his hands on my shoulders. I meet his eyes in the mirror. His nap didn't do anything to chase the shadows away.

"Thanks. So do you." Fox changed into black slacks, a black dress shirt, and, hoping I would laugh, a silver tie. He left it loose, and the button is undone at his throat. The look is sexy, not sloppy, and just for a second I picture him sitting on the bed as I wrap his tie around my hand, holding him still so I can press my lips to his.

Nothing a normal, engaged couple wouldn't do after a dinner with family and friends. Nothing I'll ever be able to do.

Darcy and Rodney are already sitting at a large table near the dining room's fireplace when we check with the hostess. There are a handful of people drinking wine who I don't know, and I prepare for an uncomfortable evening. It's not that I don't like meeting new people, but I get tired when I'm on display. It's why I treasure my evenings with Fox. After answering phones and helping Paul, it's nice to spend time with someone who allows you to be, encourages you to be, yourself.

Fox turns on his social persona, plastering a smile on his face and holding out his hand to Rodney's guests. When you're a businessman, anyone could be a lucrative contact, and I do my part as his "fiancée" shaking their hands, accepting compliments and returning them.

Rodney's a boisterous host, and the wine flows freely, an empty bottle never lingering on the table for long before a server replaces it. When our meals are served, we drool and exclaim over each other's plates, and I enjoy my beef filet and piped potatoes while I sip on a red that's a little too tart for my taste.

Fox seems like he's having a good time, chatting and laughing and telling stories. I resented the full table at first, but they save me from having to speak. Until one well-meaning woman who's married to stockbroker asks, "Have you set a wedding date yet? A ceremony like that, I would imagine you need years to plan. And the venue! A destination wedding would be so fun! Spencer and I married in Hawaii. It was fabulous, though there was some grumbling."

Spencer scoffs. "Your mother's never happy. We could've married on top of the Eiffel Tower and she would have said she was afraid of heights. No one else complained." He winks at me.

Fox dabs at his mouth with his napkin and wraps his arm around my shoulders. "We haven't set a date yet. We've been friends for years. This is new and we're savoring it."

Spencer's wife sighs and rests a hand over her heart. "That's sweet, and really, that's how people should fall in love. Spencer and I were friends for several years and we ran in the same social circles. I would go out on a date, and he would get so mad. Finally, one day I said, 'What the hell is your problem?'"

"I was sick inside when it seemed like Lynn might have found some idiot she was truly interested in, and I said, 'If you're going to run around town, at least do it with me!'"

They look at each other and burst out laughing, and I stifle my own giggle. They're adorable, and they love each other so much. My heart dips a little, though I'd never begrudge anyone their happiness.

"Luckily, I'm a needy son of a bitch and she didn't have time to date anyone else," Fox says and kisses my temple. "It was when I started daydreaming about taking her to bed that I knew I was falling in love—and in trouble."

Lynn laughs so hard she snorts.

Rodney shoots Fox a look, but I can't decipher it.

"I remember our first night," Lynn says, turning her glass of wine on the table. "We were so afraid things would change, and not for the better. The next morning, was, well, we weren't sure if we did the right thing. It took us a minute to find our footing, but it was worth it."

"Yeah, it was," Spencer says, tilting his wife's head and covering her lips with his, not caring everyone at the table watched.

I try not to be envious. It's their story, but I want it. With Fox, maybe. With Paul? No. I can't picture us being at ease with each other like Lynn and Spencer are. Fox and I are already like that—when we aren't being self-conscious about the ring he put on my finger and the lies we're telling to go along with it.

His kisses turn me to jelly. His touch sends shivers down my spine.

But I can't tip over the precipice because he won't be there to catch me when I fall.

Spencer breaks their kiss and says, "If I can offer one piece of advice, it's wait to have kids. We've been married for three years now, and we're only just starting to think about it. Enjoy each other first. There's plenty of time for babies." He lifts his glass in toast and gulps the rest of his wine.

Fox stiffens and leans away.

Darcy, who's been quiet, looks down at her plate.

Rodney clears his throat.

Lynn looks around our table in confusion, meeting the eyes of the other guests who also don't understand the sudden change in atmosphere.

"We haven't talked about having children. Excuse me." Fox throws his napkin onto his plate and pushes his chair back from the table. He doesn't spare me a glance and walks out of the dining room.

Spencer's face turns red. "I'm so sorry. I must have said something wrong."

My mind spins and a panicky sweat slides down my side. Fox doesn't know my secret. No one does. I had an employment gap before I started working at WellStone Interactive but because of HIPAA and other privacy laws, I didn't have to explain to HR unless I wanted to, and I didn't. I was fortunate they were impressed enough with my prior employment they skimmed right by the years I couldn't work.

If there's a reason why Fox is opposed to having children, he hasn't shared it with me. Darcy and Rodney obviously know something, and they look embarrassed on my behalf.

"It's fine. Fox will be forty-one this year and he's put himself under some pressure to have kids soon," I say, scrambling to explain his reaction. "He keeps saying he doesn't want to be too old to enjoy them."

Spencer frowns. "I apologize. Children are a personal choice and I'm sorry I overstepped. Let me make it up to you. Are you skiing this tomorrow? Let's meet for breakfast and spend the day on the slopes."

It's a perfect way to keep us busy, and I accept. "That sounds great. We'll meet you here, at say, nine-thirty?"

Lynn smiles, relieved the tension is gone. "Thank you for being kind. I love sleeping in."

Laughing at her grateful expression, I say, "Me too. I better go check on Fox. It was nice meeting you both." I slide my chair away from the table and pick up my purse. Leaning over, I kiss Darcy on the cheek. "Let's get together tomorrow sometime, okay?"

She squeezes my hand. "Yeah. Sure. I'm sorry, Posey."

"Nothing to be sorry for." I turn to my other side and speak across Fox's empty chair to the head of the table. "Goodnight, Rodney."

"I'll see you tomorrow, sweetheart. Look after my nephew for me."

"I will."

I nod goodbye to the other guests and walk back to the suite. Fox took our key, and when I get there, the door's propped open. He's not in the room, and I sigh.

I don't want to stay here by myself, and I change into thick leggings, put on a sweater, wiggle my feet into the winter boots I had to buy for this weekend, and grab my parka out of the closet. The second keycard is in the folder on the table and I pocket it and let the door lock behind me.

People wander the lobby, some checking in, some sitting in front of the fireplace catching their breath after a day of traveling to reach their destination, some staring out the windows like I did.

The temperature outside is crisp, and I fill my lungs with the clean air, so different from the grit and pollution of the city.

The parking lot is full, and the airport shuttle idles under the stone canopy. I keep my head low and trudge around to the side of the building. Rodney's chalet has every amenity you can think of, and on this side, guests enjoy a large skating rink, a hot chocolate kiosk, and a full outdoor bar.

Everyone's happy, enjoying time with their families.

My mother and I are close, but Walter never felt like my

dad, and because of the age gap between Claudia and me, we never bonded when we were children. Maybe, if given a chance like Darcy and Fox, we could have gotten to know each other, but after Mom and Walter divorced, I rarely saw her.

A family that's intact is a foreign concept and I resigned myself to the knowledge that a having traditional family of my own wasn't meant to be.

I walk past the skating rink and head toward a copse of trees. There's no trail marker, but I won't go far and the bright lights of the rink will guide my way back.

Tears run down my cheeks. I'm not a crier by nature, and if someone asked me what I was crying about now, I honestly couldn't say. I hurt for Fox, the way he reared back, as if Spencer's advice had physically slapped him.

I suppose whatever it is has to do with Michelle. Everything that hurts Fox does.

Even though I was lonely, sometimes I wish they hadn't broken up. He hurt so terribly, and to keep him from it, I would have gladly sacrificed the friendship I have with him.

He's been a lifeline of sorts, filling my evenings and weekends when otherwise I'd be alone. Our friendship, up until now, has been uncomplicated and relaxed, asking nothing of each other but time and attention.

It never occurred to me that we could be more, and Fox never gave me any indication that he could fall in love with me. I liked feeding him home-cooked meals, sleeping with him on my couch, and watching over him. I took pleasure in giving him whatever he needed. At the time, I didn't consider I was paying a price that eventually I couldn't keep paying, that losing his friendship, no matter how that comes to be, will be devastating.

I walk deeper into the trees, the scent of wet and foliage foreign to a city girl like me. Snow covers my boots, and I sink up to my ankles. I can barely see the sky, the trees blocking my view, but what I can see is dark, stars shining. It reminds me of the night Fox brought me to the state park to help me get our story right.

It's beautiful, but I'm not sure if it's the way I'd want a man to propose.

I settle onto an old log and rest my head against a tree. I've never let myself daydream about marriage proposals. Even if a man asks, I'd say no. He wouldn't know me, wouldn't know my secrets. I couldn't in good faith accept a proposal, but if I were free to, the way Fox did it . . . holding me on the couch, his face tucked into the curve of my neck. All that was missing was love, and a ring, of course, but love is more important. I felt safe in his arms, but not loved. He gave his to another woman, and she still has it.

All I have to do is get through this weekend.

Men and women can't be friends forever. People in general are never friends all their lives. They grow, change, move on. One day Fox will fall in love again, and it will stick. His wife won't let him have a female friend and our friendship will be over. Might as well be sooner rather than later. Besides, once he pays me, I can put my own plans in motion. I can start living my life how I want, and that won't include Fox.

I lose track of time sitting out in the cold, the weight of the ring as heavy on my hand as it is in my heart.

CHAPTER SEVEN

Fox

I can't think of anything except getting away from the table. Away from Darcy's and Rodney's sympathetic expressions and the bewildered look in Posey's eyes. I forced Darcy and Rodney not to tell her what happened between Michelle and me. I don't want her pity. She already does that enough, thinking Michelle broke my heart when she left me.

There are all sorts of places to hide, but I go back to our room. Posey's scent saturates the air, the sugary vanilla she wears both comforts me and plants a yearning for her in my heart that gouges like a barb.

Agitated, I pace in a tight circle before leaving again and going to the bar that's separate from the dining room. I order a scotch and sit at a little table in the corner, letting the shadows hide me.

I can hear Darcy and Rodney now. I should just tell Posey and get it over with. Tell her what happened, but she already feels sorry enough for me and nothing can change the past. It wasn't only Spencer's comment about waiting to have children. The night, the whole fucking night, felt too real, like something that could actually happen, and it scared the hell out of me.

What would she say if I told her I was starting to have feelings for her?

Lynn and Spencer might have been brave enough to take that risk, but if Posey didn't feel the same, I'd lose the best thing that ever happened to me.

But if she did . . . God. Could I be that fortunate?

I leave a hundred under my empty glass and trudge back to our room. Posey might still be at dinner, but the skirt and blouse she wore are laying on the floor near the bed next to her heels. I look in the front closet and her boots and parka are gone.

She went outside.

Quickly, I shove my jacket on and push boots onto my feet. I ask the front desk if they saw a pretty blonde woman walk by, but that describes a quarter of the women who walk through the lobby every minute and they shake their heads, too busy checking in guests to care about someone they haven't seen.

The parking lot is full of cars, and I stop for a second, wondering if she rode the shuttle into town, but I don't think she would have left the resort without letting me know. She didn't seem mad, or even hurt. Confused, because she knows I haven't told her everything, but in the past year since Michelle broke up with me, she's never asked, simply been the support I needed her to be.

Despite the late hour, the skating rink is packed and the bright lights illuminate the puffy snowballs falling from the sky. The powder on the slopes tomorrow will be perfect.

"Did a blonde woman wearing a white parka walk by here?" I ask the kid working the hot chocolate kiosk.

He glances at me as he fills a cup and adds marshmallows

for a little girl waiting patiently, wobbling on figure skates. "I saw a woman go that way, but I don't remember what color her jacket was. She didn't look like she was in the mood to skate." The kid jerks his head toward a line of trees. He forgets about me and smiling, serves the girl her hot chocolate. She blushes.

Once I pass the rink, it's easy to find Posey's tracks in the snow. She didn't go on a hiking trail, instead, making her own way through the trees. I don't have to go very far to see her sitting on a log, leaning against another tree. Her hair is loose, her parka's hood catching most of it in the faux fur.

Tension drains out of me.

She turns when the brush snaps under my boots, and she lifts a mittened hand.

I sit next to her on the log. "Hey. What are you doing out here by yourself?"

The snowflakes are coming down thicker and faster now, and some fall on her cheeks, melting on her skin. A couple cling to her eyelashes and she blinks them away.

"I didn't know where you were and there's nothing to do in the room. It's nice out here. I don't spend time outside in the city."

"I'm sorry about dinner. I shouldn't have left you like that."

"It's okay. I know you're still hurting, and I don't blame you for leaving. Children are a personal decision. Spencer shouldn't have told you that."

"What did you say after I left?" I ask curiously. Posey and I never talked babies, mostly because we've never had a relationship where that's been okay. A conversation like that would bring us closer in a way that wasn't part of our friendship.

Come to think of it, our friendship all these years has been casual at best and superficial at worst. We've never talked about anything important, preferring to focus on work, our social lives, or lack of them, and sometimes not even speaking when we're together. Friends share intimate details about each other, but Posey and I never have.

That has to change.

I want it to change.

I claim this woman is my best friend, and I don't know her at all.

"I said since you're going to turn forty-one this year, you were feeling your age and didn't want to wait to have kids. There wasn't much they could say to that. They asked if we wanted to ski with them tomorrow, and I said sure. They seem like nice people and Spencer was sincerely sorry he made you upset."

"Darcy and Rodney didn't say anything?" It would be like my sister to tell Posey the truth to smooth the situation over.

"No. I didn't stay at the table long after you left. I looked for you, but you weren't in the room, so I came out here."

"I'm sorry."

She puts her hand on my shoulder. "It's okay, really. Michelle hurt you, and it's not something you can get over just because people think you should. You're entitled to as much time as you need. You don't talk to me about her, but you can, you know. If you ever wanted to."

"Thanks. I don't like talking about it. Saying things out loud makes them real, you know?"

She smiles, and I search her face, hoping for jealousy though I shouldn't admit that, but there's only empathy and understanding. "Keeping the truth buried lets you hope. She might change her mind, Fox. I know you said you didn't think she would ever want to try again, but when we get back to Avondale, you should call her."

I sigh and try to think of how to say what I want to say. "Posey, you know when you're with someone, you think about all of it. The future and all it entails."

Tentatively, she nods.

"But sometimes that future, that future is something you can have with anyone. The house, the kids, the dog, the family vacations." Frustrated, I get up off the log and kick at the snow. If I tell her what I really want to say, I'm going to spook her. I need to ease into this, let her get used to the idea of us being more than friends. I'm already there, but she's not, and if I rush her, I'll do the complete opposite of what I want to do. "When Michelle left me, I missed her, yes. But this past year, I realized I missed what I could have had more than I missed what I could have had with her. Do you understand what I'm saying?"

She bites her lip for a moment and then says, "I think so."

I nod. "Okay. Good. She hurt me, yeah, but the way she hurt me is different from the way you think. Our relationship was complicated and things happened between us I'll never forget, but that doesn't mean I still love her. So please stop thinking I do."

Posey watches me with careful eyes, and I swear to God with the snow falling down around her, her coat glowing in the hazy light, she's an angel.

"Let's go back to the room. We can order dessert and sit in the hot tub for a little while before we go to bed. It's been a long day."

"Okay. That sounds good."

Holding her hand, I help her off the log, and she tucks herself under my arm like she always has. We fit together, and I was so content I didn't think to try to understand what that meant.

We take turns in the bathroom changing into our suits—the sudden modesty uncomfortable between us—and she chooses a dessert from the room service menu. I call it in while she pours the champagne Darcy and Rodney had delivered in a gift basket in honor of our engagement.

It's late and I should let Posey get some sleep, but I don't want to miss one moment of this weekend. How the rest of our time here will play out is up to me, and if I don't handle it well, she'll start dating Paul. He's made it no secret he wants her.

"How come I've never seen you in a swimsuit before?" I ask as we carry the champagne and a plate that has a gigantic piece of chocolate cheesecake on it outside. She sets the champagne flutes on a table near the hot tub, takes off her robe, tosses it to the side, and steps in. Her skin prickles with goosebumps. Moaning, she sinks onto a bench and the bubbly water laps at her chin.

"When do we swim in the city?" she asks.

"Never."

"There you go."

I chuckle and set the champagne bottle and cheesecake next to our flutes and take off my own robe. I step into the hot tub and sit, letting the warm water fight off the chill. It's peaceful out here, and I lean back and close my eyes, blocking out the mountains as they gleam in the moon's light.

Posey scoots next to me and sips her champagne. I don't open my eyes, but I don't have to see her to know how she moves. The steaming water heightens the scent of her skin, and my cock hardens under my swim trunks. Keeping my hands off her is more difficult than closing the most lucrative deal of my career and doing this right has more at stake than letting a deal like that slip through my fingers.

"This was a good idea," she says.

I don't need to open my eyes to know she's trying a bite of the cheesecake, the fork tines scraping against the plate. "I have a lot of good ideas," I say, but I'm so relaxed the words come out barely more than a mumble.

My hands sway under the water with the current, and I accidentally brush my fingers along her thigh. Maybe not accidentally. She's the one sitting so close to me. It's not all my fault.

"Sometimes you do and sometimes you don't. Do you want a bite before I eat it all?"

"Gee, thanks," I tease her, cracking my eyes open in time to watch her lick her lips.

She holds out the fork and I open my mouth, forcing her to feed me. She does, and I close my lips around the bite without breaking eye contact. Her cheeks are dewy from the steam, but in the shadows, I can't tell if she's blushing. Flirting with her is something I've never done before, and I think I'm going to enjoy it.

She looks away and sips her champagne.

"Are you feeling better now?" I ask, resting my arm along the side of the tub and playing with her hair.

"I think so. It'd been a while since I've seen Darcy and Rodney, and I forgot how nice they are."

"Don't let Darcy fool you. She's going to be looking for any way she can to get out of losing this bet. I think we should practice, just in case we need to show off a little. Lynn and Spencer will be a buffer, but everyone will expect at least a couple of PDAs."

Posey winces, and I try not to take offense she thinks kissing me is so repulsive. She seemed pretty into it the night in her kitchen, so much into it, the kiss felt real.

I'll have to change her mind.

"How should we practice?" She drains her champagne glass.

"Come here and sit. We'll kiss for a little bit, then we can head inside."

"All right. I guess it wouldn't hurt."

She sits on the sliver of bench between my legs, but I want her to enjoy this and lift her into my lap. I wrap my arms around her, my hand pressed to the bare skin of her back.

"Is this okay?" I ask, my lips hovering just above hers.

The warm water laps at us, but the cool winter air nips at our shoulders. Steam billows out of the hot tub. I couldn't have ordered a more romantic setting.

"Yeah." She rests her hand against my chest and tilts her head.

Water droplets glisten on her skin and her tender lips tremble. She parts them in invitation, but I pause. "Tell me if you don't want me to do something."

She swallows. "Like what?"

"Like anything, Posey. How you feel is more important than the bet." My voice is a little sharper than I intended, but I would never do anything she doesn't want me to do.

"Okay. I promise."

"Good." Slowly, I lower my head and meet her lips with mine. She gasps, her warm breath saturated with sugar invading my senses, and I breathe her in as I push my tongue into her mouth, tasting the chocolate and champagne. She wraps her arms around my neck, her fingers forking through my hair.

My cock can't get any harder, and I know she feels it pressed against her thigh, but she doesn't pull away.

How were we friends all these years and I never knew how sweet she tasted, how warm and pliant she'd feel in my arms? I tighten my grip, and she moans.

I can't stop myself, and gently, so gently under the water, I cup her breast in my hand.

She rears back. "Fox."

I yank my hand away and draw in a ragged breath. "I'm sorry."

"It's not that. I mean, not all of it. We can't have sex."

Resting my forehead against hers, I mumble, "Yeah."

She turns in my lap, her legs bracketing my thighs, her breasts pushed into my chest. I try to find humor in it and fail. "Posey, this isn't better."

"I know. But sometimes, late at night, when you're alone, do you ever feel like something, anything, would be better than nothing?"

I hold her face between my hands and search her face. "Yeah, I do."

"Then a little something between us, this is better than feeling like that, isn't it?"

"Why does it have to be little? Posey, what if I told you—"

She presses a finger against my lips. "Don't. Please don't say something you'll regret. As long as we don't cross the line, we'll always be friends."

I grip her wrist. "What if I want more than friends?"

"I can't."

"Can't or don't?"

"Does it matter?"

"No, I guess not." Fuck yes, it matters, and I won't stop until I find out which one it is.

"Will you kiss me, Fox?" she asks, rubbing her lips over mine, pushing her body against me as a shiver runs through her.

"I'll give you whatever you want, whenever you want it. I mean it. All you have to do is ask."

We kiss until the water prunes our skin, until we're so exhausted it's a chore to climb out of the hot tub and dry off. She uses the bathroom to change into her pajamas, and my lips tingling, I pour a drink even though it's the last thing I want.

She comes out dressed in lounging pants and a tank top, her nipples hard. Red stains her cheeks when she looks down and sees what I do, and she crawls into bed, tugging the bedspread up to her chin.

"I can sleep on the floor or the loveseat," I say, stepping into the bathroom. I've pushed her boundaries enough for now, but I won't stop. She said can't, not that she doesn't want to, and it might not mean a goddamned thing to her, but her choice of words is everything to me.

I have to figure out is why she thinks she can't be in a relationship with me.

"Don't be silly. You'll hurt your back and this bed is big enough for both of us."

I'm not going to argue with her. The loveseat would be atrocious to sleep on and there's no way I could lie on the hardwood floor, even if I used the rug in front of the fireplace for padding. I brush my teeth and change out of my swim trunks, draping them over the shower track the way Posey's drying out her bikini.

She clicks off the lamp on the nightstand, and I slip between the cool, smooth sheets. I covered myself almost head to toe in a t-shirt and lounging pants. The less of my skin that can touch her, the better it is for me.

Despite the late hour, I can't fall asleep.

Posey isn't sleeping either, her foot moving slowly back and forth under the covers.

"Did I go too far?" My voice is rocky.

She rolls over onto her side and faces me. "No, but you have to think about what you're saying. We've been friends for a long time, and just because people like Lynn and Spencer make it work, that doesn't mean we can. I . . . don't want a family. After my mom left Walter and Claudia stayed with him, I decided I didn't want to take that risk. I lost a sister. I lost a stepfather who, up until then, had been a positive influence in my life. I love my mother, but her actions hurt a lot of people. I'm not going to follow in her footsteps."

"You're going to cut yourself off from being in a relationship because your mother was selfish?"

Sighing, she says, "It's not that she was selfish. Maybe she was and could have tried harder, but maybe she and Walter truly had run their course. You commit your entire life to your partner when you decide to have children, and those children trust they're going to have parents who will love them and do everything in their power to see to it they're cared for and happy. I'm not going to make promises I can't keep."

"Then you're going to spend your life alone? Posey, that doesn't sound right." I wiggle closer and wedge my leg between her thighs. Our bodies fit in a way we've never tested, never needed to on her couch watching a movie, and her cleft is warm through the material of my pajamas. I bury my face in her hair pretending to hug her, but I count to ten, hoping to keep my cock down. The cold air after we were finished in the hot tub worked well, and I wish we didn't feel so cozy. I wish this didn't feel so right.

She doesn't balk, only shakes her head, her hair rustling against her pillowcase. "You don't understand. Your parents are still together, and when you marry, it will be for keeps. So will Darcy. You've had that example. You know it's possible. All I know is if life gets hard, it's easier to bail than fight."

Any chance of my cock ruining this moment is gone. I don't have what she's going to need to be part of a thriving relationship. I didn't know that's how she felt, and I'm too emotionally exhausted to do anything about it. Rubbing her nose with mine, I say, "One day you'll find a man who will fight enough for both of you."

"But you're saying you won't be that man."

No one can say Posey isn't intuitive, and I've always loved how talking to her is so simple. Now it cuts to the quick, a knife in my heart. I don't need to explain what she told me changes what I thought we could have had. I need the woman I fall in love with to be all in, completely, because I'm tired and I can't fight alone. "When Michelle walked, I let her go. It didn't matter how much I'd loved her up until then or what we'd gone through to reach that point. She said she wanted to leave and I let her. Because you're right, sometimes it *is* easier to let it go. I would never try to keep a woman where she didn't want to be, and maybe your stepdad is the same way."

I roll onto my back.

She follows, her upper body resting on my chest. "The woman who falls in love with you won't want to leave, if she's the right one."

"And the man who loves you won't let you go, either, but if you're counting on him to hold you together, that won't be me. I'm not strong enough to be anybody's glue."

She snuggles into my side and lays her head on my shoulder. "Friends?"

I kiss the top of her head. "Always."

I wake with my legs tangled with hers and my lips a centimeter away from her mouth. She's sleeping deeply, her eyes flickering behind her eyelids watching a dream I can't see, her face pinched with worry. Her hand grips my t-shirt, and she whispers gibberish I can't decipher.

I've never known her to have nightmares, and needing to soothe, I nuzzle her lips with mine. As she wakes, she participates and lets me in, and I slip my tongue into her mouth, deepening the kiss.

Her eyes flutter open. "Is this more practice?" she asks, wrapping her arms around my neck.

"I think I need all I can get," I say, settling on top of her and propping myself up with my arms on either side of her head.

"This looks good." Her fingers brush at the hair near my temples.

"What?"

"You have a little grey, here and here," she says, the skin around her eyes crinkling in amusement when I scowl.

"Why is forty considered old?"

"I don't think people would think of you that way if—"

"If I had a wife and kids, I know. Rodney seems to be doing okay, living the single life." My uncle never married and doesn't have kids. He was content to open the chalet using investment money my grandpa gave him, and he's been living it up ever since.

"He knew what he wanted, and what he didn't," Posey says. "It's mature, if you ask me, instead of getting married and then divorced because you made a mistake. Besides, you get a pass because you're a guy. I'm thirty-four, and if I wanted to get pregnant, I'd be considered high-risk. Technically, I'm older than you are."

"Is that like dog years?"

She laughs. "Are you calling me a bitch now?"

I smack a kiss on her mouth. "Never. You want to shower first? We're still hitting the slopes today?"

"Yeah, with Lynn and Spencer. What about tonight?"

"You've never skied before, have you?" I don't remember her saying she ever had.

"No."

"Then you might want to soak in the hot tub again, maybe get a massage at the spa. You're going to feel pretty banged up after a few hours on the slopes, but we'll have time to relax before Rodney's birthday party."

"I'm going to try to stay on my feet."

She's beautiful, her blonde hair spread out on the pillow, her eyes full of sleep, her lips puffy from my good-morning kisses.

"I'll help you."

Her smile transforms her face, and my heart lurches.

"Promise you won't let me fend for myself?"

I lower my full weight onto her and shove my hands under her pillow. "I promise, Posey. I promise."

I seal that promise with a kiss.

"You know, for just a second, I thought you asked Posey to pretend to be your fiancée this weekend just to win the bet," Darcy says, adjusting her sunglasses on her face.

Luckily, mine are already covering my eyes, hiding the guilt that would have given me away. "What made you change your mind?"

"I was worried about both of you last night, and I went to your room. You didn't answer when I knocked and I used my master key to get in. I saw you guys in the hot tub making out. There's no way you two would've been doing that if this was a sham. I'm really happy for you, Fox. Posey's wonderful."

"You shouldn't be invading our privacy like that," I say, but I'm not mad. There's nothing Darcy could have walked in on that would have ruined the bet.

The sky's bright blue without a hint of clouds. The slopes are packed with excited skiers who are happy with the snow that fell last night and the perfect temperatures. Lynn and Spencer should be around here somewhere—they went back to their room after breakfast and said they'd meet us in a few minutes. Posey's still inside, using the bathroom one more time before it's too inconvenient to stop for a break.

"What? Can't a sister worry about her brother? It's not like you left dinner in the best frame of mind. Since you and Posey are the real deal, you should tell her. She's going to want to know what happened. She has no idea, and that isn't right."

"Why? It doesn't have anything to do with us."

Her mouth drops open. "Are you serious? If that happened to her with another man, are you saying you wouldn't want to know? It's a life-changing, traumatic experience. She deserves to know."

I've heard that tone, the tone that says she's going to meddle in my life whether I want her to or not. "Don't you dare tell her."

"Somebody has to," she mutters.

"Tell who what?" Posey asks, coming up behind us.

"About the big surprise Fox planned for you at the party tonight," Darcy says smoothly, never mind that now I have to come up with something that would warrant such a huge announcement.

Posey frowns. "You know I don't like surprises."

"You'll love this one," Darcy says, her tongue tucked into her cheek.

"Why aren't you working?" I ask my sister, irritated.

She shoves me, but I don't budge an inch. "Uncle Rodney gave me the day off so I can hang out with you guys. I don't get to see you very much, you know. You're always working. Posey, you're going to have to stop him from working seventy-hour weeks."

"He doesn't now, but more vacations like this would be welcome," Posey says, gazing at the mountains towering around us.

"Let's enjoy this one, then," I say, rubbing my hands together in mock excitement.

I don't care much for skiing—I'd rather sit by the fire in the lobby and read a book—but it will give us something to do for most of the day. Lynn and Spencer are more experienced skiers, and they join Darcy and me. I give Posey a quick kiss goodbye, trusting her safety to Austin. He'll help her with the basics: finding the right sized skis, how to use the poles, and how to slow down and stop. The lesson is located at the bunny hill, a towrope available to bring them back to the top after each practice run.

I don't want to leave her alone, but she looks like she's having fun, high-fiving a little girl who was able to stop without falling over.

"You should tell her," Darcy says, needling me again while we wait for the ski lift.

"No."

"She's going to want children, then what are you going to say? That you're too scared to try again? She's going to regret she said yes, and it will be your fault. She already thinks she's your rebound relationship and this will validate her fears."

I raise my sunglasses and narrow my eyes. "She told you that?"

"Yeah, and even though I defended you, I thought it made sense. I was going to talk to you about it, but then I saw you guys last night in the hot tub and decided she's just confused. But that's another reason you need to talk to her, Fox."

"We did last night, not about that exact thing, but close enough. I know you want us to be happy, but there are some things I need to sort through myself."

"She shouldn't doubt you love her."

"I tell her all the time. I don't know what more I can do. Come on, we're next."

Racing me down the slope cuts off our conversation, and I'm grateful for the time to think.

Posey doesn't know I'm falling in love with her. The

touches and excuses to kiss her are part of her lie, but they're real to me. But I don't know what to do with what she told me last night. If she won't let herself be in a relationship, how can I get around that? Do I have the mental and emotional energy to try? I may not have a choice.

Remembering my promise not to let her ski alone for too long, Darcy and I make one last run up the hill. When I find her, she's laughing with Austin as they help a group of children down the bunny hill for the first time. She's turned from student to teacher, and I don't miss the appreciative glances he throws her way. I'd tease Darcy if she was here with me, but she went on to ski with Lynn and Spencer before she helps put Uncle Rodney's party together.

"Looks like you could teach me a thing or two," I say at the bottom of the hill where they're lining the children up at the towrope.

Posey grins. "Hey! Austin said I passed with a gold star."

He nods. "You're going to bring her to an intermediate hill? She'll be great! A little wobbly at the bottom when she tries to slow down, but nothing more practice won't help."

"You wanna try?" I ask, wrapping my arm around her and leaning in for a kiss. She tilts her head, and I press my lips gently to hers, earning a collective groan from the kids watching, and an, "Eww, gross," from one particularly disgusted little boy.

"I'd love to."

We meet Darcy, Lynn, and Spencer who are waiting for the ski lift, and we decide to do a hill that Posey can handle together. At the top, I pull out my cell and snap a selfie of all of us, and one kind skier offers to take a photo using my phone and also one with Darcy's who said she would love to use it in the lodge's promotional materials.

"Nervous?" I ask Posey, but she's poised, gripping her poles, ready to go.

"Nope. I got this," she says, and already she's pushing off, a shriek flying out of her mouth as she quickly picks up speed.

Instead of following her down, I film her with my phone, and I grin like a proud idiot as she nears the bottom without falling.

She has a difficult time slowing down like Austin said she would, and I stop recording, shove my cell into my pocket, and take off, hoping to catch up with her before she crashes into someone or something.

I'm halfway down the hill when she loses her balance and falls over, her body crumpling in the snow.

"Fuck! Posey!" I yell, and people look at me, not appreciating the expletive that shoots past my lips.

By the time I reach the bottom, a well-meaning gentleman is kneeling next to her, and I drop to my knees, my chest heaving.

"Posey?" I ask, my mouth dry. I don't want to move her in case she needs medical attention.

Suddenly, she rolls over, laughing like a lunatic. "That was so much fun!"

The guy chuckles and hefts to his feet. Posey's gorgeous—of course he wouldn't be mad—but I try to bank a rush of inexplicable anger. "You scared the hell out of me. Don't you ever do that again."

I cover her mouth with mine, shaken that something so innocent could leave me so fucking terrified. I'm bruising her lips, and she whimpers.

Darcy's, Lynn's, and Spencer's hooting echo through the air, and reluctantly, I release her.

"Get a room, you two." Spencer says, spraying snow as he

stops a couple feet away. "It looks like someone's done skiing for the day."

"Fox, I'm sorry. It was a joke."

"A bad one. I thought you hurt yourself."

She struggles to sit up, and I help her, a hand to her back.

"I'm sorry," she says again. "I'm okay, really."

I pull my glove off and touch her cheek. Everything disappears—the blue skies and blinding sun, my sister, Lynn and Spencer, even the other skiers who were waiting to see if Posey was hurt. None of that matters as I gaze into her blue eyes.

She licks her lips, waiting for me to yell at her some more.

"There are things I need to say that you're not ready to hear," I murmur, and I don't care who can hear me. "Things I'm not ready to say, but if I don't, you're going to slip right through my fingers."

She scoots back, trying to put physical distance between me and my words. I know the reasons she thinks she can't be with me, and I told her I wasn't strong enough to be the man she's going to need, but *goddammit*. I might not be that man right now, but I can be. I'll have to be because I need her in my life. I have to convince her we belong together.

"Don't pull away from me. Just don't."

"Fox—"

"Give us a chance. Please. You owe our friendship that much."

She doesn't owe me jack shit, not the way I've used her, but she nods. "Okay."

Satisfied she'll at least talk to me later, I kiss her, gently, tenderly, my fear and anger a twisted, fucked-up mess in my heart, and by the time I'm steady enough to let her go, everyone is gone.

CHAPTER EIGHT

Posey

Fox helps me detach the skis from my boots and we carry them back to the rental area.

On the way to our room, he's different, quiet in a way I'm not used to. We've always been able to spend peaceful evenings together. He's said his favorite time of day is when he could relax with me after work and decompress, but his silence now is full things he wants to say and he trying to decide if it's a good idea to say them. I can already tell him it's not.

It's not a good idea, but what does it matter now? The line I thought was there, the line between friendship and something else, that line is gone, or if it ever existed, Fox stepped right over it without one single thought to how I'd react, how I would cope.

Did I want him to step over that line? I don't know. I didn't know until he asked me to marry him, that stupid question I wished with all my heart was real.

The ring on my finger, I want it to be real.

The engagement party tonight, I want it to be real.

I want Fox to be my fiancé, but you know what, it never would have happened without this bet, and I'm angry he can't see it. That we would always have just been friends until one of us met someone else the way he was so nonchalant about leaving me behind the minute he met Michelle. Then we would have been less than friends.

Inside our room, the huge bed mocks me, the pillows plumped and the comforter smoothed, just waiting for Fox to draw it back and ruin what little friendship we have left that could be in any way salvageable.

I change out of the leggings and sweater I wore under my jacket and snow pants into a pair of yoga pants and a matching t-shirt. Fox booked me a massage and time at the salon, and I have half an hour before my appointment.

He doesn't say anything, simply changes into his own lounging clothes. He hasn't told me what he'll do while I'm at the spa, nap maybe, and he sits on the edge of the bed while I comb the knots out of my hair.

"You're mad," he says, his head tilted in speculation.

"I'm not mad."

"You're acting mad."

I meet his eyes in the mirror. "I told you I don't want a relationship."

"But you said yes when Paul asked you out. Do you prefer him over me, Posey? If that's all it is, I'll step aside, no questions asked."

"I don't know why he told you. It's none of your business."

"'Told' is putting it mildly. You could try gloat. That might fit a little better. He's in love with you and hates me for having this weekend with you, so if you return his feelings and you were just playing me for the money—"

I twirl around and face him directly. "How is this my fault?

Because I wanted compensation for the weekend? You can afford it. Hell, you can afford to let Darcy win. It was you who decided to drag me into your sibling rivalry. I like Darcy. You should tell her the truth."

"I don't want what I told her to be a lie."

"You want more than friends," I say flatly, gripping my hairbrush.

"I want more than friends," he echoes, telling me what I want to hear and breaking my heart in the process.

"What about protecting our friendship? No one stays friends with their exes. We'll lose what we have. Are you sure you want to risk it?"

"There's no chance of that. When we get married, it'll be for keeps. That's it."

"You don't even know me."

Fox pushes off the bed and walks barefoot across the floor. He stops in front of me, a tender look in his eyes that I can't let affect me.

I don't dare for one second think this could work between us. I'm broken in a way men don't tolerate. Not men who want families, and Fox will, sooner rather than later. I may have been blindly reaching last night, grappling for an excuse that sounded even remotely plausible, but men like Fox are made for t-ball games with their sons and dances with their daughters.

He skims his fingers down my temple, along my cheek and neck to rest his hand on my shoulder. "That's my fault, and I know it is. But keep this ring, turn my fake proposal into the real thing, and I promise that I'll spend the rest of our lives discovering every facet that makes you who you are."

I lift my chin, my bottom lip trembling. "No."

The light dims in his eyes and he steps away. "Okay. I won't ask you again. I'm sorry. I thought with the kisses and the—

Well, I guess I wanted to feel something that wasn't there. Do you want to leave? I can think of something to tell Rodney and Darcy."

I sniffle. "No. I'll see this through."

"Right. For the money."

I put up the shield. The shield that Audra has so conveniently said I don't need, but she knows less of me than Fox does.

"Yeah. For the money."

Fox's money is the only way I'm going to be able to get what I want, and I won't feel bad using it.

Lowering my head, I grab my purse off the table by the door and without another word, step into the hallway. Let him think what he wants. It's not my fault if he calls me a gold digger. He wasted years of our friendship when he could have gotten to know me, then maybe, had he proposed and meant it, I would have believed it.

I sit through my massage, only because Fox was right and my muscles were starting to stiffen up, and I let the stylist cut an inch off my hair and revive the blonde shimmer that hides the lifeless color of my original shade. After she dries and curls it, she pins it into a pretty updo that I would have had a difficult time doing on my own. She calls me Mrs. Caldwell, and I don't correct her.

When she's finished, she hands me off to a cosmetologist who applies my makeup and accentuates my eyes with a dark grey eyeliner that will go well with the evening dress I brought for the party.

I linger in the hallway outside the spa, reluctant to go back to the room. I can't be afraid of Fox or avoid him. We have one more show to put on tonight, and in the morning after breakfast, we can pack up our things and leave.

I take my time walking back to our room, but Fox isn't here.

There's a magnum of champagne sitting in an ice bucket and two sparkling flutes waiting on the table near the sliding glass doors that let out to the hot tub. On cream card stock, Fox wrote in his masculine script, *I'm sorry. I know apologies aren't enough, but they're all I have to give you. I'll see you tonight in the ballroom at seven. Fox.*

He's changing elsewhere. Maybe he'll arrange to sleep somewhere else too.

Sipping on the champagne, I change into my dress and remember all the fun Fox and I used to have. Singing in my kitchen while cooking a meal. The weekend sleepovers when we would fall asleep on my couch. But during all those hours we spent together, we never took the time to get to know each other.

He didn't deny there was more to him and Michelle than simply breaking up, and he didn't offer any explanation. He doesn't want me to know. I can't blame him for that. There are things I've kept from him too. He doesn't know I go to therapy. He doesn't know I keep a journal. He doesn't know the real reason I've cut myself off from having a relationship. My mother certainly doesn't help, but she's only part of it, the part I felt most comfortable telling him. I don't have the role models he and Darcy do.

But he never once asked me over dinner, "Hey, Posey, do you want children someday?" and I could have said, "Yes, I'd like to have a couple of kids." That would have led him to ask, "Then why haven't you started a family?" and I would have said, "Because I can't." I can imagine the conversation we would have had after that and he could have asked someone else to pretend to love him, except I don't have to pretend.

There's a chance he could still want me after he knows, but I'd like to hang on to some semblance of friendship after this weekend and not lose it over the could-have-beens.

I can hear the music before I reach the ballroom. The large dance floor is empty except for a few balloons that skitter when someone cuts across it, and the tables along the edges are crowded with people. A band plays on stage, a Bruce Springsteen song if I'm guessing correctly, and the lights are dim. Not too dark, but dark enough the room feels intimate despite being packed with guests who want to wish Rodney a happy birthday.

A set of French doors lets out to a stone terrace, and a couple is already taking advantage, leaning against the balustrade, kissing, the mountains a majestic and romantic background.

"There you are," Darcy exclaims, Austin following her and looking handsome dressed in a suit. "Fox said you'd be a little late."

"I spent too much time at the spa," I say, accepting a glass of champagne a passing waiter offers me. Holding the flute will give me something to do with my hands. I didn't bring a purse. I didn't think I'd need any money and if I need to get into the room, I can use Fox's keycard or we'll end up leaving the party together the way a happily engaged couple would.

"It was worth it. You're gorgeous, but are you okay? You look peaked."

"Skiing wiped me out. I'm going to sleep well tonight."

Fox joins us, and I tilt my head, asking for a kiss. He pecks my cheek and says, "I don't want to ruin your lipstick."

"That's thoughtful," I say, but my tone sounds like I didn't think it was thoughtful at all.

Darcy hears it and narrows her eyes.

"Do you want to dance, Posey?" Fox asks over the silence that could turn uncomfortable quickly.

"Give her your surprise first," Darcy says. "I want to see her reaction."

"Oh, you don't have to—" I start. I don't want Fox to give me anything else. Nothing else he could turn against me and probably will.

"I want to," he says, sliding out a long, black velvet box out of the pocket of his suit coat. He flicks it open and inside lays a beautiful platinum and aquamarine necklace that matches the ring on my finger. The necklace must be worth thousands of dollars.

I shake my head. "I can't accept that."

He frowns. "Why not?"

"It's too expensive."

He laughs, catching Darcy's and Austin's eyes. "She's not used to the fact that my money is her money now."

"It's a lot to wrap my mind around," I admit, skimming my fingers over the stones.

Darcy squeezes my arm. "That's why you're perfect for my brother. I'm so happy for you both."

Fox fastens the necklace around my neck, his fingers brushing my skin, and heat simmers in my belly. Looking over my shoulder, I say, "Thank you."

"You're welcome. Dance with me."

The band begins to play a slow song, and I have no choice but to set my empty flute on a table near the dance floor and step into his arms. Fox holding me is as natural as breathing, but it's painful, too. Nothing that feels this good should hurt.

"Posey, tell me what I should do. I hurt you and I don't know how or why or how to fix it."

I don't want him to fix it. I don't want him to try. He'll only make things worse.

"I want us to be friends. I want us to go back to the way we were before you asked me to do this."

"Why? I don't understand. I know you feel what I do when

I kiss you. You feel it right now while I'm holding you. Why are you fighting it?"

I turn this on him, because it's him too, isn't it? This isn't all me. I'm hiding only half our secrets. "I'll stop fighting what I feel for you if you tell me what happened between you and Michelle."

"I *have* told you. She wanted to leave me and I let her go. I loved her and it was hard on me, but I'm over it, Posey."

"No, you're not, because that's not all that happened. If you can't tell me, you have no business trying to start something between us. You want to think you're over it but you're not, and I have my own problems to deal with, okay? I'm not . . . I'm not emotionally available. I can be your friend, but that's all I can give you."

"Then I guess I'll have to be happy with what I can get."

"I guess you will."

We finish the dance, me resting my cheek on his shoulder, him trailing his fingers up and down my spine, two people so in love they've blocked out everything else.

The second the last note fades, I excuse myself, and not stopping to talk to anyone, walk out onto the terrace. The temperature is too cold to be outside for long, but I need the fresh air and a break from Fox's musky cologne. The sun has set and the mountains glow under the moonlight as I try to calm my nerves and find peace. It's easy to forget there's a huge world out there and I am just a small, insignificant part of it.

"Posey, are you having fun?"

Rodney steps out of the shadows holding a cigarette, the orange tip glowing in the dark.

"Yes, thank you. I'm sorry we didn't find you earlier. Happy birthday."

"Thanks. The years have a way of sneaking up on you."

"Yeah, they do. Especially when you feel like you haven't done much with the years you've been given."

He chuckles. "That's true. I've been accused of partying my life away. No obligations but to the people I employ, no close family, though I love Darcy like my own daughter. They think being unattached is a bad thing, but I think it means you don't run the risk of letting anybody down."

Leaning against the ice-cold balustrade, I ask, "Is that why you never married? Because you're afraid you'll let your wife down? People do, you know. That's just life."

Rodney takes another puff from his cigarette, stamps it out under his dress shoe, and wraps the butt in a tissue. He pockets it, saying, "I was in love once, 'bout thirty years ago."

"What happened?"

He rests his arms next to mine and stares out over the mountains. "She wanted to get married. I didn't. I didn't know what a piece of paper had to do with us being together, being happy. She couldn't accept it and gave me an ultimatum. We get married, or she'd leave. I let her go."

"Do you regret it now?"

He gestures to the moon in the sky, to the resort and all his guests. "Would you, if you had all this?"

I pause and think. What can fill a hole in your heart? "Yeah, I think I would."

He blows out a breath. "I don't know why it mattered to her so much. She could have been here, standing where you are, right now. We still could have had the life we wanted. We wouldn't have been any more in love with a signed piece of paper."

"Did she ever marry?"

"Yeah, 'bout three years after she left me. Popped out a couple of kids and got a divorce a few years after that."

"That's too bad."

"I was bitter for a long time. I'm a petty bastard when I want to be and I thought she got what she deserved. Now I just feel sorry for her."

I nudge his arm with mine. "Maybe she feels sorry for you."

He looks at me in surprise. "Why would she do that?"

"Because she took a chance, and even if it didn't work out, she still tried. You could have found a compromise. A non-denominational minister and married her here at the resort or found a justice of the peace in town. She wanted it legal so she could have your name because she loved you. You denied her that."

"What about what I wanted?"

"She should have compromised, too. A long engagement, maybe. But it sounds like she wanted kids and sometimes a woman can't wait."

"The years slipping by thing, huh?" he asks.

"Yeah, something like that."

"Posey, can I ask you something?"

Lifting a shoulder, I say, "Sure?"

"I know you and Fox aren't engaged."

I swallow. "That's not a question."

"No, I guess it's not. I just wanted to put it out there. You might be able to fool Darcy into believing she lost the bet, but I know Fox. He loves you, I can see that whenever you're together, but he's not ready and wouldn't have proposed. Not for real. What I want to know is if you're going to wait for him or not."

"I've told him I only want to be friends. He'll announce our breakup in a few weeks."

"Okay," he says, sighing. "Fox is lonely. He doesn't let many people in—"

"Including me," I point out, maybe a little defensively, but it's not my fault Fox won't talk to me.

Rodney tilts his head in acknowledgment. "And I wanted to know what to expect after you two leave tomorrow. He had you when Michelle left him. He won't have anyone when you do the same."

I scoff. "Rodney, you can't leave a place if you're not already there. You just said he's not ready, and he treats me like he's not. I'm not going to let you make me feel guilty for protecting myself. Before we flew out, he was talking about moving to Seattle and opening a branch of the company there. I told him it was a good idea. I'm sure he still sees Michelle everywhere he goes, and a new city will help him move on. If this engagement was real, it'd only be a crutch. Once he's healed, he won't need me anymore, and that's not a position I want to be in."

"That's fair, it really is, and you could be right. I wouldn't ask you to do anything you aren't comfortable with, but when you're back in Avondale, can you do me a favor?"

"Maybe."

"Don't stop being his friend. It will be a natural thing to hide, but don't let him, and don't do it to him, either, because I don't think he's strong enough to fight. Not right now."

"If he tells me to leave him alone, I'll have no choice."

"We all have choices, but sometimes we don't pick the right one. You mean something to him, and he'll listen to you."

"Then why won't he tell me about Michelle? Why won't you? You know what happened. So does Darcy. You're deliberately keeping me in the dark."

"Because sometimes terrible things should stay buried. Digging up old bones doesn't do anything but keep skeletons in the closet."

"You're right, and that's why when Fox asks for more, I can't give it to him. I've been trying for years to keep my own skeletons buried. And I can be petty too. I'm not going to give him mine if he can't give me his." I pause. "Happy birthday, Rodney."

"Thanks. You got the birthday part right."

He steps into the ballroom, and it's only after I'm alone do I realize how cold I am standing out here in the dark, snow starting to fall.

"Hey, there you are. Rodney's going to cut his cake, come on," Darcy says, poking her head out the terrace doors. "You must be freezing without a coat."

"Thanks. I don't want to miss cake." I try to sound cheerful but come across tired and in a poor mood at best.

"Can I ask you a question?" she says as we weave our way around Rodney's guests toward the front of the ballroom.

There's a lot of that going around. "Yeah, sure."

"When you and Fox get married, can I be a bridesmaid? I think it's kind of customary for the bride to ask her fiancé's sister, but I wanted to check with you."

My heart aches, and I'm mad at Fox all over again. So many people are going to get hurt after this weekend. "Of course, Darcy. I would love to have you stand up with me. Your approval means a lot, it really does."

She grins. "Awesome! This is going to be so much fun. It's wonderful seeing Fox so happy again. You did that, and I'm grateful."

"He would have found someone, eventually. You know that."

"Yeah, but I'm glad it's you."

"Thanks."

Rodney's standing at the front of the ballroom, and Fox is already there. He didn't come look for me, so maybe Rodney told him I needed a minute alone. I slip to his side and casually, he puts his arm around me. I lean in.

Sparklers burn on the top of a three-tiered chocolate cake,

and we sing Happy Birthday while they fizzle out and die. Rodney looks happy, and if we wouldn't have had the conversation we just had ten minutes ago, I never would have suspected he carried around a broken heart.

While the waitstaff passes around more champagne, he rattles off a quick speech, thanking us for being here and helping him celebrate. "But tonight isn't just for me," he continues. "My nephew brought his fiancée to the party. Fox, Posey, come over here and let everyone get a look at you."

I glare at him, but he ignores it, gesturing with a quick roll of his hand for us to join him in front of his guests.

"Sorry," Fox mutters in my ear, but I don't have time to reply.

We stand at the front of the ballroom with Rodney who raises his champagne glass in our direction. "Like many of us, Fox has gone through some shit."

Fox freezes, and I reach up onto my toes and kiss his cheek. "Easy. It's okay."

I might be mad at him for keeping secrets and for sucking me into his lies, but that doesn't mean I want him hurt.

"Sometimes you wonder if Fate has it in for you or what you did in a past life that turned Karma into such a bitch," Rodney continues.

The crowd laughs.

"But then something happens, and all the misery is worth it. You meet someone. You fall in love, and that person, who you love with all your heart, they give you the ultimate gift. They love you for who you are. Not what you can do for them or the material things you have, but they love you for you." Rodney runs his finger through the frosting on the top tier of his cake and holds it up to the crowd. "And the icing on the cake? They not only love you for you, but they gather all your flaws, buff them and shine them up until they aren't flaws anymore. They're diamonds made out of coal because those flaws make you who you are, and that person you were fortunate enough to meet, that person loves all of you. That's what Fox found with Posey. She loves every bit of dirt on that boy, and trust me, there's a lot of dirt. But she loves him, and I know she won't try to change him into something he's not meant to be. Thank you, Posey, and welcome to the family."

He kisses my cheek, and the microphone picks up my "Thanks, Rodney. That was beautiful."

"Now, let's eat some cake and get drunk!" Rodney hollers, and everyone in the ballroom cheers.

Fox and I find a place with Lynn and Spencer at their table, and I sit in Fox's lap, resting my elbow on his shoulder. He wraps his arms around my waist and whispers in my ear, "Christ. I am so sorry about that."

I rub my fingers along his scruffy jaw and say, "It's okay. He's happy we're together."

"Yeah, he is."

Tentatively, I lower my head and press my lips to his, barely moving in case what I said earlier changed his mind about us. Rodney's speech touched my heart. I *do* love Fox, and would knowing what happened between him and Michelle destroy what we have? What Fox wants us to have?

The secret I keep tucked away will ruin us, but no one said I need to say anything. At least, not right now. Why can't I have this small sliver of time before I have to tell him?

Fox breaks the kiss. "Don't do it if you don't mean it."

"There are things we don't know about each other. I'll accept yours if you accept mine."

"Posey, there's nothing you could tell me that would make me change how I feel about you."

"Don't say it if you don't mean it."

His arms tighten around my waist. "I mean it."

He can't possibly, and that will be my burden when he knows the truth.

I kiss him again, and he groans against my lips.

"How long do we have to stay here?" he mumbles, his hand moving from my waist to my leg where he plays with the edge of my stocking.

My heartbeat quickens. Tonight we'll do more than pretend to be engaged. "This is our last night here. We should be polite."

"Yeah, you're right."

We eat cake and chat with Darcy and Austin and Lynn and Spencer. Rodney stops by to say a quick hello before moving on to speak with his other guests. As the night goes on, the crowd gets tipsier and tipsier and the band becomes louder and louder. Darcy and Austin hit the dance floor, and Lynn and Spencer throw their manners aside and make out at our table between bites of cake and sips of champagne.

All the while, my sense of anticipation grows, and it's part excitement and part apprehension. I want to make love to Fox, but once we do, I can forget about any line, blurred or otherwise. The line will completely disappear, and nothing, *nothing*, will bring us back to this point in time, when right now we're only two people figuring out how to love each other and if the outcome is worth the risk.

"Let's head out." Fox has to yell in my ear for me to hear him, and I drain my glass. I haven't had that much to drink but my blood hums.

He sweeps me into his arms like a bride, and several people hoot and clap. It's a little unnerving because I can't remember him ever picking me up before, but I snuggle into his chest, not taking a single second of tonight for granted. There's no easy way out of the ballroom, and he has to walk around the dance floor to reach an exit. It's a relief to get away from the band. My ears are ringing and my throat's scratchy from having to raise my voice to be heard when I spoke to Lynn and Spencer.

He carries me down the quiet corridor to our suite and sets me on my feet. Trapping me against the wall, he rests one arm over my head and braces his other hand over my shoulder. "I want to make love to you, but if you don't want to, then you have to tell me."

His green eyes are solemn and serious. Stubble covers his jaw, and in his suit, he's delectable. I could say no and he could go back to the ballroom and have his choice of women, but that isn't why I say yes.

I want him too, no matter the consequences, and my heart knows there will be many.

"Please, Fox."

He blows out a breath and brushes his thumb over my cheek. "I won't hurt you. I promise."

"I know."

He opens our door with his keycard, and we step into the dark room lit only by the moonlight glowing through the window.

Trepidation and desire swirl around my stomach, and my hands tremble when I pour more of the champagne I drank while I dressed. Fox steps behind me and places his hands on my shoulders, rubbing his lips against the side of my neck. I tilt my head to give him better access, and as his lips linger, he pulls the zipper of my dress down.

I don't stop him, yet it seems with every rasp of every tooth he's waiting for me to tell him this is all a mistake.

The zipper runs out of teeth. He pushes the thin straps down my arms and the dress slides to the floor in a cloud of navy satin and tulle. I still look out the window, the mountains shimmering silver and there's nothing else but snow.

"Look at me," he rasps, helping me step out of my dress,

and I turn and stand in front of him wearing nothing but panties, my garter and stockings, a strapless bra, and the jewelry he's claimed me with. "You're beautiful."

"Thank you."

I look down at the floor until he raises my head with a finger under my chin. He covers my lips with his, pulling me to him, a hand pressed to my back.

One summer a few years ago, I bought a pint of strawberries. There was one in the middle of the plastic carton, huge, bright red, and it looked delicious. I took a bite, but the center was rotten, and gagging, I threw the rest in the trash.

That's how I feel when Fox looks at me. He sees perfection, but I'm not, and one day he's going to nibble away enough to uncover the truth and like the strawberry, he'll throw me into the garbage.

I try to stop thinking about it and undo his tie, letting the ends hang down his chest as I unbutton his shirt. He's not wearing an undershirt, and I splay my hands over his bare chest that's sparse with hair. His skin is hot, and his heart thumps erratically under my palm.

Fox's body is like a road I've traveled many times in the daylight. I know the curves, the potholes to avoid. I know where the shoulder is too narrow to pull over if I need to stop. In the dark, the road turns into something I can't navigate, and I have to slow down or I'll go too fast and crash and burn.

"Do you want to go to bed?" he asks, toeing his dress shoes off his feet.

"Yes." I finish my champagne and set the glass near Fox's note.

If he wrote one in the morning, what would it say?

I sit on the edge of the bed and he kneels at my feet and unbuckles my heels. Once he's tossed them aside, he unsnaps my stockings and rolls them down my legs, his gentle touch setting my skin on fire.

I skim my fingers through his hair, over his cheeks and down his neck. I've never touched him this way before, and now I eagerly memorize every inch. I need to remember.

It's almost as if he needs to do the same. Gripping my ankle, he trails kisses from my calf to the inside of my knee, to my thigh, where he stops at the edge of my panties. "Will you stand up?"

He's on his feet now, but instead of following, I undo the buckle of his dress pants. He's wearing boxer briefs, and this is familiar territory. I don't know when we dropped the modesty —sometime before he asked me what I wanted to eat while I was using the bathroom—and changing in front of each other has been a common occurrence for many years. I know the brands he favors, know without looking how they mold to his tight butt, how his thighs strain the material. But I've never glimpsed what another woman would see, never been privy to what he uses to give a woman pleasure during the most intimate act two people can share.

He guides my hand to his hard shaft, and it surges under my touch. It shouldn't, but his size surprises me. Nothing about Fox is small. Not his body, nor his personality. Not his ideas, or how much he enjoys life. He even mourns bigger, harder, more intensely, than anyone I have ever known.

"Don't be scared. I promised I wouldn't hurt you." He nudges me to my feet. "Do you trust me?"

The truth spills unbidden out of my mouth. "No."

"Then I'll have to earn it."

He crushes his mouth to mine, our teeth clicking together with the force.

It's been so long since I've been with a man, I've forgotten what to do. Gingerly, I push my hands under the waistband of his briefs and cup his cock in my hands. He hisses. His skin is so soft and the tip of his cock is already wet with pre-cum. Up and down, I glide my hands over his erection as he unhooks my bra and cups my breasts in his hands. His thumbs graze my nipples and arousal shoots straight to my core, my clit throbbing with an ache that's so unfamiliar my legs shake.

Whimpering, I stroke him faster.

Gently, he clasps my wrists, slowing me down. Desire and moonlight glitter in his eyes, filling his features with affection as well as a primal need. "Posey, wait. We have all night, sweetheart."

Now that I've decided this is what I want, I want it as quickly as possible. "I'm sorry. I want—"

"I know. I do, too."

He takes off his pants and shirt. It doesn't occur to me to be self-conscious standing half naked in front of him. This is Fox, and despite him changing the dynamic of our relationship, I'm comfortable around him. Kneeling, he finishes undressing me, and only when I'm standing completely naked in front of him does he tug off his briefs.

His erection is long and thick, brushing against abs I've only felt through his shirts and sweaters.

He's gorgeous, and I don't know how I could have missed it, unless I was deliberately keeping myself from noticing. If anyone had asked me a month ago if I thought this would ever happen, I would have laughed and said they were crazy.

"This looks good on you," he says, brushing his fingers over the necklace he gave me. The only thing I'm wearing now besides his engagement ring. "I hope you keep it."

"If that's what you want."

"I do."

"Okay."

Tenderly, Fox rubs his thumb over my bottom lip. "I love

you, Posey. I know you think I don't know you well enough to say it, but I think I do. This isn't just sex for me, do you understand?"

"I know you believe that's true, and I won't argue, even if I don't agree." My voice is low, raspy with tears I'll cry tomorrow. "But I've seen the way you love, and we don't have that."

"No. What we have is better than anything I've ever let you see."

His eyes smolder, dark and hot, and a zing of apprehension shoots through me. Better than love? What do we have that could be better than how he loved Michelle? He crowds me until the backs of my knees hit the mattress and then more until I have no choice but to lie down.

"Scoot up."

I do what he says, and we crawl under the sheet and comforter.

He moves slowly, his hands roaming over every part of my body, from my shoulder to the curve of my waist, to my hip and back again. His cock presses against my thigh, and he sucks one of my nipples into his mouth. I gasp when he bites.

"Too much?"

"Maybe. Fox, it's been such a long time for me." I want to cry and hope he doesn't want to know just how long it's been.

"Then I should ask if I need a condom because I didn't think we'd be doing this and didn't pack any. We'll need to, I mean, I'll have to . . . I don't have an STD. So I can pull out if you're okay with that. If your cycle is, you know. In a good place."

I swallow. I forgot we'd have to have the birth control talk. It's something I stopped thinking about. This would be a good time to tell him I don't need birth control. That I haven't for nine years and never will again, but it would kill the mood and I want tonight, no matter how much it's going to hurt me. I want to remember what it feels like to lie in the arms of a man who thinks he loves you.

I try for something in the middle. "I can't get pregnant now, and I don't have anything, either."

"Good. I want you to enjoy this, without worrying about anything."

Except our secrets, I want to say, but that would kill the mood as surely as telling him the real reason why he doesn't need a condom.

He turns his attention back to my nipple, sucking it into his mouth, and the delicious hint of pain makes all my muscles quiver.

I've turned off this part of myself. This sexual, sensual, part of me. Fox is wakening something inside me that's been dormant, no, suppressed, and desire is threatening to claw its way out.

I arch my back, encouraging him to give me more even as I'm so scared the feelings he's bringing out in me will shatter my entire existence.

Wiggling down the bed, he sprinkles kisses over my belly and settles between my legs. "Move your knees up for me, sweetheart," he says, nudging my thighs apart.

"Fox, no." I can't. That level of intimacy will destroy me. He'll do more than expose the physical part of me, he'll knock down any emotional walls I have left, and I'm not ready for that. I'll never be ready for that.

He meets my eyes in the dark, the tips of his fingers finding my slit. "I want to make you feel good. I want to taste you."

"No. It's been years, and I'm—"

"Scared. I'll never hurt you, Posey."

A sob breaks out of my throat. I'm not scared, I'm terrified, but I bring up my knees, giving him permission to touch me. The very thing I crave will kill me.

He dips his head and spreads me open, revealing my arousal. Lightly, he barely pushes a finger inside me, and I moan and whimper at the same time, my lips blocking the harsh shriek.

"You're so wet, sweetheart," he murmurs.

"Fox," I cry.

"I know. Shh. I know."

He moves his hand and covers me with his hot mouth. I want to jerk away, but my body does the opposite and my hips push my cleft against his lips, increasing the pressure. I claw at the sheets and my heels dig into the bed. God, I need him, need him to show me he wants me as much as I want him.

My muscles clutch greedily at his tongue as he licks a part of me no other man has, and my whole body trembles when he replaces his tongue with two fingers. He hooks them, finding the exact spot to urge me to fall apart. His teeth scrape over my clit and sends me over.

I come, my body burning brighter than the sparklers on Rodney's cake, pleasure setting every nerve on fire. Tears drip down my temples, and I can't stop them, my fingers gripping the sheets so tightly my hands ache.

He licks at me until I can't stand it, and I jerk away, my chest heaving, a mist covering my skin. The room smells like me, like my want for him, my need, and I'm embarrassed I exploded so easily.

"That was exquisite," he says, covering my body with his, his lips close to my cheek. "I could listen to you come every day for the rest of my life and I would never get tired of it. The sounds you make are so fucking sexy."

I laugh weakly. "I don't feel sexy. I feel like an overcooked noodle."

"Find a little more energy, because it's my turn and I want you along for the ride." Fox dries my tears. "Don't cry, sweetheart. You should be happy we found each other and what we have between us."

What we have is going to break my heart, but I turn my head and kiss him.

He fists his cock and the tip nudges where his tongue had been only minutes before. "This is going to change things for us. I want to be sure you're with me."

What could I say now? That this charade hasn't destroyed our friendship? That after we have sex, we can go back to the way things were? That there won't be damage? I tried to tell him and he didn't listen, didn't believe he was throwing away seven years of friendship to win a bet he could afford to lose.

"I'm with you," I lie.

"Tell me if this hurts and I'll stop."

"It will hurt, Fox," I say, but no matter the warnings, he'll do it anyway.

"I'll go slow."

I'm wet, and his fingers have loosened me. There's no resistance as he slides inside me, inch by inch. Letting me adjust to his size, he stops and kisses me, long, slow licks, his fingers tangled in my hair. I don't want him to stop, and I wiggle impatiently. "Fox."

Chuckling, he starts moving again, and when he's as far as he can go, he rests his weight on top of me and continues the urgent exploration of my mouth. I bring one of my legs up and wrap it over his ass, pushing him farther until the tip of his cock hits the center of my body. Once again, my nerves spark in delight.

Nibbling at my neck, he pulls out and pushes back in. "I guess I don't have to ask if you're doing okay?"

"I'm okay," I whisper, playing with the hair at the nape of his neck. The feel of his body is delicious, the friction of his cock encouraging me to explode all over again. The bed moves with every thrust, the frame creaking as he plunges inside me over and over again.

He increases the tempo until a groan rips out of his throat, and with a hand to my ass pulling me as close to him as a woman can be to a man, he comes. Hot streams of cum shoot inside me, and his cock empties for several moments, twitching and jerking.

Finally, he quiets and lowers me to the bed. I don't let go, hiding my face in the sweaty curve of his shoulder, and with a huff of amusement, he cuddles me to him.

"I hope that was as good for you as it was for me," he mumbles.

It will be one of the most memorable experiences of my life. "Yeah, it was."

"Good. I need to get up. Do you have to use the bathroom?"

"I can wait until you're done."

"Okay."

His cock slips out of me as he untangles our arms and legs, and he rolls off the bed. Sighing, I turn onto my side. I can't let him see that I'm sad or he'll think I have regrets. I *will* have regrets, but not right now. Right now, I'm holding on to how magical the experience was for me. He helped me come first and didn't hurt me. And because I know Fox, he'll want to spoon all night. He's always liked to snuggle and I bet having sex beforehand, he'll be even more sentimental.

I never let myself think about his relationship with Michelle. How they'd cuddle when she slept over, which was a lot the year they were dating, or him bringing her coffee in bed, the way he sometimes will for me when we fall asleep on my couch and he wakes up first.

I never wanted to be jealous. I didn't know what to be jealous of. She had his time when it used to be mine, but beyond that, I didn't know what it would be like to be in a physical relationship with him. Now when he moves on to another woman, I'll know what there is to be jealous of. A tear runs over the bridge of my nose. I wipe it away before he steps out of the bathroom holding a washcloth.

"Let me clean you up," he says, sitting on the edge of the bed.

My cheeks burn. "I can do that, you don't have to—"

"Let me. I want to. It's my mess." He smiles, teasing.

Reluctantly, I roll onto my back and he nudges my legs apart. This is almost as intimate as having sex, and he blots at the skin between my legs, my cum and his running out of me and onto the bed in a warm trickle.

"What's this?" he asks, his fingers tracing the vertical scar down my abdomen. It's barely visible and he wouldn't have seen it if he hadn't left the bathroom light on.

"I had a procedure done a long time ago. You've seen it before," I say, though, I don't think he has. At least, if he had, he never asked about it. Now that he thinks we're more than friends, maybe he'll have more of an interest in my life.

"What happened?"

"Some issues with my ovaries, nothing to worry about," I say, but there's plenty to worry about. I don't think there's a day since the surgery I haven't worried about what it's done to some aspect of my life.

He frowns. "But you're okay?"

"I'm okay as I can be with what I had to have done. Can we not talk about it anymore?"

"Posey, if you're sick, I want to know." He finishes dabbing and moves on to wiping the cum off the insides of my thighs.

"I'm not sick." *Anymore.* "Do I look sick?"

Resting his warm hand on my leg and kissing my knee, he says, "No."

"Okay, then. I'm tired. Can we go to sleep?"

"Yeah, sure. I'm sorry."

He throws the washcloth onto the vanity in the bathroom and turns out the light. The moonlight leads his way back to the bed, and just like I thought he would, he spoons me, his chest pressed to my back.

I try to find comfort in his arms around me, but I can't enjoy it now while I'm worried about later. Fox found a happy place between what he thinks he knows about me and what he's decided to keep me from knowing about him.

I'm surprised he thinks he can maintain the balance.

No one can thrive in a relationship built on secrets.

Even so, I promised to cherish what I could get and hide it away for the lonely nights when I'm living without him. I roll over and kiss him, wrapping my hand around his semi-hard cock. He doesn't need much persuasion to harden the rest of the way, and he slides inside me, moaning.

We make love all night and into the morning, the sun rising over the frozen mountain peaks.

I'm sore when he comes inside me one last time, rubbed raw by a bout of vicious, almost desperate, lovemaking, as if Fox were saving me up in preparation for a drought. "Don't leave me," he gasps, holding me close, our bodies sweaty. "I'm not strong enough to ask you to stay." He chokes and buries his face in my hair, knowing our time at the chalet is almost gone.

"The right woman won't want to leave." I don't claim to be that woman, and maybe Fox hears it, maybe he doesn't, but he doesn't answer me, only fights for control, his body trembling and his shuddery breath hot against my skin until he can lift his head without crying.

"I love you, Posey," he says against my lips.

For once, since the start of this whole weekend, I tell him the truth. "I love you, too."

I wake to the scent of coffee permeating the air, and I crack my eyes open. Fox is sitting on the bed, holding one mug and sipping out of a different one. "How long have you been sitting there?"

"Not long. Five, ten, minutes. Maybe twenty. Okay, an hour. I lost count watching you sleep."

He forces a light tone to his voice, but it clashes with the haunted look in his eyes. I sit up, and wanting to comfort him somehow, give him a kiss good morning. He loosens up a little, but I get resentful. It isn't my job to ease his mind about something he insisted he wanted when he should have left well enough alone. Now we're both in it up to our necks hoping we don't drown.

I smile and hold out my hand for the mug I assume is mine. "Creeper."

"Yeah, but I blame you."

"Hmmm." I sip the warm coffee, fixed exactly how I drink it. I guess that's one thing about sleeping with your best friend. He knows what you like.

"Posey, I don't know how things are going to go once we're back in Avondale."

Staring into my mug, I say, "I don't know, either. We'll have to figure things out as we go along. I haven't been in a relationship for a long time. I've held myself back thinking I couldn't, and I still think it because of reasons you say you don't want to hear. You insist they don't matter, but that's not true and it leaves us at an impasse. I'm not going to beg you to tell me what happened between you and Michelle if you don't want to tell me."

"You knowing would do nothing."

"We're not special because we were friends first. Couples

share information with each other. They don't hide. This will blow up in our faces and we'll deserve everything we get."

I slide out of bed, tugging the sheet with me. I've always wanted to do that, thinking it looks sexy in the movies, but I hold it tightly to my breasts now because I'm tired of baring myself to him. I'm tired of him stripping me naked only to reject what he finds underneath the layers of protection he doesn't want me to wear.

Standing under the hot spray, I don't cry. I should think of Fox's stubbornness as a gift, a rare gift. I know what will happen when we're back in Avondale, and we'll be over before we begin. I'll go on a couple dates with Paul, tell him thanks but this isn't working out, and after Fox pays me for this weekend, I can continue with my plans.

Fox, if things go well, will move to Seattle and leave me alone.

When I come out of the bathroom, Fox is packing his bags. In silence, I dry my hair and put on a little makeup to hide the pallor. It'll be a relief to be back home and we can drop the act. It's exhausting to pretend things are okay when they aren't.

We eat breakfast with Darcy and Rodney in the resort's dining room before we leave. Rodney keeps a close eye on us, noting how Fox pours me more coffee without me asking, or touching my hand, or smoothing my hair. Little things he did before we made love that we pretended meant more. Darcy chatters excitedly about last night, the wedding, and a bridal shower she wants to throw for me here in the spring.

I make all the appropriate, appreciative noises, and she doesn't suspect a thing, caught up in plans, coffee, and pancakes and bacon.

"Come back soon," Rodney says, dressed in his signature leather blazer and jeans as we wait under the canopy for the lodge's valet to put our luggage in the courtesy van. "Don't be strangers until the wedding. You'll need at least a year to plan something that large."

Darcy holds up her clipboard. "I'll help you get it all done. It's what I do."

"That'll be great," I say, kissing her cheek. I offer my hand to Rodney. "Thanks again for having us. You know, maybe you should look her up. Invite her for coffee."

Fox frowns. "Who?"

"Just an old friend," Rodney says, ignoring my hand and hugging me instead. "Maybe I will."

"Good luck."

"To you, too."

I stand off to the side as Fox says his goodbyes to his family. Darcy shakes her head, smiling wistfully. "I'm going to miss that beach house, but I'm so glad you found her."

"Thanks, Darce. Catch ya later."

Rodney hugs his nephew and slaps him on the back. "Have a safe flight."

"We will."

Fox helps me into the van and the door slides closed. Rodney and Darcy wave at us until we can't see them through the back window anymore, and it's only when we're out of their sight do we collapse into the cushions, tension and pretense rushing out of us.

I turn on the bench. "You won the bet."

He scoffs, but he's grinning. "That I did. You know, whatever it is you wanted to buy with the money I said I'd pay you, I'll buy it for you. A house, a vacation home, whatever it is, I'll help you."

He doesn't understand that what I'm buying isn't a thing, but a life.

"No, thanks. I prefer to take care of my own business."

"You're not going to tell me, huh?"

"Oh, you know, it's part of that pesky little secret you don't want to know about."

He holds my hand and asks me to look at him, a finger under my chin. "It's not that I don't want to know, it's that you want to know mine in exchange, and I don't think it matters."

"When you love someone, everything matters."

Closing his eyes, he leans his head against the bench. "I'm still dealing with it, okay? I need time to work up to telling you."

His misery cuts me to the quick, just like it always does. I hate seeing him sad, and I hate knowing the only person who can do anything about it is Michelle.

The jet's waiting for us at the airport, and in the cold, the ground crew works quickly, transferring our luggage and helping us board. Air traffic control instructs us to wait for clearance, but the pilot assures us we won't be waiting long, and we don't.

I sit in the same loveseat I did before, but this time Fox sits behind me and urges me to rest my back against his chest. I can't journal this way, and even though I try not to, I revel in his embrace. How quickly he's gone from being my friend to the man I love. I *do* love him, but there's a difference between loving with your whole heart and choosing to love with only bits and pieces. We love each other in a way that will never last long-term.

His hands are busy as I stare over the clouds, his fingertips smoothing over my belly, lightly skimming over the scar he saw last night, and then lower, to my panties.

"What are you doing?" I ask, twisting slightly to look at him.

"I want to make you feel good," he mumbles into my ear, his hand dipping between my thighs.

I stiffen, but my body betrays me, heat flooding between my legs in delighted eagerness. "Not here."

"Why not here? There isn't a flight attendant on board, and I hope to God the pilot has something to do."

I can't help but laugh. Everything is so simple when Fox is involved.

I'm wet, and gently, he pushes a finger inside me. I'm still tender from last night, and my low laugh turns into a whimper. He anchors an arm around my stomach. "Shh, I've got you."

"Fox."

"You're so wet for me, Posey. When did you start thinking about me like this?"

He rubs my clit with his slick fingertip, and heat gathers in my belly. I was quick to get wet when he started to play, and I'll be quick to come. "Last night."

"Do you want to know when I started having feelings for you?" He slides two fingers inside me and presses the heel of his hand to my clit. Greedily, my muscles grab onto him, and I roll my hips wanting more.

"No. Fox, I need you to touch me."

"I am."

"No, like this." I tug at his wrist until he understands what I want, and he rubs my clit with his fingers again. "I'm going to come."

Fox pinches one of my nipples through my thin t-shirt, and that spark is enough to send me over. Pleasure courses through me, and my heels dig into the leather loveseat. He chuckles into my ear, and I don't know which would get me off faster, the sexy sound of his voice or his skilled fingers in my panties.

"I knew something wasn't right the night we went to the park."

"What wasn't right? What do you mean?" I pant, trying to catch my breath and keep track of the conversation.

He lazily swirls his fingers around my swollen clit, and

little aftershocks hum through my veins up into my brain leaving me almost thoughtless.

"That something was going on, something more than friends."

"Oh." I buck away from him and with another chuckle, he pulls his hand out of my yoga pants and discretely wipes his fingers on his sweatshirt.

"That's it? Oh?"

I turn on the loveseat, kneel between his legs, and wrap my arms around his neck. "Do you think you would have fallen in love with me without the bet?"

He brushes a piece of hair out of my eyes. "Yes."

"How do you know?" I'm skeptical, but I don't want to be.

"Because the night in the park, I knew things were different, and that's when I figured it out. I didn't say I fell in love with you then. Posey, we've been friends for as long as you've been Paul's PA, and I think, on some level, I've been in love with you all this time."

I open my mouth to respond, but he cuts me off with a kiss.

"I've been in love with you for years, I just didn't know it."

Fox drifts off and it gives me the chance to write down my thoughts. Audra's going to want to talk to me about this, and more than once I've thought about stopping my sessions. Maybe I could if Fox would be willing to listen to me, if he wanted to be half of a committed couple. The sounding board I pay my therapist to be.

I understand he doesn't want us to share our secrets on the chance they'll destroy what new love we've found, but what he won't see, and what I already know, is keeping those secrets will be what ends us. If he would just be willing to sit down and talk, tell me that he still loves me despite everything and let me to do the same—because I would love him no matter what he had to say—then I could believe him.

Rusty's waiting for us at the airport when we deplane, leaning against the car like the subzero temperature isn't bothering him at all. The wind's sharp and hurts my cheeks, and I lower my head to protect my face and step down the stairs to the tarmac.

"You guys look good together," he says, grinning and opening the door for me.

"We don't look any different," I say, amused. Rusty always puts me in a good mood.

"Engaged, I mean," he says.

Getting into the car after me, Fox stops mid-crouch. "How do you know?"

"Said so in the *Avondale Times*. Could've told me. I would've kept it on the down low." Rusty slams the door shut and trots around the hood.

"The *Times?*" I ask Fox.

"I wasn't going to bother with an announcement, but I guess Darcy contacted the paper. It's fine, but I don't want to know what photo she used."

"What do you mean, 'it's fine?'"

He turns to me, his eyes bright and his jaw scruffy. "I love you. I want our engagement to be real."

"That's a bit presumptuous."

Quirking an eyebrow, he asks, "It's presumptuous to assume that the woman I love, and who says she loves me too, would want to marry me?"

"What happened to dating? Getting to know each other?"

"We've been friends for years. We're more comfortable around each other than most newlyweds, but if you want me to court you, I will."

Rusty climbs behind the wheel and drives away from the plane.

"You make me sound like a shrew," I grumble, looking out the window. "I need time to get used to the shift in our relationship."

"I agree. Move into my penthouse."

"No."

Fox lets out a long, loud laugh. "You say that a lot."

"Because no one else dares to say it to you. You always get what you want, Fox Caldwell, but it's not always what you need."

"I think the lady's got a point," Rusty says, glancing at us in the rearview mirror.

"No one asked you," Fox says, but he doesn't look mad, only vaguely amused we're ganging up on him.

"Thanks, Rusty," I say, leaning forward and patting his shoulder.

Rusty grins. "You bet, Posey. A couple more minutes."

There isn't anyone on the sidewalk on this cold, dreary, Sunday afternoon, but the street is full of cars and Rusty has to double park in front of our building to unloads our bags. I keep my purse and carry-on, and after we tell him goodbye, Fox carries our suitcases through the lobby and to the elevator.

He backs me up, pressing me against the wall. "Let me spend the night." Cuddling me to him, he nuzzles my neck with his lips. "Please."

"Since when do you ask?" I bury my fingers in his hair, damp from the snow, the scent of his shampoo making me dizzy. I wish I could enjoy what we found together. I wish I wasn't expecting the end before we could start.

"Since I started courting you."

"*Pffft.* Okay, but we'll have to order in. I don't have anything in the fridge."

"That works. I'm going to unpack and check my email, then I'll come down."

The elevator bumps to a stop on my floor and the doors slide open.

"I need to check on Peaches and put some laundry in the wash, so, whenever you want." I step out of the elevator dragging my suitcase behind me.

Unexpectedly, Fox pulls my hand and tugs me back into the lift. "Hey." He brushes his fingers over my cheek.

My heart turns over as he stares at me. He's never looked at me like this before. Like I'm a miracle, like I'm the eighth wonder of the world. "Hey," I whisper.

He blows out a breath. "I'll see you in a couple of hours."

"I'll be waiting."

I step out of the elevator and look over my shoulder, and the desolation and despair in his eyes almost drop me to my knees.

Blocking out his pain, I turn and shuffle tiredly toward my apartment.

I thought we'd have more time before things crumbled around us.

I was wrong.

We pass the evening in a pleasant haze of laughter, food, and wine. Sometime between the elevator doors closing and when he stepped into my apartment, he lost his sad aura. We eat while we watch TV and he helps me clean up the kitchen like he always has.

He feeds me tiramisu, and instead of spooning and watching a movie after dessert, we turn the TV off and make out like kids. I'm surprised to find the intimacy adds to our friendship rather than takes anything away. I love the feel of his scruff against my jaw, and the way his hand skims over my skin as if he can't go a second without touching me.

"Let me give you a little more," he says, tucking me against his chest and shoving my pajama shorts down to my ankles. He pulls his cock out of his sweats, and widening my legs, he pushes inside me from behind, filling me as he rubs my clit with his fingers.

It brings back the nasty words Paul said to me at the awards dinner, and I try to block out the filthy feeling they gave me while Fox thrusts deep inside me.

Our relationship isn't dirty. Love between two friends isn't dirty. He lashed out in jealousy and anger, and I won't let it hurt me.

Shuddering, Fox comes, squeezing my breast as he gasps, "I love you," into my ear. I twist the upper half of my body enough to kiss him and he desperately licks at my mouth as if our lovemaking wasn't enough to calm him.

"You didn't come," he mumbles.

"I lost focus," I admit.

He slides out of me and nudges my shoulder until I'm flat on my back. "Here. Let me help you." Trailing his hand along my thigh, he spreads my legs, and I kick my pajama shorts on the floor and rest one leg on his hip.

"I'm all wet," I say, his cum leaking out of me and onto the couch cushion, his cock pressed into my hip.

"All the better." He kisses me and rubs my clit.

I wrap my arms around his neck and burrow into his chest.

"You're so beautiful," he whispers against my lips. "Come for me, Posey. I want to watch you come."

His request is all I need, and I sob his name as the orgasm shivers through me, tensing every muscle until it feels like I could shatter. When I'm done quaking, I loosen my arms and he lies on top of me, his face in my hair.

"I'll never get tired of this," he says.

"Fox—"

He tenderly holds me in his arms, cradling me like a child who needs consoling. "Don't get melancholy on me now. We're going to be happy, I promise."

I force a smile. "Do you keep your promises?"

He kisses the tip of my nose. "Every. Single. One."

CHAPTER NINE

Fox

I've shared many mornings with Posey in her kitchen. I know her space better than I know my own. Where she keeps her coffee, how many grounds she uses to make a pot. I've fed Peaches while I let her sleep, and I bring in the paper the paperboy leaves in front of her door.

All of those things I have done many times, never fully realizing the place I've created for myself in her life. I lean against the counter, and I know every small appliance and storage container behind me. I know her microwave needs to be cleaned. I know the dishwasher needs to be emptied.

I know she's missing the whisk in her drawer.

I know what happened to it, and I know she doesn't.

This morning, while I sip on coffee while Posey sleeps, I wonder if I barged my way into her life, or if it was more subtle than that, a transition that can't be measured. All I know is the mornings I've had like this, the mornings where I've assumed I was welcome, those mornings are gone.

I will never take one second with Posey, or my place in her life, for granted ever again.

She pads into the kitchen, yawning, her hair a tangle down her back. Before the bet she would have put lounging pants on, but now she's wearing nothing but her panties and a navy blue tank top. She steps into my arms and rests her cheek against my chest, her eyes still partially closed in sleep.

"You didn't need to get up," I mumble, pressing my lips to the top of her head. "I wanted to get an early start."

"Just a minute." She cuddles into me, and I wrap my arm around her back and rest my hand on her hip.

We made love in the middle of the night, turning to each other in the dark. I felt her trepidation, her need, her urgency, and I wanted to tell her to go slow, go easy, but nothing I would've said would have calmed her down. I let her push her fear onto me as she positioned herself over my body. She rode me hard, and she fell asleep sated but not secure.

I did that to her, but I won't say I'm sorry. I'm a selfish prick just like Paul said I am, and I'll trade the security she had in our friendship for the shaky ground she stands on in our relationship. Because I want her, and this time what I want is what I need.

"Lunch today?" I ask, savoring her touch as she runs her hands over my skin under my t-shirt.

"I don't know. I'll need to ask Paul if he can spare me. He might have me working through to make up some of the time I missed on Friday."

"He's been talking about a new game. All the market research indicates a huge portion of gamers are women, more than we thought. We want to focus on developing a game women would like to play, characters that don't have their boobs hanging out and with more on their minds than finding a man."

She looks up at me, her mouth hanging open in mock shock. "You mean we think about more than that? Wanting a man to cook and clean for?"

"None of the women in my life have ever needed a man. You all can take care of yourselves." I sip my coffee noting how true that is. My mother does her own thing while being half of a whole with my father. Darcy has always lived life on her own terms, and Posey has proven time and time again she doesn't need a man's support to achieve her goals.

"And Seattle."

"Seattle?" My heart stops for a second. Seattle. Fuck. I forgot all about it.

"Won't he want to talk about the new office?" She blinks, her eyes gritty with sleep.

"Yeah. Ah, that's a ways down the road, I think, but something that will probably happen."

"It's a good idea. To expand, I mean."

I clear my throat. "First things first. I'm going upstairs to shower. I'll send Rusty back for you. You're going in at eight-thirty?"

"Yeah. Thanks." She kisses my cheek and heads down the hall to the bedroom, her panties clinging to the delicate curve of her ass. She can get another hour if she can fall asleep, and by the looks of it, she'll have no trouble.

In the penthouse that feels even emptier after spending all weekend with Posey, I shower and dress for work. Rusty's waiting for me downstairs, Monday morning traffic already clogging the street. The sun's beaming over the horizon, as if it knew my spirits needed a lift, and the sky glitters with pinks, oranges, and purples, but I can't get on board with its effort.

My phone starts buzzing with congratulation texts and emails, invitations to dinners and parties to show off Posey and her ring, and offers to let me brag about the Starlight Award. To anyone else, it would seem like I'm on top of the world, and I am. Well, I should be.

I don't like that Paul and I are fighting over Posey, and he's waiting for me at the elevator when I step onto the freshly waxed tile.

He assesses me for a heartbeat, meeting my eyes, and then says, "You slept with her."

With the early hour, we're the only two on the floor, and I bet he came in before everyone else just to confront me.

"I don't see how that's any of your business, but I love her and yes, we slept together," I say, giving him a wide berth on the way to my office, clutching my briefcase in my hand.

"You *think* you love her," he says, following me. "I think you're using her to get over Michelle."

"I don't want to argue. We've been friends for a long time and I don't want Posey to ruin that. I love her. She loves me. Our engagement might have been fake, but it's real now. You can either accept it or not, but don't be pissed off at me, and don't be pissed off at Posey. She doesn't deserve it."

Paul scoffs. "Do you want kids?"

I set my briefcase on my desk. The cleaners were in over the weekend and there's a faint scent of lemon in the air. "No. Maybe." I swallow hard. "I don't know. It'd be difficult. You know that. Posey and I haven't talked about it. Why?"

Shaking his head, he says, "You have no idea what you're getting into. You're going to break her heart, but you know what? I'll be there to pick up the pieces. She deserves a man who will love her exactly how she is."

I frown. "You're right, I have no idea what you're talking about, but whatever comes up, Posey and I can handle it. Together. I'm sorry you have feelings for her, but this isn't a competition."

He sets my nerves on edge when he laughs. "No, it's not,

because I've already won. Slow and steady wins the race, my friend, slow and steady." He rubs his hands together. "Meeting with research and development at one today. We gotta keep the momentum going."

"Yeah, you're right."

I make my own coffee, and intending to work, sit at my desk with a fresh cup and the day's schedule, but all I end up doing is waiting for Posey to come in. Rusty messages me that they're on the way, and I force myself to stay at my desk when I hear the elevator ding and Posey's heels click across the floor. I don't care when my own assistant arrives, setting a box of donuts I didn't ask for on my desk and wishing me a good morning.

It requires a tremendous amount of effort on my part not to poke my head out the door and see what Posey's wearing, how she did her hair, how she's acting, or how Paul's treating her. I've already turned her personal life upside down. I need to leave her alone at work or she'll quit.

Paul keeps her through a working lunch, and I grit my teeth. I know they're working on what we're going to talk about at the meeting, but I don't know if Paul planned it or if it was a convenient way to needle me.

Probably a little of both, knowing Paul. I could sit in on their meeting, but I don't want to. Unless it's necessary, I don't think the three of us occupying the same room is wise, even if Lydia would be there to take notes. Paul can't stop gloating about something I don't understand, and I can't overestimate my control not to punch him in the face.

After lunch, Paul and I ride the elevator down to research and development. The guys are high on the Starlight win, and we waste twenty minutes slapping each other's backs and listening to how the team will spend their bonus money. Then it's down to business, and I forget about everything while we go through marketing numbers and statistics, finding the sweet spot that will launch our next game.

Paul mentions Seattle at the end of the meeting, and the guys perk up. Some of them are from the Seattle area, and a chance to go home creates a wave of interest. I'm angry he brought it up when it wasn't in the meeting notes, but I don't say anything until we're in the elevator and the guys are buzzing with characters, plots, and Pike Place Market.

"You could have warned me," I say, angrily jabbing at the number for our floor.

He shrugs, not the least bit contrite. "Why? You were excited about it before the weekend and nothing's changed. It's a good move for the company, we agreed on that. Why wait?"

There's a gleam in his eye as he leans casually against the wall, his suit immaculate, his tie the color of Posey's eyes. I wonder if he did that on purpose.

"Why are you doing this? Do you hate me now that Posey and I are together?"

"I don't hate you, Fox, but I *am* concerned. I don't think you're ready to be in a relationship with her. You haven't come to terms with Michelle and what happened. You didn't see a therapist, you didn't talk to anybody. You buried it, and that's not the way you deal with grief. Now you think you can sweep it under the rug and no one will get hurt."

Just as I open my mouth to object, Paul presses the red emergency stop button on the panel. The elevator bumps to a halt, and immediately the phone rings, the shrill noise bouncing off the walls, security wanting to know what the problem is.

We ignore it.

"I know you think you're fine, and maybe you are," he continues, lifting a hand and acknowledging my want to interrupt, "and if you are, then there's no harm in being fine in Seattle, is there?"

He knows I can't argue with him, especially since Seattle was my idea. What I don't want to admit is the fact that I'm scared Posey won't come with me.

I'm trapped.

"No."

"And it sounds like half the team will want to transfer. That'll keep HR busy here. There's a lot to consider, a lot of things to do to get the ball rolling." He lowers his voice as he presses the button to make us move again. "I think it'll be good for you."

"Everyone keeps saying that."

"Then listen."

I let my gaze wander toward Paul's office where Posey sits at her desk answering phone calls and typing. She's wearing a black skirt, a black and blue sleeveless blouse, and a black blazer hangs off the back of her desk chair. Her hair is pinned away from her face, but I can't see if it's a French twist, chignon, or a bun. I want to pull the pins out one by one as I kiss her neck and hide from the world.

She flicks a glance at me and I turn away.

Lydia thrusts a handful of messages at me as I walk by her desk, and I sift through them, uninterested, intending to waste the next two hours until it's time to go home.

My relationship with Posey is so new, I don't know how tonight will play out. I know what would have happened before. Before my fake proposal, before the awards dinner, before our weekend at the resort. I would have gone up to the penthouse after Rusty dropped us off, showered, changed, grabbed a bottle of wine, and proceeded to spend the evening at Posey's.

Today shouldn't be any different, except I don't want to have to go to the penthouse to shower and change. I don't want to have to go upstairs for wine. I want us to share the same space. Her apartment has always felt like home, and I resent any time I have to spend outside of it.

Four o'clock rolls around and I'm restless as hell. If I want to go home with Posey, I have to wait until five. I can slip out early, say I'll finish the workday at home, but Posey's stuck until Paul says he doesn't need her or he leaves. He doesn't want us together, and I bet he milks every second he can with her from here on out.

At five after four I give Lydia permission to go home, and she eagerly accepts the unusual Monday order, grabbing her coat and purse and calling, "Have a nice night!" over her shoulder before I can change my mind.

I sit at my desk, brooding.

Someone knocks on my door, and I answer with a gruff, "Come in." I'm not in the mood to troubleshoot or go over paperwork, and it better not be Paul telling me he wants to keep Posey after hours and to go home without her. If he booked a business dinner and needs her with him, I'm going to explode.

Suppressing a growl, I look up from my blotter and stagger to my feet. "Michelle."

She smiles, chagrined. "Hello, Fox."

"What are you doing here?" I regret sending Lydia home early. I could have used the warning, the few minutes Michelle would have sat in reception paging through a magazine waiting for my okay, rather than barging in, and me being unprepared to face a part of my life I thought was over.

"I hoped we could talk."

Pain, swift and sharp, jabs at me like little scalpels into my chest, slicing deeper and deeper into my heart. Tears burn behind my eyes, and my hands start to tremble.

"You look good." It's almost an accusation. Her dark brown hair shines and bounces around her shoulders in thick waves. Her brown eyes are clear, unlike the last time we saw each other, and her skin is free from the lines grief etched into her face. She's slim, maybe a little slimmer than when I first met her, but her heavy coat hides most of her figure. Her legs are long and lean, and she's wearing black leather boots that stop at her knees.

"Thank you. So do you. Do you have a minute?" Her voice is calm, cool and collected, adjectives I never would have used to describe her before.

Tersely, I nod. "Shut the door."

I don't know who saw her come in, and I hope to God Posey doesn't know she's here.

Michelle quietly shuts the door and slips off her coat, revealing a black dress. She hangs it on the coat rack next to mine, her motions graceful and unhurried.

"I missed you," she says, stepping over the carpet to where I still haven't moved from behind my desk.

The words fall out of my mouth. "I missed you too." The words aren't lies. I *have* missed her, but the missed is past tense. I used to miss her. I don't anymore.

She smiles and stands in front of me. "I wasn't sure. I . . . saw the announcement in the paper. You're engaged."

"Yes, I am. You told me to move on, and I did."

Her face falls. "I tried to, too. I really did."

"Did you get some help?" I'm frozen, memories of meltdowns and uncontrollable sobbing flooding my brain, outbursts and unreasonable demands. Then the days after, dealing with the aftermath, darkened bedrooms, begging her to eat or shower.

"Yes. I've been seeing a therapist who specializes in loss, and I joined a support group. It helps to know that other women have gone through what I did. What we did." She drifts away from me and stares out the window. The sun is setting and it casts shadows between the skyscrapers. Windows twinkle and from up here it doesn't seem so cold, but winter is desolate and bleak and Michelle brought those feelings with her.

"She said it was wrong I made you grieve alone, and I've come to apologize."

"Did you get help for your other issues?" I ask, trying to be kind. Paul called her crazy. Darcy called her unhinged. I said she was mixed up, but no matter how anyone described it, she'd been unstable.

"I'm on medication, and I'm feeling a lot better now. Fox, I know when we were together I didn't make it easy, and I know you don't believe it, but while I was acting out, I knew what I was doing. I just couldn't stop."

"I'm happy for you. What have you been doing for the past year?" I join her at the window. I've wanted this moment for a long time. Needed the closure, I guess you could say, and one day, I stopped needing it because I thought I would never have it. I moved on without her apologies or explanations and dealt with my grief alone the best I could, using Posey to prop me up when it wasn't her job.

"Working on my mental health, mostly. I let my apartment go and moved in with my mom and dad. I try to surround myself with people. I feel safer that way, not so alone. For months after I left you, I went to a support group meeting almost every day. It was my anchor, like my grief and loss weren't so bad if I could share it with others who understood. I spent a lot of time talking to my therapist. I'm in a much better place, but I should have taken you with me to get there." She reaches for my hand and links our fingers. "I'm sorry."

I squeeze.

She looks up at me, tears glistening on her cheeks. "I still love you."

I need to let her down easy, and, if I can, stay on civil terms with her. We have a lot to talk about, a lot of things to say to each other, things that could help my relationship with Posey go smoother.

"I loved you too, or I thought I did. Made myself believe I did. Your pregnancy only postponed the inevitable."

"Fox." Her lips tremble as she says my name.

"I know. I'm sorry."

She steps toward me, and just as she does, my door clicks open. "Fox, I'm ready— Oh."

Posey freezes in the doorway, her eyes locked on Michelle's hand holding mine. Posey's a class act. She doesn't burst into tears and run away. She doesn't spit profanities. Her eyes dim, the joy of going home with me and spending the evening together gone, but she forces a smile and walks into my office holding out her hand. "Hi, Michelle. It's nice to see you again."

Smirking, Paul stands outside my office. He knew Michelle was here, maybe even sent Posey in to tell me she was free to leave.

"Hi, Posey. You always look so nice. I love your style," Michelle says, untangling our fingers and shaking Posey's hand.

"Thanks. You're looking well." Posey turns to me and stares over my shoulder, avoiding my eyes. "I'll go on ahead."

"Rusty's downstairs waiting."

Posey flashes a smile at Michelle. "Have a good night."

"You too."

I wait until Posey's gone and the door's shut before rubbing my eyes. Undoubtedly this will create problems. Problems I stupidly hoped to avoid.

"Posey didn't seem upset I'm here, but if I had a ring that huge on my finger, I wouldn't worry either."

"She's not entirely convinced I'm over you. She thinks we should be together."

The corner of Michelle's mouth lifts up. "I think she's right."

"I don't."

Her smile wavers, but she moves closer. I let her, the damage already done. "We could try again."

Sweat starts to trickle down my back. She might have faced her grief, mourned properly, but I ran from mine as fast as I could and I mourned in a way I shouldn't have. "No."

She steps into my arms and rests her cheek against my shirt, eerily similar to how I stood with Posey this morning in her kitchen. "Why? I'm strong enough. I want to try again."

"You know we weren't right for each other. Not the way you were. I put so much energy into being with you, into trying to keep us together, and when you left, I could finally breathe. I'm sorry if you thought we could pick up where we left off." I pause. "I need to go."

"Chasing after her?" she says, but she's not mean about it, not the way she would have been, attacking me because I didn't act the way she thought I should act or say what she thought I should say. Maybe she really has gotten the help she needs.

"I love her, Michelle."

"You didn't love me at all, did you? You only said you did."

"I wanted to, so damned bad, but it was too difficult. You were out of control, and you weren't doing anything about it. I took a beating staying with you, letting you scream at me when you were low because the highs were worth it. I was worried about you, God, you have no idea how worried I was, but I was relieved when you broke things off. I didn't have the energy to take care of you anymore. I'm glad you're okay. Thank you for coming by and letting me know." I tuck a piece of hair behind her ear. We were lovers. Barely friends. Almost parents. We were never enemies.

She looks out the window, the day giving way to twilight. She doesn't tear into me, but my muscles don't loosen. I'm so used to being on the defensive, waiting for something to happen, that when she only sighs, it sends my flight or fight response into a tailspin.

"I deserve that. Then it's too late? I'm too late."

I sit on the armrest of a loveseat and try to relax. "I'd like to be friends. I haven't handled things as well as you have, and it would be nice if we could talk through what happened. It might help."

She bites her bottom lip. "Will you go to therapy with me? She suggested I ask you."

"I'd like that. Thank you."

She steps between my legs and brushes her thumb over my jaw. "You would have been a great father, Fox. You will be, one day. Don't let our tragedy keep you from that."

"That means a lot," I say, rubbing her arm, but her compliment slides over me like water on a duck's back. I'm not a father, might not ever be, and her words mean little. "My number hasn't changed. Give me a call."

Her hand falls to her side and she leans away. She knows she's being dismissed. "Are you sure you don't want to try again?"

"I'm sure. You'll find someone new, someone you won't share bad memories with."

"Maybe you're right. Thanks for not throwing me out of your office," she says wistfully.

I hold her coat and she slides her arms through the sleeves. I miss Posey and our end-of-the-day routine. She went home without me tonight. Paul might have helped her with her coat, might have went down to the lobby with her to walk her outside, maybe sent her home in is own car. I clench my teeth. Michelle coming here gave him exactly what he wanted.

She tugs black leather gloves onto her hands.

"I wish you the best. I always have," I say, opening the door, gently encouraging her to leave. I want to go home. I want to see Posey and explain. I want to stand in her kitchen and drink wine while she cooks dinner and pretend this afternoon never happened.

"I know, but I had the best. With you. Maybe one day I'll find it again. Take care, Fox."

"Let me know about therapy times."

She nods. "I will."

I lean against the doorjamb as she walks past Lydia's desk and waits for the elevator. Posey's chair is empty, Paul's door is shut, and our receptionist has gone for the day. I'm alone on the floor.

Feeling like I'm trying to tread water in a turbulent storm, I put my jacket on.

I don't know what I'm going to find at Posey's, but I know, without a doubt, the current is going to suck me under and I'm going to drown.

I force myself to pretend everything is normal and don't beat on Posey's door the second I step inside the building. I shower and change my clothes. I don't know what she's making for dinner and I grab a bottle of red and white to cover my bases. Chances are good she's not cooking anything. Hell, she might not even be home. Rusty said he drove her to the building and watched her go inside, but what she did after that is anyone's guess.

Ella Fitzgerald is crooning when I walk down the hallway to Posey's apartment, and I knock when before I would have just gone in.

Posey opens the door with a hand towel draped over her shoulder. She changed into yoga pants and a tank top, and the normalcy slows my heartbeat down just enough that I don't feel like I'm going to have a panic attack.

"Hey, come in." She opens the door wider and steps aside.

"I didn't know what's for dinner," I say, holding up the two bottles. "We can order in if you don't feel up to making something."

"The red works. I stuffed shells with cheese. They're baking in marinara sauce, and I had breadsticks in the freezer."

"Sounds good." I set the bottles on the counter, and like always, she has the corkscrew waiting and the wineglasses ready. The kitchen is warm with the oven on, the tangy scent of tomato sauce in the air. She watches me uncork the red, and I pour.

She's teased me about how uncouth that is, not letting it breathe, and I would always laugh, but tonight she watches me with solemn eyes and wraps her hand around the wineglass I give her without saying a word.

"Are you going to let me explain?" I ask, swirling my wine around the glass. Might as well get this over with.

"I don't think there's anything to explain. Not on your part, at least."

I frown. "What do you mean?"

"I mean," she says patiently, staring into her glass,

"Michelle is a better match for you, and if she came back asking for a second chance, you should give her one."

Anger rips through me, my blood boiling hot, and I force myself release my grip on my glass or I'm going to break it. "Why the *fuck* would you say that? Posey, you know I love you. Haven't I said it enough? Don't you feel it when we make love? Honey, *I love you*."

She tilts her head. "Yet you refuse to talk to me. You refuse to listen to the things I need to tell you."

"We have time. We have time to share those things. Why does it have to be now?"

"Because it's important, Fox!" she yells, flinging her arms into the air, her wine close to sloshing out of the glass. "Because what I need to tell you will ruin what you want us to have. I tried to warn you. I tried to keep my distance, but you drew me in and now I'm stuck. Can't you understand that? I don't want to be with you like this."

"You don't want to be with me like what?" I ask carefully, watching her.

Her face turns a pasty white and tears shine in her eyes. "I can't have babies."

A tear drips down her cheek, and I step toward her wanting to brush it away and comfort her. She stiffens, and I stop. "What do you mean?"

"The scar you saw at the resort. I had ovarian cancer. They removed my ovaries, and I went through chemo and radiation. My hair fell out. I couldn't eat anything for months. My mother moved in with me for two years because I was too sick to be alone. My doctors say I'm lucky to be alive, but while I was in treatment, all I wanted was to die. I can't have children, and I don't want to be with you like this. We had our fun. You gave me a little taste of what it could be like between us, but that's all we'll have. *Don't you get it?*"

I scramble for something to say, anything that will ease her pain.

But the words won't come.

"I want you to go." She sets her glass on the breakfast bar and leans against the sink, blocking me out.

The scent of melting cheese wafts from the oven, Ella still crooning away, the soundtrack to what is turning out to be the second worst day of my life.

"Posey. Don't do this. It doesn't matter."

A whine unlike anything I have ever heard comes from the back of her throat. *"Doesn't matter?* I can't have a family. It's all I've thought about for *nine years.* There's not a day that goes by when I don't see a mother and her baby and think that won't be me, or get invited to a baby shower, or get coupons in the mail for baby formula that can't belong to me. I'll never experience pregnancy, I'll never feel a baby kick. I'll never buy a book of baby names or suffer through morning sickness. I'll never have a baby that's half me and half the man I love. It doesn't matter? It's the only thing that matters. We're done, Fox. Please leave."

I step behind her, and she braces against the counter. I don't touch her or I think she'd turn around and slap me. I have to tell her something, that I still love her, that we can make a life despite what she just told me, but she wouldn't believe a word of it.

I don't know if I believe it myself.

I'm processing, and my mind's stuck on the image of an empty crib, the same but different somehow, from the one that was in Michelle's apartment before I hired someone to take it away.

"The money." I latch onto something. Anything. "I transferred the money into your account today."

"Thanks." A tear drips off her jaw and hits the bottom of the sink.

I don't want to hurt her anymore, and doing what she asked, I leave and stand uncertainly in the hallway. I'll go back inside if I hear her crying, but there's nothing except Ella and the snick of the lock as Posey engages the deadbolt.

And for the first time since we've been friends, she secures the chain to keep me out.

CHAPTER TEN

Posey

I stare into space long after Fox is gone, the only thing forcing me to move is the timer screeching on the stove. I take the shells out of the oven and turn it off. Our wine is still on the counter, but I ignore it, flick the kitchen light off, and tell my home device to shut down.

There isn't anything unusual about a night I spend by myself. When Fox was dating Michelle, I got used to it, resigned myself to it. Almost convinced myself I enjoyed my evenings free again.

Peaches winds around my ankles, and I stumble over her little body on the way to my bedroom. I climb into bed, pulling the comforter to my chin. Fox's scent still lingers in the sheets and on his pillow, and the musty odor of the sex we had last night turns my stomach. I should get up and wash the bedding so I don't have to smell it all night, but I don't have the energy.

This doesn't change anything, not really. Maybe Fox won't

hang around my apartment every evening, but I was going to need my evenings free soon anyway. Now that I have the money I need, I can buy a house and move out of this building. It would be a smart thing to do, even if I didn't already have plans. I don't need to see him in the lobby or get trapped with him in the elevator. Until then, I'll have to figure out rides to work. I'm not going to use his car if we're not together, not as lovers or as friends.

He didn't waste any time, did he? Probably rushed out of here as fast as he could to call Michelle. It was a surprise to see her in Fox's office, but not a surprise to see them holding hands. He took her leaving so hard, and I wasn't stupid enough to think I could replace her.

All Fox and I were ever destined to be was friends, and now even that's gone.

I reach for my phone that's in the side pocket of my yoga pants and bring up my therapist's number. At six-thirty on a Monday evening she'll still be at her office, sitting at her desk and finishing up client notes. I connect the call and the line rings only once before she picks it up herself. Her secretary leaves every day at five. "Audra Stanley."

"I told him."

I don't introduce myself or ask how her day was. I don't have the mental capacity for it. I need to get this off my chest before it cracks my ribs open.

"What did he say?"

"Nothing. He left."

"Because you asked him to or because he wanted to?"

"Because I asked, and he didn't try to stay."

She's silent, maybe scribbling a note or two, observations on my even tone, the lack of tears in my voice. What direction she might need to go with me during our next session.

"I'm sorry," she says. "I know you wanted a different outcome."

"One I knew he wouldn't give me."

"You can't always think the worst of people."

"Even if I always get it?" I ask, but not too bitterly. I knew this was coming, and yet I believed Fox when he said things would be okay. Believing him was my own mistake.

"Not always, Posey." She's patient. I've spent a lot of time with her, and she knows if she waits, I'll draw the appropriate conclusion the situation calls for myself.

I suck in a deep breath and think of all the people who haven't let me down. My mom put her life on hold for two years to take care of me. The human resources department at WellStone Interactive hired me, even with a gap in my employment. Fox has always been a good friend up until now, and Paul's been a decent boss, never once propositioning me until he heard Fox was going to fake propose to win a bet.

"No, you're right. Not always."

"What are you going to do now?"

"The same thing I planned to do before. Fox paid me. I can look for a house. I can quit my job, though my time at work will look better on the application than being unemployed or between positions. I have vacation time saved up, maybe I'll take a few days off."

"Come see me tomorrow. I'll stay late and ink you in at five-thirty."

"I'm okay, Audra."

"Posey, you haven't been okay since the day you lost your ovaries. Come see me."

She hangs up, her old rotary phone clunking as she drops the receiver into the cradle.

I flop onto my back, stunned by her bluntness. She's wrong.

I was okay, for a little bit, in Fox's arms. I thought he meant it when he said he'd love me no matter what.

His love was situational.

Situational love.

I've never heard of that before, but that's what it is. The bet, the resort. Our situation called for it, for him to love me, and he did. The minute he didn't have to anymore, he left.

I'll miss the evenings with him. The weekends.

But soon I'll have other things to replace that time, and I need to look forward to that. Women don't wither away and die because a man leaves them.

I'll be okay.

With or without Fox.

With or without my ovaries.

I'm alive, and I'm healthy.

The rest is a bonus.

I can do without situational love.

I deserve better, but it's nothing I'll ever find.

I force myself to get out of bed and eat. I'm too skinny, the chemo and radiation doing something to my appetite that never bounced back. I sip on the red wine Fox left behind and shove the bottle of white into a cupboard behind a carton of old taco shells. I never want to look at it again. I store the leftover shells in the fridge and turn on a movie that I watch by myself with Peaches purring on my lap.

I try to find comfort in the solitude. Many of the women I work with complain about their lack of free time, their lack of privacy. Children watching them pee, husbands bothering them because they can't find the ketchup in the fridge. Dogs that have to go out but no one will walk them. I would always shake my head and *tsk*, commiserating with them over their perfect lives. Then they'd admire my life, my singleness, my wardrobe and shoes, my disposable cash to afford those things. My lack of obligations. What did they know of my life when their husbands show up in surprise at the end of the day to grab an early dinner or when their children call from daycare because they miss their mom and their teacher said it was okay to use the phone for a few minutes?

I scratch Peaches under her chin.

It's nice to have the whole couch to myself, not only a sliver of the cushions. Fox needed so much space, and I would lie pressed against his chest, his arm wrapped around my stomach to keep me from falling on the floor. This is much better, and I stretch my legs under the throw that smells vaguely of his cologne.

It will be a while before all the traces of him are gone.

I'll probably end up moving first, but that's okay, too. With the money, I can afford new furniture. I can start fresh.

I need new friends anyway.

The next morning, dressed in my usual skirt, blouse, and blazer combination, I pause at my door. I didn't think this morning would be any different than any other morning, but of course it is. I won't be riding with Fox, and Rusty won't be driving me to work. I want to avoid both of them, and instead of catching a taxi in front of the building, I order a car and wait for it in the alley. Much to my relief, the elevator's empty and I don't see Fox in the lobby. It would be nice if he tried to avoid me as much as I'm going to try to avoid him. Work doesn't bother me. I can hide behind my computer, pretend I'm on a call, and if things get really bad, I can talk to Paul and ask to be transferred to a different department.

He didn't want me dating Fox and he'll be happy to agree when he hears we're no longer together.

Fox's office door is closed, and I give a slight wave to Lydia before I settle at my desk. Paul pauses on the way to his own office. "Lunch today?"

Fox didn't tell me how he'd publicly end our engagement, or when he would. I don't want this to be any harder than it needs to be, especially since I like Darcy and Rodney and they're going to be innocent bystanders in this mess.

Paul sees the hesitation on my face. "Don't worry. I'll keep it discrete."

"Okay."

He smiles. "Good. Send my nine o'clock straight in."

I nod, the phone going off the second I adjust my headset over my ears. If someone can get past reception, I field their call and determine if Paul has the time to talk to them or not. Usually, I take a message and let him decide when to return the call. I'm in the middle of one such message now when Fox steps out of the elevator. I focus on my computer screen, my heart slamming and my fingers tripping over the keyboard as I type out the message.

He doesn't look my way, simply opens his office door and closes it behind him.

I blow out a sigh and press my lips against a cry. He looked good in his coat, his hair ruffled.

Nothing about this is going to be easy and I'll have to harden my heart more than I ever have before. I already knew he wouldn't want me damaged and broken. That he proved me right shouldn't be such a heartbreaking disappointment.

The morning goes by quickly, and not once does Paul leave

his office until it's lunchtime and he pokes his head out the door. "I can leave in five."

"Me too."

My stomach's queasy, some of it from hunger, some of it from expecting Fox to leave his office to go to the breakroom or down to research and development, but he never did.

I didn't think I'd need to ask for a transfer, but now I know it will be easier, and if the new position doesn't stick, I can look for something else. I'm qualified to work in any office in Avondale.

I log off and put my headset aside. Paul meets me at my desk and helps me into my coat. "Thanks."

"You're welcome. The car's waiting."

At that moment, Fox steps out of his office, and I feel his eyes on me as Paul and I walk toward the elevator, my hair brushing the back of his hand that's hovering near my shoulder.

If it wasn't so cold we could have walked to the little deli Paul chose for lunch. Near the WellStone Interactive building, Fox and I have eaten at the corner deli many times, and their potato salad is one of my favorites.

Today, I order soup and a turkey sandwich, and Paul and I sit at a table near the window. I want to ask him how discrete this is, but we've been spotted having lunch before and even if a gossip columnist or rag blogger happens to see us, they aren't going to wonder what we're doing.

The animosity Paul gave off at the awards dinner is gone, and in its place is a cheerfulness I appreciate. I relax and enjoy my lunch, nibbling on dill pickle chips.

We chat about work, and he asks about Peaches. I don't have a lot to contribute that doesn't have to do with Fox, and my answers are short.

We're both done with our food and sipping coffee and I think Paul's not going to ask me uncomfortable questions about

Fox, but he says, "I know you and Fox aren't seeing each other anymore."

Disappointment and bitterness prickle my skin. "He was quick to tell you."

"He knows I want to date you, Posey," he says, pushing our trays to the side and reaching for my hand.

I quirk my lips in distaste but don't pull away. His touch is warm and soft, and I'm human, okay? I need something, someone, solid until I'm on my feet. "Is that like a bro code? Honor among thieves?"

"Nobody's stealing anything from anyone as far as I know," he says, leaning closer, his voice low despite the loud conversation around us. "He wants you to be happy, and he thought maybe you could be with me."

"Because I couldn't be with him? Charming. Passing me off like an unwanted dog."

"Why did you break up?" He rubs his thumb over my bare ring finger. If anyone asks, I'm having the stone cleaned. I couldn't bear to wear it anymore. It's a symbol of a fake promise Fox had no intention of turning real.

I don't answer. I can't because I don't want to admit the reason Fox threw me away like a used tissue.

"He wants kids, doesn't he, Posey?"

Startled, I meet his gaze. "What do you know about it?"

"All of it. I know you had cancer, I know you can't have children." His voice is earnest, and there's nothing in his eyes but compassion and kindness. "I know, and I don't care. If Fox can't be with you because you can't give him what Michelle can, then that's his loss and he deserves it."

I try not to shake from anger and embarrassment. I didn't tell anyone because I don't want people to feel sorry for me. "How do you know about my medical history?"

"The director at Peace Valley Hospital is a friend of mine. He looked into it when I asked."

I try to yank my hand away, but he hangs on, his fingers digging into my wrist. "That's illegal."

"I know it is, but when HR sent me your personnel file for approval, I was concerned about the gap in your employment. I didn't know if it was something that would interfere with your position. That's all. I fell in love with you despite it. Fox is stupid and blind. He doesn't understand that you don't need children to be happy." Eagerly, his eyes bright, he leans farther across the table, and it's difficult not to get caught up. He's saying everything I wish Fox would have told me last night.

I need a moment to think of what to say, and I look out the window.

Rusty's stopped at a red light and Fox is staring at us from the backseat.

Our eyes collide for a few excruciating moments before the light turns green and Rusty inches into the intersection.

Then he's out of my sight.

Paul watches the entire exchange.

"If I saw you talking to another man, you can bet your ass I'd be out of the car and my fist in that asshole's face," he says, jerking my attention away from the cars on the road and back to the deli, the red trays and red and white checked paper lining them too bright in a haze of grey.

"You two are friends."

"Were."

"Paul," I say, wrenching my hand out of his grasp, "I don't want to be responsible for that."

"You're not. The way he's handled this past year is."

"It's not your place to judge him. He was hurting."

"Yeah, he was bleeding fucking everywhere, and you were

the gauze. Now when you need him, he leaves? How fair is that? And why am I the only one angry about it?"

I tell him the truth because the truth is all I have left. "I'm too tired to care."

"Then lean on me. He used you to get over Michelle and the minute she crawls back, it's like you don't exist. I would never do that to you."

I shouldn't sit here and listen to him talk like this. He's pouring whiskey all over my wounds, and it hurts so badly I can't breathe. "We should go. Lunch hour is over."

"I love you, Posey."

"Yeah, I'm hearing that a lot lately," I say, gathering my trash to throw away on the way out.

"Let me prove it to you."

I lift my chin. "Fine. Start by approving my transfer to a different department. I can't stand to see Fox every day. Living in the same building is bad enough, and I'm planning to fix that as quickly as possible."

Satisfaction gleams in his eyes, and I don't care if I'm feeding into his war against Fox as long as I get what I want. I've been used, maybe it's time I start using too.

"Done. I'll miss you. I don't mean looking at you, though there is that. You're a damned good PA."

Trust Paul to tell it like it is. "Thanks."

"Come on. We'll start the wheels turning when we get back to the office. No point in waiting."

"I appreciate that."

"I don't care how long and hard I have to work at it, Posey, I'll prove I have your best interests at heart."

We'll see about that. It seems these days the only interests people have are in their own wants and needs.

The ride back to the office is quick, and true to Paul's word, we stop on the twentieth floor and begin my transfer. The office manager in legal just put in her two week notice, and even though I don't know a syllable of legalese, I'm approved to take the position effective immediately. Thankfully, she can train me, and I'll try to learn quickly, even if it means enrolling in a class or two online to catch up. I heave a sigh of relief. It will mean my employment dates won't be broken, even for a few days while I looked for something else.

Fox is standing at Lydia's desk, glaring at the elevator when we step out. Paul stiffens, but I don't let Fox bother me. I've had years of practice, and his bark is worse than his bite.

I hang up my coat and settle at my desk, putting my headset on and turning off my voicemail that told callers I was away for the lunch hour. I resume my day's duties while focusing on organizing Paul's schedule, email inbox, and files for the temp who will replace me until interviews for a permanent position begin.

Paul knows I'm broken. I don't have feelings for him, but I'm grateful for one thing. He proved a man could love me the way I am. He fell in love with me knowing the truth, a truth he's known for several years.

Fox and I were friends for those same years, yet he never bothered to ask me about my life.

What does that say about Fox, or about me?

We were never close.

Now we never will be.

I stay past five knowing I'll be late to my appointment with Audra, but it doesn't help me avoid Fox, who stands by Lydia's desk glaring at me, his hands shoved into his coat's pockets, a red scarf hanging around his neck. I don't remember if he wore it this morning. Did Michelle stop by and give it to him while I was in meetings with Paul earlier? He steps in my direction and stops.

We have a childish staring contest, and I narrow my eyes, daring him to talk to me. *Come on. Tell me the things you were too chickenshit to say last night.* He's with Michelle now, but he still wants to be my friend. That my infertility doesn't matter, that he'll always love me in his own way.

He swallows, and even from here I can see his eyes grow hot.

I don't blink, and he turns away.

"Can I take you home?" Paul asks, stepping out of his office, unaware of what just happened.

"No, I'm fine. Thank you. I need a minute to clean out my desk, and then I have an appointment."

His smile falls. Maybe he wanted to ask me out to dinner or hoped I'd invite him up to my apartment for a drink, but he says cheerfully, "Goodnight, then. Be safe."

"Thanks. You too."

I box up the few personal items I had sitting on my desk, relieved Paul didn't push. I'm too disheartened and short-tempered to explain why my evening isn't free. He's like that—unrelenting—until he gets what he wants, and I don't want to fight. Even if I'm in the mood.

I don't have time to stop by my apartment and drop my box off before seeing Audra, and I don't dare cancel. She would never let me forget it, and she'd double down on me even more than she already is. Her receptionist is gone for the day, and she's sitting in her office doing paperwork by the light of a lone lamp on her desk.

She doesn't look up as I step inside and set my box on the floor, nor does she when I pull off my coat and lay it across the armrest of a chair neither of us uses during our sessions. She's still scribbling as I kick off my heels and drop in an exhausted heap on the couch.

"Coffee?" she finally asks, closing a file and setting it aside.

"No, thank you."

"What's in the box?"

"Things from work. I'm transferring to a different department."

"I cut myself once," she says, pushing away from her desk, the wheels of her chair grating against the plastic mat covering the carpet. "The cut was so deep, and it happened so quickly, I didn't know I hurt myself until I was dripping blood on my clothes."

The thing with therapy is if you listen as well as they do, you learn some things about them, too. I know Audra and what she's getting at. "You think I'm hurting and don't know it yet. Trust me, I do."

"Close. I think you know you've been hurt, but you aren't aware of how much, and once it hits you, you're going to go into shock. I don't want you to be alone when that happens."

I lift a shoulder. "I'll get used to being alone again. I was alone last night." Except Fox hadn't been gone an hour before I had to call her, reach out to someone to hear their voice.

She sits in the chair in front of me, kicks off her shoes, and props her feet on the little coffee table between us. She doesn't have her pad and pen.

Her hair is short and wavy, brown mixed with a little red, and her glasses frames are a dark green that highlight her eyes. She looks like a trendy older mom whose children visit on the weekends. Audra does have people close to her—the happy photos on her bookshelves mock me every time I come in—but she's never explained who they are or what they mean to her. I only guess at her family situation.

She folds her hands in her lap. "How did your weekend in

Colorado go? Was your mother happy about your engagement?"

"I haven't heard from her."

"You mean you haven't told her you're engaged."

Bristling, I say, "Why would I? It was fake."

Audra taps a finger against her lips. "Was it?"

"The engagement, the proposal, our friendship. It was all fake."

Saying it out loud brings tears to my eyes. How had our friendship disintegrated into nothing? When did the time we spent together start to mean less and less, until we were just using each other to avoid being alone? That's what it was. We were using each other. He hid from Michelle. I hid from trying to find a man who would love me as I am.

"How do you feel about that?" Audra asks.

If I had a friend, a real friend I could spill my guts to during a girls' night out, I wouldn't need Audra. I don't have any close girlfriends, only acquaintances I go to lunch with two or three times a year at best because I devoted all my time to Fox. I wasted my time, now instead of having a close friend who would talk to me if I needed her, I pay someone to listen to me whine. That's not all Audra does, and she'd be offended if she could read my mind, but I'm angry I invested so much time and energy in Fox and got nothing out of it except a broken heart.

"Used. Stupid. Lonely. A lonely fool. I thought he cared about me."

"He wanted to marry you. What changed?"

"You have to ask? It's why I'm here. The weekend was great. He told me he loved me and said he wanted our engagement to be real. We made love, and it was . . ." I stand and wander around her office, the carpet soft under my stockinged feet. "It was lovely. And when we came back, we slept in my bed, and it felt *real,* you know? Like the fake had turned real somehow. Then yesterday at the work I walked in on him and Michelle. They were holding hands." I stop at a set of French doors that let out to a small balcony. I love sitting out there in the summer drinking coffee while we chat about how bleak my life is. With the sun shining and the birds chirping, it never seemed so bad.

Resting my forehead against one of the doors, the cold glass cooling my skin, I skip over who Michelle is. I don't have to explain. Audra heard plenty while Fox was dating her. I don't need to tell Audra how hurt that made me, their fingers linked together, how close they stood next to each other. I don't have to tell her I expected it, encouraged it. It didn't matter how many times he said he wasn't in love with her. I saw it when he looked at her yesterday, and I saw it in her eyes, too. She seemed different. Friendlier than I remember her being, not as hard. Pleasant, a word I never would have used to describe her before. Beautiful. She's come a long way, and she's ready to give Fox what he needs for their relationship to grow into what it should have been the first time they were together.

"Last night he came over like he always has, and I told him. I told him to go back to her because I couldn't have kids and couldn't give him what he wanted."

"What did he say?"

"Nothing."

"He didn't console you, hug you? He didn't want to talk about what that would mean for your future?"

"No." I whisper to the snow outside. "I made dinner, but he didn't stay and eat. He uncorked the wine he brought, but he didn't drink any of it. He looked like a guppy, and I threw him out."

"So you made the decision."

"The decision was made. I saw it on his face."

"How many minutes passed between you telling him and throwing him out of your apartment?"

I shrug. "Three? Five? Ten? What does it matter?"

"It matters because people process things differently and you didn't give him the time and space, the *understanding,* he needed to do that. You had already decided he was going to take the news poorly and you didn't give him a chance to prove you wrong because you're scared."

"There's no other way he could have taken it."

"Posey, you don't even know if he wants children, do you? You're so worried about what your infertility could mean you haven't talked with him to figure out what it *does* mean. To him, to the both of you. I've been in this business for a long time, and rarely does something like this keep people apart."

"Then what does?"

"Fear. Stubbornness. Feelings of inadequacy. An unwillingness to bend. It isn't the problem, Posey, it's how you handle it."

"You're saying I was wrong."

"I'm saying you were wrong."

I wipe a tear off my cheek. "He left me."

"He did."

The chair creaks as she stands up, and she stands next to me.

Tears burn the back of my throat. I *am* scared. I'm terrified.

Audra turns and pulls me into her arms. She's crossing the line from therapist to friend, but I let her and drag her to the floor, crying into her shoulder.

She kneels with me as I sob.

"It's not fair. What did I do to deserve this?"

"I don't know, sweetie. I really don't." She brushes her hands over my hair, maybe like she does to her own daughter, if she has one. I haven't seen my mother in a while, and the kindness in her touch breaks me.

Audra holds me for a long time, rubbing my back.

She doesn't need to tell me what I already know. This was a conversation for me and Fox to have, that *his* arms should be the ones to hold me while I cry.

Now I've ruined that chance and there's no way in hell I'm going to do anything about it.

What's done is done.

There's only so much pain I can take.

CHAPTER ELEVEN

Fox

I toss and turn all night, and finally, at three in the morning, I take the elevator to the fifteenth floor and sit in front of Posey's apartment. The lights in the corridor are too bright, and I press the heels of my hands against my eyes. It's stupid, sitting out here, and I didn't check to see if she chained the door again, the scraping still scratching my heart. I don't want to know, because if she didn't, I'd be slipping into bed with her right now, holding her and making promises she's not going to believe.

It's better to stay out here and figure out just what the fuck I'm going to do. I have a difficult time getting past the pictures in my head: Posey hunched over, vomiting into a toilet, lying in bed too weak to move, the doctor's appointments, the utter despair she would have gone through knowing she'll never have children.

It's confusing as hell I keep shoving myself into the pictures, holding her as she throws up, lifting a soup spoon to her mouth, encouraging her to eat a little. Driving her to appointments and being the emotional support her mother had been. It doesn't make sense because I didn't know her, but it doesn't stop me from wanting to be there for her.

All the years we've been friends, and she never once mentioned it. Hid it away like a dirty secret, praying it wouldn't exist if she never acknowledged it, much like me never telling anyone except Paul, Darcy, and Rodney that Michelle and I lost our baby.

"Fuck." The word rasps from between my lips.

I haul my ass off the floor and go back up to the penthouse. I need a plan. I need to get my shit together so when I plead my case, she'll know I'm serious, know that what I'm saying is the truth. I let her have her way, but she better not get used to it because it was only going to happen that one time.

Posey's my best friend. She's also my lover, my fiancée, my other half. All the sappy shit men say about the women they love. I don't care if she can't have children. It doesn't change one goddamned thing about the way I feel about her. Without her love, I have nothing.

I need to find the strength to be the glue that holds us together.

I lie in bed as the sun comes up, formulating a plan. There are things I have to do before I talk to Posey, and if I need more time, then I have no choice. What's three or four more days when we're talking about the rest of our lives?

Posey thinks she can throw me out.

She can throw me out, but fuck if I'll stay gone.

The first thing on my list is to confront Paul. He knew about Posey, goaded me with it, and I was too dense to question him.

He hasn't been a friend, always keeping his eye on her and what he could get out of her, and I'm done.

A hot shower doesn't loosen the tension or relieve my headache, and guzzling a carafe of coffee only sharpens my already jagged nerves. In the car, my foot bounces on the floorboard, and I'm buzzing with caffeine, itching to get things started. Rusty's navigating the snow and traffic the best he can, and I grit my teeth, impatience rubbing me raw.

My phone dings with a text and I slide it out of my pocket. *My therapist had a cancellation this morning. In twenty minutes. Can you be there?* Michelle asks.

I scowl. I don't have time for this and respond with a terse, *No, I'm busy,* but then I change my mind before pressing Send and type, *Yes. I'm in the car right now. Give me the address.*

A second later an address pops up, and I tell Rusty, "Change of plans. We need to go here," and I toss him my phone.

This wasn't the way I wanted to spend my morning but if I'm serious about moving forward with Posey, I can't keep hiding from the hard shit. That's been my problem all along. Letting Michelle leave before we'd talked through our loss. Lying to Darcy to win a bet instead of confessing the truth. Letting Posey kick me out rather than forcing her to listen to me.

I'm a coward.

No matter how much it hurts, that has to end. Today.

The building Rusty stops in front of is stone and nondescript, full of doctors' offices. "I don't know how long I'll be," I say, opening the door and twisting to get out.

"No problem, boss," he responds in his good-natured way.

Michelle's waiting in a beige and cream lobby, and I let her lead me to a bank of elevators. Classical music fills the lift, and she studies me. "You look different."

"Well, I'm not," I say, but I'm apprehensive and nervous. I've never seen a therapist before, never talked to one or anybody who wasn't a close friend or member of my family.

"Hmmm," she says, but there isn't time to ask her what that means. The elevator doors open, and she strides down the hall in the same boots she wore to my office, confident, her hair swaying down her back.

The therapist's office is cozy, decorated in white, mint green, and grey, and the scent of coffee and pastry sugar permeates the air.

I help Michelle take her jacket off and then hang up mine, the wool damp with melting snow. I'm uncomfortable, and it doesn't help knowing this will probably be the easiest thing I'll go through this week.

"Pour yourselves a cup of coffee, if you'd like," a pleasant woman says. "I know it's early."

I fix Michelle a mug from the service sitting on a coffee table positioned between two loveseats. When I have a plain white mug in my hand, I shift my attention to the therapist who'll be conducting our session. She's a little on the young side, and it puts me on edge. Not enough that I want to leave, but enough that I question how much of her life experience, if any, she can layer into her advice. Sighing, I admit I shouldn't judge. I never would have guessed Posey had gone through something so traumatic at such a young age, and I try to swallow back my bias with my coffee.

"Good morning. My name's Emily," she says, holding out her hand.

"Fox."

"Hello, Fox, nice to meet you. Thank you for joining Michelle and me this morning. I know it means a lot to her that you're here."

I force a small smile. "It was a surprise when she came to my office yesterday."

Emily's pen glides over her pink legal pad. "Did you not expect to see her again?" she asks, jumping right into it.

"No, I didn't. The way she left me was so abrupt, so final, I spent the last year scrambling to come to terms with it."

"And did you?"

Michelle stares at the floor.

"I thought I had, but then she showed up, and I hurt just as much as the day she left."

"You must have done better than you thought, being engaged and all," Michelle mutters, her lips pressed to the rim of her coffee cup.

"There's some resentment there," Emily notes, tilting her head in Michelle's direction. "You left him, something we've talked about many times during this past year, and you wanted him to move on. Why are you resentful he did what you asked?"

"Is it a crime to want a man to miss you?"

Emily meets my eyes. "Did you? Miss her?"

"No. Yes. I needed more than what she gave me when she told me she didn't want to be with me anymore." I turn to Michelle. "A week after we lost our baby, you said we were done. I didn't have time to mourn with you. I'll never forget the day in the ER, when they told us there was no hope. The days after when I tried to help you cope but I could barely function myself. We needed more time."

Michelle starts to cry, but I can't comfort her. Talking about the days after we lost our baby drags me to a place I'm trying to leave behind.

Emily directs her attention to Michelle. "If you needed him, why did you break it off?"

"I felt guilty. I couldn't look at you knowing it was my fault.

Our baby died because of me." She covers her face with her hands and sobs shake her shoulders.

I rear back. "I never blamed you. Things like that happen. I *never* blamed you."

She lifts her head and tears drip down her cheeks. "It doesn't matter. I did plenty of blaming for myself and I couldn't bear to be in the same room with you anymore. I couldn't . . . It was easier breaking it off."

Cupping my coffee mug in my hands, I blow out a breath. Is that how Posey feels? Guilty her body betrayed her? Guilty she can't give me children if we stay together?

"Fox, if you didn't want Michelle to leave you, why did you let her push you away?"

I give Emily a hard stare. "You can't force someone to let you be with them, and I was carrying around my own guilt." Standing, I set my coffee cup on the table and roll my shoulders, hoping to ease some of the tension. "Michelle was hard to live with, very hard to live with, and when she told me she was pregnant, I was scared. I was scared of what kind of parents we would be with her issues and me trying to do damage control every second."

I focus on a watercolor of an ocean beach, the seagulls floating in a pristine blue sky. I've never told anyone what I'm about to say right now, but it's important if I want a future with Posey that I admit what I was feeling. I have to face the terrible things that were going through my mind when Michelle lost our baby.

"I felt trapped, and after she miscarried, I was relieved when she broke it off. It gave me a way out. I'm sorry, Michelle, but I never wanted children with you."

She bolts off the couch. "You son of a bitch." She slaps me, the sharp sound echoing through the quiet room.

"Hey, that's enough," Emily says, dropping her legal pad

and pen on the floor and standing between us, palms facing our chests, but her mild manner is no match for Michelle's explosive temper.

"I deserve that. I know I do. But you didn't want to get help and I couldn't have been a good father when all I was doing was taking care of you and protecting myself. You can hate me for how I feel, but at least own up to your share of the blame."

The fight drains out of her, and she sinks down onto the loveseat where I was sitting. "You're right. Now that you've said it, I know you're right. There's no way I could have been a good mother with my mental health out of whack. But you should have told me that."

"Are you cra—" I press my lips together. "Michelle, when you were low, you were *low*. You didn't listen to anything I said, and if I tried to talk to you about it on the days you were feeling good, there was no faster way to bring you down. There was no reasoning with you, and you will never know how guilty *I* felt, when all I could feel is free after you lost the baby."

Emily cuts in, clearing her throat. "I think it's important to bring up the idea of birth control. You're both consenting adults, but you didn't talk about children before Michelle got pregnant. That's not responsible, for either of you, and while you both acknowledge her miscarriage might have saved you, it's worth exploring the fact she could've had a healthy pregnancy and you could be co-parenting an infant right now. How did that happen?"

Heat rises to my face. "For better or worse, Michelle has always been passionate, and our sex life was like that. There were nights when we would go at each other, and condoms weren't on our minds."

"I understand getting caught up in the intensity of the moment, but you saw each other for at least a year. An accident could have happened a lot sooner. Michelle, I suggest you think about going on the pill, getting an IUD or something similar, and Fox, have a heart to heart with the next woman you start a relationship with and be open to a vasectomy if you think children aren't what you want. You both need to learn from this experience." She picks her pad and pen up off the floor and sits in her seat, crossing her legs.

"I agree."

The three of us fall silent, Emily jotting down notes, Michelle drying her face. My cheek stings, and needing something to occupy my hands, I sip my tepid coffee.

"Where do we go from here?" Michelle whispers.

Emily pauses, her pen pressed to the pad. "Where do you want to go?"

Michelle looks at me out of the corners of her eyes, and I step back. "I'm in love with someone else," I say firmly. I can't let her think there's even a ghost of a chance of us reconciling.

Emily smiles sympathetically at Michelle. "I know that's disappointing for you."

"Yes, it is."

Turning to me, Emily asks, "Does the woman you're in love with know about your history with Michelle?"

I shake my head. "Not all of it. It wasn't until this morning, at this session, I admitted out loud how relieved I was when Michelle miscarried and broke up with me. I've carried that guilt and shame all this time. I was hoping when she left she'd take my feelings with her, but that didn't happen."

"That's fair, and brave of you to admit. Miscarriages are a natural part of life, but even though that's true, they're still devastating. I went through one not long ago, so I understand how it feels, but I also know my body was doing what it was supposed to do if something wasn't right. You can say it's God's will, or science, or even Fate, whatever you need to help yourself understand that it wasn't meant to be. Be sad about it," she says, nodding at Michelle, "or be relieved," she says, nodding at me, "but acknowledge it's no one's fault and no one's to blame."

I sit next to Michelle and cover her hands with mine. "I'm sorry."

"Me too. I'm sorry I slapped you." She lightly touches my cheek, my skin still burning.

"I deserved it."

"No, you didn't," Emily says firmly. "Expressing your true feelings shouldn't be cause for punishment. That forces people to keep their feelings to themselves, and a relationship can't thrive under those conditions. I recommend both of you see a couples therapist if or when you're in another relationship, and plan a way to be open with each other without the fear of consequences."

There's a lot of work ahead for Posey and me. We've been friends for several years, but we never talked about things that mattered, pretending, instead, that spending time together was enough. If we don't start, if we can't accept and love each other for who we are like Rodney said in his birthday speech, our relationship will never last. I still love her, flaws and all, and I can only hope that after she hears my secrets, she loves me too, flaws and all.

"Now try again," Emily says.

I frown. "What?"

"Repeat what you said just a moment ago."

I humor her and stare into Michelle's dark brown eyes. "I'm sorry for everything that happened."

"Me too. I'm sorry I slapped you."

I fight a grin. I won't say I deserved it this time. "Apology accepted."

Emily claps her hands. "That's better. Let's meet again soon, Fox, if you can give Michelle a few more hours of your time. I think your involvement is an important part of her recovery."

"That's fine." I don't think Posey will mind if I help Michelle deal with our baby's death. It will help me, too.

I kiss Michelle on the cheek and shrug into my coat. Shaking Emily's hand, I say, "Thank you. This was a big help."

Her eyes are full of compassion, and still holding my hand, she says, "You're a good man. You proved it to me by showing up when Michelle asked. You're struggling to believe that, but we're all human. Our imperfections don't change the fundamental core of who we are. The woman you're in love with, if she loves you back, then she understands that too. Fox, monsters under the bed aren't monsters to anyone but us. We're scared of them because we think they're there, but when someone else looks, what do they find? Remember that when you tell her those scary things." She finally lets my hand go.

I jerk my head in a quick nod of dubious agreement and step out of her office.

It's still snowing, and I suck the cold air into my lungs to clear my head. I'm worn out and it's only nine. I still have a lot to do before I'm ready to offer Posey my heart again.

Rusty's waiting at the corner, and even with the lighter traffic, I'm late to work by half an hour. I expect Paul to be on my ass when I step out of the elevator, but only Lydia greets me and hands me a cup of coffee and a stack of messages. Muttering thanks, I glance quickly at Posey's desk, just to see what she's wearing, and a brunette is sitting in her place.

I don't stop to think, don't stop to reason with myself. I drop my briefcase in my office, set my cup of coffee on my desk before I fling it against the wall, and in a haze of anger so thick I can't see anything but red, I stride across the floor to Paul's office.

The new girl sitting behind Posey's desk stands up in objection, but I wave her off. She doesn't know who I am and I ignore her indignant sputtering.

Paul's sitting at his desk, his feet up, cool, talking on the phone, the receiver tucked between his cheek and shoulder while he plays with a stapler.

I want to clock the smug son of a bitch and almost do it too, but I stop. He's not worth the broken bones. Mine, that is. My hands wouldn't come out of a fight like that unscathed.

He hangs up and regards me through narrowed eyes.

"What did you do with Posey?"

"What did I do with her?" Paul echoes, sneering. "I didn't do anything with her. She requested a transfer so she wouldn't have to see your sorry ass day after day and I granted it."

If I had an IQ bigger than my shoe size, I would have anticipated that. I tried to keep my distance hoping she wouldn't feel the need to give up a position she enjoyed, but either I didn't do a good enough job and she still felt threatened, or she had other reasons for leaving that have nothing to do with me.

Yeah, I'll believe that never.

"Fuck. I'm sorry."

He shrugs. "I would've been angry if she quit, but she didn't. Is that all you wanted?"

"You knew about her cancer."

He stands, the chair squeaking. "Yeah, I did. I did because I cared enough to find out, and I told her I love her anyway. Much to my regret, I can't say we're a couple, but she knows how I feel and I'll give her time to decide."

Struggling to keep my face smooth, I try not to let his words hurt me. He cared enough to find out and I didn't. "I love her, Paul."

"You have a funny way of showing it. Leave her alone."

Like hell I will. "I'm flying out to Seattle to look at property for the new branch. I'll be gone the rest of the week."

Paul crosses his arms over his chest. "What should I tell Posey?"

"Why are you asking me? You'll tell her whatever the fuck you want. I don't know when we became enemies over this, but Posey's mine and she said she loves me. You can try all you want to take her away from me, but it will never happen."

"You did that on your own. For the past year all you've done is use her, and she's sick of it. I watched it, every day, knowing she deserves better. Supporting you, giving you all her time, everything she had. Do you know how many men would have killed to be in your shoes? And you didn't even appreciate it."

My heart sinks. If he hates me that much, we can't run a business together. Eventually the animosity will destroy us. "Maybe we shouldn't be partners anymore."

He cracks his knuckles. "Maybe we shouldn't."

"I'll go down to legal and let them know. Contact your attorney and I'll get a hold of mine. I'm still going to Seattle. I think I've worn out my welcome in Avondale."

"I'm sorry it's come to this. I really am. But I've been in love with Posey for a long time and I knew, just knew, I never stood a chance. You're a son of a bitch who has to have it all. You always have, without regard to how anyone else feels. We built a solid company with your ruthlessness and selfishness, but I can't be a part of it anymore."

"Enjoy the millions in your bank account," I say, opening his office door. "And find your own woman."

I walk by Posey's desk that's no longer Posey's desk, and as I stand in the elevator, I fight back bitterness and resentment. I'll let our attorneys know that we're splitting up the company. I'll take my half to Seattle, and Paul can do whatever the fuck he wants with his. The split will be easy, at least. We both worked hard and we earned everything together. He'd never try to keep more than what he deserves. He's got integrity, and maybe that's what destroyed our friendship and WellStone Interactive. His misplaced honor and allegiance to a woman who didn't ask for it.

The elevator lets me out on our legal team's floor. We don't have a large team by any means, but the attorneys we do have are always busy fighting trademark and copyright battles and sending out cease and desist letters and notices of infringement. From huge toy companies trying to create knock-off characters to the mom sewing and selling baby blankets online using fleece stamped with our characters, it's never ending.

I pass the receptionist's desk and Barbie watches me go by, her eyes wide. Unless there's a huge court case that has a high-stakes outcome, Paul and I rarely come down here. We employ smart, competent attorneys, and we don't need to look over their shoulders.

Rounding the corner, I trip over my own feet.

Posey's standing next to the legal team's office manager, Tameka Jones, and she's holding a stack of files and nodding at whatever Tameka's saying. She looks lovely wearing a sheath dress the color of her eyes, her blonde hair coiled in a bun at the back of her head. So this is where she went. I never would have known if I hadn't wanted to start the split myself. I could have asked HR, but Posey transferred without telling me. She obviously didn't want me to know.

Tameka looks over Posey's shoulder and catches me gawking. Posey follows her gaze and flinches when she sees me.

I wave them off and walk down the carpeted hallway to Rob Peterson's office, our lead attorney, and I spend more than an hour warning him about what's coming. I should do the same in HR, but that will save for another day. The split won't happen overnight. Hell, I don't even have office space yet, or a company plan. I love gaming, I always have, but do I want to continue? It's all I know but that doesn't mean I can't go in different direction.

Rob doesn't appear too worried about any of it. "Another one bites the dust," he says, tapping a pencil on his desk, his ankle propped on his knee. "Do you want to grab lunch later? Hash out a timeline, or aren't you and Paul that far yet?"

"We decided this morning. Our partnership ran its course and I wanted to give you a heads up this was on the way." I stand and inch toward the door.

"Okey dokey," he says. "You guys made a good team. It was fun while it lasted."

"Yeah, yeah it was. I'll keep you posted."

Posey's waiting for me at the receptionist's desk. Well, maybe not waiting for me, she's talking to Barbie and their conversation could be job-related, but she breaks away when she sees me walking toward the elevator.

"What's going on? You never come down to legal. You always ask Rob to go up to your office."

There are shadows in her eyes and she's frowning. I hate it when she worries. I hate she thinks bad things are going to happen, that I don't love her, that I'm not going to fight for what we have. But like any war, I need to plan my strategy and I swallow back all the love and pleading and begging and everything else that wants to spew out of my mouth before I'm ready.

"Paul and I are going our separate ways." That's safe and true. Nothing to do with us.

She wilts. "Fox. I'm sorry. Is it because of me?"

I rub her arm, her skin soft under my palm. "No. Don't think for one second it is. We outgrew each other, that's all, and we thought it'd be better if we do this now rather than drag it out. We're still friends. At least, we're not enemies."

That sounds a lot like what's going on between Posey and

me, too, but she doesn't say anything. "Then what are you going to do?"

"Seattle, like I planned. I'm heading out today, actually, so don't worry if you don't see me around for a few days. And you can stop catching an Uber in the alley. Rusty will drive you to and from work."

Tears fill her eyes, and she blinks to clear them. "Fox—"

Unable to resist, I rub my thumb over her trembling bottom lip. Barbie pretends she's not listening, but she is, and it keeps me in check. "I'd do anything for you, give you anything you need. You don't know that because all I've done is take, especially this past year. I didn't see it, and maybe I can thank Paul for that, but it's too late. I know it is, Posey, and you don't have to be sorry. I'm the one who's sorry. I have to go. Be good."

I jab the Down button and the doors slide open.

Posey steps forward, her heels quiet against the carpet. A tear runs down her cheek. "Fox."

Flashing her a grin and holding the door, I say, "Things will work out. Do you trust me?" I love her so much, and I can't stand the thought of her being unhappy. I want to sweep her off her feet and kiss her tears away.

She stares at me, gripping the thick stack of folders close to her chest. "No."

I try not to let her answer disappoint me. I haven't earned her trust, or if I had it, it's gone. Even if I'm disappointed, I should be grateful she hasn't started lying to me. If she starts lying to me instead of telling me how she really feels, then we don't stand a chance.

"One day, you will. I promise."

I let the doors slide closed, blocking out her troubled features.

I just need a few days. A week at the most. Enough time to figure out what the hell I'm doing so when I offer Posey a life with me, she'll know what she's getting into. But that's only if she can see past my flaws as easily as Emily did in therapy this morning. My darkest secret, the one I hid in the deepest corners of my heart since Michelle miscarried, passed off with an understanding squeeze of my hand. How is it possible? I would have been more comfortable if she would've called me evil, despicable, a heartless human being who didn't have a soul. After all, it's what I've called myself.

Bad things happen. How can anyone with a conscience find good in such tragedy?

Posey will be my judge and jury, but I need to do a few things first before I plead my case.

CHAPTER TWELVE

Posey

I feel like a zombie for the rest of the day, and Tameka's irritated when I ask her to repeat things. I can't help it. How can I keep my mind on memos and meetings and court dates and cases when Fox is going to Seattle to look at property? When he dropped that bomb on me? Splitting up Well-Stone Interactive.

I can't help but think it's because of me, but I shouldn't take the blame for the company's crumbling. Maybe Fox was telling the truth. Maybe he and Paul decided to go their separate ways while they're still friends and it has nothing to do with our fake engagement. I want to go up to Paul's office and demand answers, but then what? Fox didn't invite me to go to Seattle, to look at property or otherwise.

The minutes creep by until finally the workday ends, Tameka giving me a "get it together" look before logging off and grabbing the elevator with Barbie and a handful of others.

I waste time straightening my desk and putting my coat on.

I don't believe Fox asked Rusty to take me home, but he's there in front of the building, waiting for me.

"Hey, Posey," he says, opening the car door, the bitter wind biting at both of us.

"Hi, Rusty. How's it going?" I ask, climbing in.

"Good, good." He slams the door shut and trots around the hood of the car.

I relax against the warm leather, Fox's cologne hanging in the air. I try not to breathe him in, but it's no use and I tip my head back and pretend he's sitting with me, that we're going to spend the evening together like we always have.

The loneliness of it threatens to tear my heart in two.

Rusty doesn't have much to say either, tapping his fingers on the steering wheel, his head bobbing to the low beat playing on the radio.

Three blocks from the WellStone Interactive building, a fender bender slows traffic to crawl, and it's a full hour before Rusty reaches my street. "Tomorrow morning?" he asks, letting me out onto the sidewalk.

I smile weakly. "Are you sure Fox doesn't mind?"

"He told me to drive you to work and then home again. You'll be doing me a favor if you would. He'll call and check, and if I can't tell him what he wants to hear, he'll chew me out."

I doubt Fox would do that because he knows I'll make my own choices regardless of what he wants, but I say, "Okay. Eight-thirty. Thanks. Goodnight, Rusty."

"Goodnight." Grinning, he tips his imaginary hat. I wonder if he'll move to Seattle with Fox. I don't know much about Rusty except that he's married and has a little boy. He and his wife may not be willing to relocate.

I don't have anything planned for dinner, and I don't set out the corkscrew and the wineglasses. I don't play the music Fox and I enjoy listening to. The missing pieces of my routine remind me of what I'll be living without if Fox isn't in my life.

I change into yoga pants and a tank top, and in the kitchen, fix a salad. Peaches winds around my ankles, and I put fresh water in her bowl and feed her dinner. The apartment's eerily quiet without Fox here, and to break the silence, I listen to my voicemail. A real estate agent called me back, offering to email me listings of properties for sale. During my lunch break, I filled out a couple of online questionnaires about the type of house I'm looking for, the kind of financing I would need, and where in the city I'm looking.

I want my house to be close to good schools, and I won't be living in the heart of the city like I am now. The commute to WellStone Interactive will be longer, but who knows, I might not have a job depending on how Paul and Fox's split goes.

That's still a shock, and one I didn't see coming. They've been friends for so long and I enjoyed the cheerful and friendly vibe in the office. All that changed when Fox asked me to marry him. Would Paul have acted the same way if the proposal had been real? He looked at it as me saving Fox, again, and maybe that's true, but during the past few years, Fox also saved me from spending evenings alone or trying to date knowing I'd fall short to any man who wanted a serious relationship.

Call that hiding if you want because it was. I was hiding and using Fox's friendship as an excuse not to admit how lonely I was or what kind of future I'd have by myself. I didn't have to acknowledge it when I was with Fox. Except for the year he dated Michelle, he seemed happy enough with me, and I didn't question it, too scared of what would happen when he met someone else and left me again.

My phone rings, and my mother's name flashes on the screen. She travels a lot with her new husband, but their home base is in Florida, on the opposite side of the state where Walter and Claudia still live.

"Hey, Mom, how are you?" I tuck the phone between my ear and shoulder and carry my plate to the sink. Peaches wanders around the apartment, no doubt looking for Fox.

"Why didn't you tell me you're engaged, and to Fox, too? You should fly down and we'll go out to dinner and celebrate."

"You're in Florida, then?"

"We have been for the past few months. Everywhere else is so cold, and Nolan's arthritis flares up."

Rinsing my plate and putting it in the dishwasher, I say, "I'm sorry to hear that."

My mother laughs. "Don't get old, honey. Once your body starts going to crap, it doesn't stop. Now tell me about your engagement! How did he do it?"

"We were on my couch watching a movie. It was a surprise, really. I had no idea he'd been planning it."

"All the years you've been friends hadn't clued you in?" Mom asks, her tongue pushed into her cheek.

"No, and why would it? It hasn't been that long since he broke up with Michelle. Now, if he would have asked *her* to marry him, *that* wouldn't have surprised me. They were attached at the hip from the second they met."

"Hmmm. Some people are not good matches, but I have a feeling he knew she wasn't you." She pauses. "Then he knows about the cancer?"

I dry my hands and lean against the counter. I can't let her think we're still engaged. I don't have to tell her it was all a sham from the beginning, but I don't need her planning weddings that will never happen.

"I told him, after he proposed. I didn't tell you we were engaged because it didn't last long. I broke it off, and he's planning to relocate to Seattle. He didn't ask me to go."

Saying it out loud hurts me more than I thought possible, and I double over in pain, holding my arm to my stomach.

"Posey Ann Palmer, I'm ashamed of you."

I bobble the phone, almost dropping it on the floor, her angry tone surprising me. "What? Why?"

"You let your insecurities ruin a good thing. Baby, nobody's perfect, yet you keep punishing yourself. So you had cancer, so you can't have babies. *So fucking what?* You're beautiful, kind, and compassionate, and you'll be a good mother no matter how you and Fox make a family."

"He didn't want me damaged, Mom."

"Posey, how old are you?"

I frown. "Thirty-four."

"That's right. Thirty-four. I've known you for thirty-four years, and if I know anything about you, it's this. This doesn't have anything to do with what Fox thinks or if he'd love you without your ovaries. This has nothing to do with him at all, but it has everything to do with how you perceive yourself. He'd love you, scars and everything else, but you don't want him to have you that way. You want him to have you only if you're perfect, but trust me, sweetheart, there's no such thing."

"That's not true." My voice is weak. Haven't I always described myself as broken and damaged? In his arms, I felt beautiful and special, but after I told him, I didn't feel like I deserved his love and kicked him out.

"If it wouldn't have been your ovaries, it would have been something else. Weight gain, a bad haircut, God forbid you're in an accident and you need his help for the rest of your life. What would you do then? You love him, Posey, I understand that, and you want to give him your best. He loves you too and loving you means every part of you. Even your broken parts. That's what 'in sickness and in health' means."

"I didn't give him a chance to say anything. I didn't want to face him, and I made him leave." I walk into the living room and sink down onto the sofa.

"Then he might not come back. A man like Fox listens. You'll have to apologize. Tell him you love him and every dirty secret he's ever going to tell you. Nobody's perfect, Posey," she repeats, "and when you tell Fox you love him, that's what it means. All the imperfections, all the blight." She sighs. "I know it's hard, but you have to understand that he might have things to tell you, too, and if you don't want to hear them, then you shouldn't be with him, with or without your ovaries."

"You're right, and it was my own self-esteem issues that kept me from listening to what he really thought." I pause. "He's moving to Seattle."

"I think it will do you good to see a new place. I dragged you around for a while, and Minnesota is the longest you've stayed anywhere."

"Because of Fox. He's home."

"Then it doesn't matter he's moving."

"No, it doesn't. When you and Walter decided to get a divorce, were you upset Claudia didn't go with you?"

"She loved her father beyond all reason, and she still does. She's proud of him, and he's a good man. It hurt when she didn't want to come with me, but she didn't want to change schools or leave her friends and I didn't take it personally. Why?"

I shrug and prop my feet on the coffee table. "I'm trying to come to terms with the idea that maybe I'll never be a mother."

"Would that be the end of the world? Some couples choose not to have children, whether they can have them biologically or not. You and Fox would have a full life if you decided not to share yours with a child. He's filthy rich, honey. Travel, see the world. Enjoy him. You almost died. I'd think you'd have more of an appreciation for the things you have, not wallow in the things you don't."

"I guess you're right." That's all I can force out of my mouth. I never thought of my situation that way. I've always been fixated on what the cancer stole from me, not everything I had left after I recovered. "Audra never said anything like that."

"I'm sure she did, but you weren't in a place to hear it. Falling in love with Fox changed you. It opened you up to a new way of thinking. I need to get going, but let me know how things turn out. I want to be there for your wedding. Don't you dare elope."

"We won't."

"Good. I love you, Posey, just the way you are, and so does Fox. Apologize, and when he asks for grace, it will be your turn to give it to him. Love isn't the only thing that makes the world go around. It also takes patience, understanding, compassion, and empathy."

"Okay. I will."

"Get some sleep."

"You too. Goodnight."

I hang up with a renewed sense of purpose. Fox didn't say he wanted me in Seattle, but he didn't say he *didn't* want me there, either. I'll ask Paul if he knows where Fox went. He probably won't want to tell me, but there's not much I can do. I love Fox and Paul will just have to accept that.

Lying in bed, I make new plans. Fox may decide he doesn't want children, and if that comes to be, then I'll make peace with that choice. I've been obsessed with becoming a mother since I lost my ovaries, never once thinking that a deep, emotional, loving relationship with a man would be just as satisfying. Fox and I can enjoy life without kids.

As long as we have each other, we'll have everything we need to be happy.

CHAPTER THIRTEEN

Fox

The flight to Chaska isn't long, and we're descending into the little airport before I can decide what I want to say to Darcy. No matter what kind of consequences I'll have to pay to my sister for lying, I should tell her the truth.

At the airport, I order a car instead of waiting for the chalet's courtesy van. I don't want to rent a vehicle—I won't be here long enough to need one. I'll spend the night, sleep on Darcy's or Uncle Rodney's couch if there isn't a room available, and then go on to Seattle. I have a lot to think about when it comes to the company. Splitting down the middle sounds fair, until I think about the employees I'd be stealing from Paul. Just because it's fair doesn't mean it's right.

The driver lets me out under the canopy, the valet waiting near the glass doors for guests to arrive. It's a beautiful day for skiing, but I'll never be able to enjoy staying here again without Posey. We weren't here long, but I see her everywhere: at the large windows in the lobby looking out over the slopes, standing at the front desk chatting with the reservationist, sitting by the fireplace sipping spiked hot chocolate. The weekend we shared ruined this place for me, and after today, I won't be able to come back without her.

"Can you track Darcy down for me, please?" I ask Tara, the woman working the front desk. I don't know her, grabbing her name off her nametag that's shaped like a diamond, and she grins at me.

"Sure thing, Mr. Caldwell."

"Thanks."

She speaks into a walkie-talkie, and after a burst of static and a voice warbling in response, she tells me, "She's in one of the meeting rooms. Do you need directions?"

"No, that's fine, thank you."

I take my jacket off and drag my carry-on and briefcase behind me.

Darcy's just finishing up a meeting with the head chef, head of housekeeping, and the resort's maintenance director. They walk out of the conference room chatting about weekend plans, and I plop my ass into a vacant seat across from her and help myself to some leftover coffee and a ham and Swiss cheese sandwich.

"What are you doing here? Is Posey with you? How was your flight?" she asks, filling her mug and leaning back in her chair. She doesn't seem surprised I'm here again after such a short time between visits, only curious.

"The flight was fine, and she's not with me. That's why I'm here. You didn't lose the bet. Our engagement was fake."

She blinks. "I don't believe it. I saw you together. You love each other."

"We love each other, but we didn't figure it out until we were already here. I asked her to be my fake fiancée so I would win. I'm sorry."

I open my briefcase and pull out the deed to the beach house and the transaction receipt for the money I transferred into her account. "Here's the money and the deed." I slide them to her across the table that's sprinkled with breadcrumbs.

She looks at the papers but doesn't touch them. "But you won. You love each other. You're getting married."

"I don't know, Darcy. One doesn't mean the other." I stand and look out the window. The mountains will never cease to amaze me. Minnesota's so . . . flat.

"I don't see why not."

"She can't have children. After she told me, she broke it off."

"I don't suppose you told her about Michelle."

"No, I didn't. She stopped by to see me, and I went to a therapy session with her. She's doing better and wanted to try again."

Darcy jumps to her feet, outrage shining in her eyes. "I hope you told her no."

"She knows I'm in love with Posey."

"Good. She had her chance with you and she blew it. I'm sorry, I know her mental health issues weren't her fault, but you tried to reason with her several times. You shouldn't feel guilty for protecting yourself, and even if she's doing better, that doesn't mean she's always going to be. You tried. Leave it at that."

"She asked if I'd keep going to therapy with her, and I agreed. I owe her that, at least."

"You don't owe her anything, but I can see where you're coming from. Now what are you going to do?"

"I'm flying to Seattle after this. Paul and I are splitting up the company."

Her lips part in surprise. "Really?"

"He's in love with Posey and we can't work together anymore. It's causing too much friction."

"Oh. Why Seattle?"

"Because that's where I thought I'd open a new branch of WellStone Interactive."

"Oh," she says again and worries her bottom lip between her teeth. She sidles up beside me and tucks herself under my arm. "You know I've missed you since Mom and Dad decided to cruise around the world a hundred times."

Her exaggeration makes me smile but she's not that far off. Mom and Dad are usually unreachable because they're floating around on a body of water that may or may not be on a map. I love that they're having fun and I've never missed them because I've always had Posey and quick access to Darcy and Rodney.

"Yeah, I know. Seattle's not that far away and I'll try to visit more. I thought I'd keep up with gaming, but I'm not sure now."

"What if you moved here?"

"Moved here? And do what, Darce?" I laugh, picturing Posey and me in the little touristy town of Chaska.

She shrugs and moves away.

Shit. I hurt her feelings.

"I don't know. Do whatever you were going to do in Seattle. It's not like you need to work—"

"Wait—"

"I know you'll want to eventually, but what's wrong with buying a house and bumming around for a year or so after you and Posey get married? You could have the ceremony at the resort this summer and enjoy a long honeymoon."

"You're forgetting one thing. Posey dumped me. She doesn't want to marry me."

"Not right now because I bet when she told you she couldn't have kids you didn't handle it very well and she saw it all over your face. And that's your fault for not being honest with her in the first place. You can't expect her to want to marry you if all you did was whittle her existence down to her uterus. Jesus, Fox."

"She didn't give me time to—"

"Time to what? Untie your tongue? You needed two seconds to wrap your arms around her and make her listen to you. You did neither of those things or you wouldn't be here right now telling me you lost the bet. Go home and apologize, tell her about Michelle, and hope to God she forgives you for being an ass. I want her to be my sister and it would be great if we were neighbors, too. I'm *lonely,* and I want my family with me."

I sigh. "Why didn't you say something sooner?"

She presses her lips together and looks out the window. She's trying not to cry and I feel like a jackass.

"I don't want Uncle Rodney to feel like he's not enough, but he's been spending time with Elaine—"

"Who's Elaine?"

"An old flame. I don't care about that. Austin started seeing a girl in town and I was stupid and didn't see it coming."

"You're not stupid. Men are assholes. I should know. Come here."

I hug her and rest my chin on the top of her head.

Well, damn, this changes things. I don't need to go to Seattle if I'm not going to relocate my half of WellStone Inter-active there. I don't have any ties to the area, it just seemed like a good place to do business.

My half of WellStone Interactive. Maybe I should let Paul buy me out. He can rename it Gladstone Gaming and have the entire thing.

Where would that leave me? Lazy mornings waking up with Posey. Puttering around the house. What house? A house we buy here in Chaska? Eating dinners with Uncle Rodney and Darcy. Posey wouldn't be satisfied with that kind of life for long. She's driven—it's one of the things I admire most about her—but she's also had a hard time and I know for as long as she's worked for us, she's never gone on a proper vacation. I could convince her to relax for a while.

Hmmm.

She loves me. She said the right woman would never want to leave me, but that's a load of bullshit. I can't expect her to put up with how I treated her. I said I couldn't be the glue that holds us together, but that's bullshit too. A successful relationship needs two people who will never back down, and I need to stop pretending keeping my secrets isn't hurting her.

I take my phone out of my pocket, and Darcy looks at me, her eyebrows raised in question.

"Hey, Rusty, can you do me a favor?"

"Yeah, boss, what's up?"

I explain what I want him to do and end the phone call with, "And how do you feel about living in Colorado?"

CHAPTER FOURTEEN

Posey

Spending the night without Fox is lonely, even more so knowing he's not upstairs, let alone in the same state. The look in his eyes when he said goodbye . . . he wanted to ask me to go. He wanted to ask me to toss my whole life here in Avondale to be with him, and he didn't ask because he knew I would say no.

But I wouldn't have.

Not now. Not after speaking to Audra and my mom. Not after realizing what a stupid fool I was to throw way what we had because I was too scared to keep it.

I saw my entire life in Fox's eyes when we stood by the elevator, his thumb rubbing my bottom lip like he couldn't keep his hands off me just for one second.

That's the passion I crave, the love I need.

I flop around in bed, Peaches getting crabby at me for disturbing her and finally jumping on the floor in search of a calmer place to sleep.

Fox and I need to talk. Sooner rather than later.

The next morning, groggy and nervous, I shower, and while I shave, wrack my brain to think of a plan. Mom's right. I can't wait for Fox to come back to me. It's too risky. If I want this, I'm going to have to go to him.

I call in sick, the lie scratching my throat, and I sound like I have a cold. Tameka will be upset about the lost training time but it's better than telling her that depending on how things go with Fox, there's a good chance I won't be back.

After that, I book a flight to Seattle. Fox would let me use his plane if it was in the city, but commercial will have to do.

I laugh at how snobby that sounds.

Dressed more casually than I would for work in jeans and a blouse, I go down to the lobby. People crowd the sidewalk, and I step to the curb and hail a cab. I called Rusty and told him I wasn't going to work, but it would've been nice if he was here to drive me to Paul's office. It's just another reminder of how close Fox and I have been, rarely going somewhere without the other.

"The WellStone Interactive building," I tell the cab driver, then sit back and wait while we inch through traffic.

Tameka will be ticked off if she finds out I'm in the building, but I'll have to cross that bridge if I come to it. The driver double parks and lets me out, and I trot up the concrete steps that separate the skyscraper from the sidewalk. Everyone is already clocked in for the day and there's no line when I walk through security.

I don't have an appointment, but Paul will talk to me without one. He hasn't contacted me since our lunch . . . since he knew Fox would see us at the deli. Maybe he bribed Lydia into telling him where Fox was spending his lunch hour that day, but however he found out, I'm disappointed Paul would be that unkind.

"I'm here to see Paul," I tell his temp.

"He's on the phone. You'll need to wait, please."

"That's fine," I say, but I walk by her desk and open his door.

"Miss—"

I slam it shut, cutting off her objection.

"I'll have to call you back," Paul says, lifting his feet off his desk. He hangs up his phone and regards me with a contemplative gaze. "Posey, it's nice to see you. How's legal? Aren't you working today? Are you having an issue?"

"No, no issue. I called in sick to talk to you."

"You didn't have to do that. I could have given you time off—"

"Not only that. I'm flying out to Seattle to see Fox. I don't want to wait until he comes back."

He stands and leans against his desk. Narrowing his eyes, he crosses his arms over his chest. He's handsome, in a young Paul Newman kind of way, but I see the edge now when I didn't before.

"You still don't know everything, do you?" he asks.

Lifting my chin, I say, "No, I don't. He hasn't told me, and I don't care. We love each other, Paul. I've let a lot of things get in the way, and I won't anymore. It doesn't matter what happened between him and Michelle. That's in his past and I'm going to be his future."

He nods. "That's fair. But when you find out, I'll be here to wipe your tears away, because there will be tears, sweetheart, there will be tears."

I don't believe him. Nothing could be that bad or I'd already know about it. Fox and I have been good friends since I started working here and there's not a secret that terrible he would have been able to hide from me. I don't know everything, I admit that, but no matter what it is, it won't have the power to break us up.

Paul steps in front of me but I don't back down. I'm not scared of him. He rubs my arms through my coat and gently places his lips on mine. I don't flinch or move away. I stand still as stone and wait for him to finish.

I'm not going to let him threaten me.

"Why are you here if you're going to chase after Fox like a little hound?"

Embarrassment heats my cheeks. "First, I wanted to tell you that there's no chance for us, and second, I don't know where he's staying. I was hoping you do."

He chuckles. "Why would I help you find him when I want you for myself?"

"Because you used to be someone I admired and respected and you two used to be friends."

"That doesn't mean anything to me, not anymore, but I'll tell you because I don't think I've done anything that deserves losing your respect. He booked a suite at the Four Seasons. He flew in yesterday."

"Thanks." I turn to go.

"Remember, this all started with a bet. He didn't care about you until he was going to lose ten million dollars."

I want to zing off a retort, something that will make me smile in satisfaction years later, but all I see is a man who's lost his best friend because of jealousy and the impulse dies on my lips. Paul's handsome and rich. He could have any woman in Avondale, but he had to choose me because he hated that Fox and I spent so much time together.

"I'm sorry," I murmur.

Closing the door, I ignore the temp who glares at me.

I'm not going to be able to work here anymore. I hoped transferring to the legal department would be enough, and maybe it would have been if the problems were between only Fox and me, but working for Paul will be impossible. The money Fox transferred into my account will keep me going until I can find a different job, and stopping at human resources, I turn in my resignation.

I stand and look at the skyscraper until the blustery cold threatens to turn me into an icicle. I have a lot of good memories working for this company, and, of course, I wouldn't be where I am right now if I hadn't met Fox. He's been a good friend for a long time, even if we haven't shared all there is to share with each other.

Before my flight, I feed Peaches and call down to the concierge's desk and arrange for a pet sitter to keep her bowl full, her litter box clean, and to play with her for an hour every day while I'm gone. When I'm finished, I throw a few last-minute things into my suitcase and pack a small carry-on.

I have no idea how long this will take. My trip could be as short as an overnight stay if Fox and I decide we aren't right for each other, or it could be weeks while I help him find office space and a place for us to live. I'm hoping for the latter, but the former is a possibility, a fear I didn't confess to Paul. I have to be confident. I have to believe the look I saw in his eyes yesterday.

I hail a cab, and to keep myself busy on the way to the airport, I check my email, send a text to my mom telling her what I'm doing, and bring up my boarding pass on my phone. I fly out at three, and it's a four hour flight. With the time change, I'll land in Seattle around five o'clock local time, and I'll head straight to the Four Seasons. I've never been to Seattle before and my hands sweat in my gloves as anticipation and apprehension flutter around in my stomach. At least there isn't a layover. I don't know what I'd do if my flight was delayed and I was stuck in Denver or something. I'm nervous enough as it is.

The driver unloads my suitcase and carry-on, and I tip him extra for giving me a friendly smile. There is so much riding on this trip—the rest of my life, as a matter of fact—and his kindness goes a long way.

Just as I step into the airport, I hear my name over the PA system. I stop and look up at the ceiling in confusion, and people mutter as they go around me. "Posey Palmer, please visit the courtesy counter. Posey Palmer, please visit the courtesy counter located at the east wall."

Crap. What happened? I check my phone, but I don't have any missed calls or voicemails, and the only text I've gotten is from my mom wishing me good luck.

I glance around the busy airport, people heading toward their chosen airlines to check their bags. I can't say which direction is east, but I don't need to know. Huge white letters on the navy wall spell out "Customer Service" and point everyone to a long counter. Four airport representatives are helping guests three deep and I stand in line and anxiously check the time. I don't want to miss my flight.

"Posey! Hey, come with me."

I whip around.

Rusty's running toward me, his eyes bright and that cheerful smile on his lips.

"Rusty! You scared the crap out of me. What are you doing here?"

"The concierge at your building told me where you were going and I drove like a mofo to get here before you went through security. Come on."

I shake my head. "No, you don't understand. I'm flying to Seattle to see Fox."

He grabs my suitcase and starts to roll it across the shining white tile. "Boss isn't in Seattle, he's in Chaska, and I'm supposed to ask you if you want to meet him there. I'm assuming you do, so we gotta get moving."

"Wait, stop," I say, running after him and trying to grab his arm. "What about the courtesy counter?"

"That was me, hoping to stop you from boarding. Good thing, too."

"What's Fox doing in Chaska?" I struggle to keep up with him. He's better at dodging people than I am and I'm out of breath. I clip a lady's shoulder and she shoots me a dirty look. I don't have time to apologize.

"I think he'd rather explain that to you himself."

Rusty leads me through the VIP lounge and out the back to one of the private airstrips where Fox's plane is waiting. "He sent his plane for me?"

He gives me a look full of disbelief. "He'd do anything for you, Posey. You don't get that yet?"

"I . . . think I'm beginning to." I swallow back a relieved sob. I didn't ruin things. He still wants me, and he wants me how I am.

The flight crew stores my bags on the plane and Rusty urges me up the stairs, a hand to my back. "Aren't you coming with me?" My breath puffs out white in the cold.

"Not this time. Have a good flight." Relieved he caught me and he was able to do what Fox asked him to do, he playfully salutes me.

The pilot beckons me into the plane and says, "We're waiting on clearance to take off, Miss Palmer."

He looks familiar but I don't remember his name. "Thank you."

"Make yourself comfortable."

"Thanks, I will."

I settle into the same loveseat I sat on when Fox and I flew to Chaska, and I text him to let him know Rusty found me and that I'm on my way to see him. The text shows delivered, but he doesn't answer.

His silence increases my nervousness, and I'm a nauseated mess by the time we land at the small airport. The chalet's luxury shuttle isn't waiting for me, instead, a sleek black town car is parked on the snow-covered tarmac and a distinguished older gentleman wearing a chauffeur's uniform is standing in the cold. He's holding a sign that reads "Palmer" written in black block print.

I want to laugh as I'm the only one who's deplaning and the private airstrip is empty except for Fox's plane, but this is Fox's way of showing me he's expecting me and my giggle turns into a thankful cry.

"Miss Palmer, it's a pleasure to meet you. I trust your flight was uneventful?"

"It was fine, thank you."

"Mr. Caldwell has instructed me to drive you to meet him. Is that all right?"

The familiar mountains loom behind him, and the remaining apprehension I felt meeting Fox in Chaska disappears. There's nothing that feels more right or natural. "Of course. Thank you."

The nameless driver opens the door for me, and a ground crewman loads my suitcase and carry-on into the trunk. The interior's warm, and I sink into the sumptuous leather. I catch hints of Fox's cologne and the woodsy, earthy scent steadies me. I miss him. I miss his smile, the way he touches me. I miss the laughter in his eyes and the way he wraps his body around mine. I was a fool to think I could live without him, that a house and children would fill the hole he would leave behind if we were no longer together.

The small town of Chaska goes by, and I watch with interest out my window. When we visited Darcy and Rodney, we never explored the tiny town, and the quaint main street enchants me. A gentle snow falls, and tourists excitedly enter and exit the little shops. The picturesque scene reminds me of a snow globe just shaken, the perfect town safe and protected.

The car winds up the side of the mountain, but I don't recognize the road or know where we are in relation to Rodney's chalet. Abruptly, we come to the top of the slope, and a huge house that appears to be made entirely out of glass and cut into the rock surprises the hell out of me. I hadn't expected the house, but instinctively, I know this is where Fox is waiting for me.

The driver parks and leaves my bags near a four-stall garage. "Take care, Miss Palmer," he says, touching the tip of his hat and climbing back into the car, leaving me standing uncertainly in the driveway.

"Posey."

Fox's rich voice carries to me through the frozen air, and I turn toward it.

He's standing in the doorway dressed in one of his usual suits, days of scruff covering his jaw, strain and fatigue pulling at his eyes. "Would you like to come in?"

"What's all this?" I ask, my voice raspy. I missed him. Not only the couple of days we weren't speaking, but I missed what our friendship used to be and what our relationship no longer was when I kicked him out of my apartment.

He smiles ruefully. "Sorry about the fanfare. When Rusty told me you'd booked a flight to Seattle, I had to scramble like mad to catch you."

"I wanted to surprise you."

"You did. Come inside. It's cold."

He holds the door open for me, and I leave my suitcase and bag in the driveway. I don't want to deal with it now, and no one is around to steal them. I step into the house and hide my face against his chest. "I'm sorry," I squeak. It's impossible to speak through the tears clogging my throat.

He wraps his arms around me and presses his lips to my hair. "You don't have anything to be sorry for. This fucked up mess is my fault. We'll talk this out and then you can decide."

I lift my head and look into his sad green eyes. "I already know what I want."

"Don't be too sure."

He leads me into a large room that's too elegant to be called a laundry room. The washer and dryer look state of the art, and there's a separate sink next to the appliances. Built-in storage cabinets look brand new, their handles gleaming, and empty hooks and crannies near the door beg for someone to use them. "Should I take off my shoes?" I ask, snow melting off my shoes and dripping onto the floor.

"If you'd like."

I nudge the wet flats off my feet and immediately slip on the hardwood floor in my socks. "Careful," he says, gesturing for me to follow him. We walk down a short hallway to a huge kitchen that's connected to an enormous living room. The walls are nothing but floor-to-ceiling windows, and the mountain view leaves me breathless. I've never seen anything so beautiful. "Whose house is this?"

"Mine, sort of. I put a deposit on it so the realtor couldn't sell it. I wanted you to see it."

"It's gorgeous."

"I thought so. It has three bedrooms, two baths, and a deck upstairs—" he says, pointing to a winding staircase I didn't notice until just now— "and a sitting room and den on this floor. Also a couple more bathrooms and a patio that has a hot tub built into it."

"I don't want to know how much it costs," I say in awe.

He shoves his hands into the pockets of his slacks. He's careful to keep his distance, letting me look around the living room without getting too close. "You don't have to worry about that."

"Why Chaska? I thought you were moving to Seattle."

He sighs, his shoulders slumping. "I don't think I'm going to keep half of the company. What's the point of splitting it up? Our game developers work best when they're together and the whole team can't go with me. I thought I'd let Paul buy me out and I could start fresh somewhere else. I don't know what happened, but we're going our separate ways."

I rub my hands over my coat. "Because of me."

Fox's eyes glint with anger. "No, it's not. If he wanted you, he should have asked you out a long time ago. I don't know why he kept how he felt about you to himself, but he did, and our friendship turned into more, even if we didn't see it."

"He should have asked when you were dating Michelle. I would have gone out with him then. I missed you, but I didn't understand what it was." I didn't understand until Fox asked me to marry him and offered me everything I wanted in that simple, four-word question.

"I didn't know what I was doing. All I knew was that I was looking for something, and when I met Michelle, I thought I found it in her vibrancy, her . . . passion. She had an excitement about her that consumed me. But nothing ever felt right when I was with her. I always felt just on the edge of disaster, and not only because of her mental health issues. I missed you too, and I tried to figure it out by spending more time with her. It was only after we broke up and I went back to my normal, safe, untroubled routine with you that my life turned right again."

I blow out a breath. I never felt like I was Michelle's equal, and it had nothing to do with her being able to give him children when I couldn't. I never felt like I could match her fire. I'm quiet, preferring a small, simple existence rather than gobbling up everything life has to offer. Choking, I've never been able to handle that. Sampling little tastes of this and that has always pleased me more.

"You don't know how happy I am to hear you say that, but you never answered me. Why Chaska?" *And why are you still across the room like you're afraid to touch me?*

"When I saw you in legal and said goodbye, this is where I was headed first. I told Darcy the truth and I wired her the money she won. When I mentioned Seattle, she said she wanted us to move here because she misses her family. I'm all she's got besides Uncle Rodney since I don't think Mom and Dad are going to settle down unless they have to. After I talked to her, I scrapped Seattle and contacted a realtor. This house had just gone on the market. It's big enough."

I look around. The living room is almost romantic now, the setting sun glowing through the windows, and it's easy to picture us sitting in front of the fireplace, talking and drinking wine. Making love.

"Big enough for what? I can't have kids, Fox."

"I know, but that was never important to me. That night in your apartment, you took me by surprise—"

I inhale and open my mouth to apologize for not giving him time to think things through, but he stops me.

"—and that wasn't your fault. You were insisting I tell you every detail of my breakup with Michelle, and after you told me about your cancer, there was no way in hell I was going to tell you anything."

The blood drains from my face. "Why? What does Michelle have to do with my cancer? You *did* want children with her, didn't you?"

His whole body sags, weighed down with something I don't understand. "Do you want to see the upstairs?"

Silently, I nod. It's difficult to keep my emotions under

control. I want to scream at him to tell me, force him to admit that he's accepting less by being with me.

He leads me toward the stairs, and we walk up, his hand hovering near my back, protecting me from falling.

The second floor is as pretty as the lower level. The bedrooms have a spectacular view of the mountains, there's a ton of closet space, and the floors gleam. It's modern, but in a cozy way, and my mind is full of pure white comforters and sleek, but comfortable, furniture. I could scatter fluffy rugs on the floor and hang gauzy curtains in the windows.

Fox walks into the master bedroom and I follow. The rooms are empty, feet upon feet of cream walls that are all but begging for paintings and shelves crowded with knickknacks and pictures to fill up the space.

It would be so easy to turn this house into a home.

"You thought when Michelle left me, she broke my heart because I loved her," he starts, looking out the window at a view I would never tire of.

"Of course I did. Why wouldn't I think that?"

I force myself to calm down. This is a conversation I've been wanting to have with him since he and Michelle broke up. It was difficult to respect our boundaries—the boundaries created by our friendship-only relationship—and when he gave off hints he didn't want to talk about it, I didn't ask. Our friendship is more now, and I have a right to ask. I have a right to know, but being defensive, being afraid, won't help.

"You had no reason to, and I knew it hurt you. I wanted to tell you the truth. So many times when you caught me tearing up, or unable to sleep because of a nightmare. There were so many times, Posey, that I almost came clean. I didn't want you to hate me, and after you told me about your ovarian cancer, I didn't think there was any way for you to hear this and not despise me."

I take my place next to him. Hasn't that always been my place? By his side? Nothing he can tell me will change that. I squeeze his hand.

"You know Michelle was volatile. I tried to convince myself she was passionate, but it wasn't only passion. She had mental health issues she didn't do anything to control. When she was feeling good, everything was amazing, but when she was down, she was abusive and didn't listen to anything I said. One evening when she seemed okay, I was going to tell her we weren't working, but before I could, she told me she was pregnant."

My body rushes hot and cold, and I jerk my hand away. He and Michelle were going to have a baby. *Of course,* I think bitterly, *she has a working body, a body that could give Fox the family he wants.* Jealousy swamps me. I knew they were sleeping together, and because Fox and I were only friends, it didn't bother me. Not on a conscious level. I thought any woman who was lucky enough to date him wouldn't wait to sleep with him, and I was the same. I fell easily into bed with him at the chalet, let him have me all night. I couldn't blame any woman who would do the same.

"I wasn't happy, and she saw it on my face. It completely derailed what I was going to tell her. I wanted my child to have two parents who were together, and I tried to make it work. I went to her appointments. I spent even more time with her than I had before. I encouraged her to find a therapist, but she refused and said since she was pregnant, she couldn't take medication. I believed her and let it go."

I can't pretend to know anything about pregnancy. My knowledge is limited to the fact that I will never know how it feels, and I say lamely, "That's probably true, but talking to someone would have helped."

He steps away from me and sits on a wooden window seat.

He's still wearing his jacket and shoes, but he doesn't look out of place.

"Maybe, but she didn't even try. Her mood swings got worse as she went through her first trimester, and I kept trying to think of a way to leave her but still be a part of my baby's life. She was too much, and my mental health was suffering dealing with hers."

"She never would have let that happen."

He stares at the floor. "It would have gotten ugly," he agrees. "I would have needed to sue her for custody. I didn't want to have to use her mental instability in court, but the way she was then, she wouldn't have been a good mother. Not without a lot of help, so I stayed because there wasn't anything else I could do."

"I'm sorry. What happened? She had the baby." She must have, but after she and Fox broke up, I lost track of her and never saw her again until the day I found her in Fox's office.

He shakes his head and tears fill his eyes. "She miscarried at fourteen weeks. We would have had a little girl. When Michelle was well enough, we buried her in the Avondale Catholic cemetery. Having a funeral made Michelle feel better."

I don't know what to say. I want to go to him, comfort him, but I can't force my feet to move. He and Michelle had been so close to starting a family, and if that baby had lived, I wouldn't be standing here now, looking forward to a life with a man I desperately love.

Dread weighs me down. That's not the worst of it, not the way Fox hasn't relaxed now that he's told me, or the way he can't meet my eyes. I know his every movement. The past few days of pretending we weren't together haven't erased seven years of history. "Why do I have the feeling there's more?"

"Because you know me." His voice is sad, subdued. "I was

able to keep all that from you, God knows how. Paul, he was a good friend back then, and he was there at the burial to support me. I asked him not to tell you, and he didn't. I kept waiting for you to lash out at me, to, I don't know." He shrugs. "Tell me we couldn't be friends anymore, but he never said anything."

I lick my lips and step forward. "Fox—"

He scoffs. "What? You think we would've stayed friends if you'd found out I got Michelle pregnant? You would have resented the hell out of me, because you know as well as I do that we were always more than friends. We've always been more, Posey, even if we didn't acknowledge it, and rather than admit what I'd done with another woman, all I told you was that she broke up with me. I had to, or you would've wondered why I suddenly had my free time back. I couldn't lose our friendship. I couldn't. Not because I needed you, though I did, desperately, but because you're an important part of my life."

"You weren't the one who broke it off? Because you were free to do so?"

He turns on the window seat, props one foot onto it, and stares outside. "No, she did it. She said looking at me reminded her of what we lost. When she was at the office the other day, she asked me for another chance. For the past year she's been going to therapy, and she's on medication. She wanted to try again."

My mouth dries. It's my worst nightmare coming true. "It's what you want."

"No! It's not what I want!" he explodes, lurching to his feet and raking his fingers through his hair. I've never seen him so angry. "From the second I asked you to marry me, all I've wanted is you."

His words should have made me warm inside, but they don't do anything. "Then why keep Michelle's miscarriage a secret? When I told you about my cancer, why didn't you tell me? I wanted to know."

"Because when we lost the baby, I was *relieved.* I didn't want to be with her, I didn't want to be attached to her in any way. I had visitation and custody battles, court hearings and child support arguments ahead of me for the next eighteen years. I wasn't happy she lost the baby, but *goddammit,* I should have been a lot sorrier than I was."

He meets my eyes, but I don't reach out.

"Now you know. Now you know my filthy secret, what I've kept from you this past year. I wasn't heartbroken because Michelle left me. I was mourning our baby and drowning in guilt. Your secret doesn't seem so dirty anymore, does it?" He pauses. "The car's downstairs. I told him not to go far. He'll drive you back to the airport."

"Fox . . ."

"What?"

It's unfathomable he'd feel anything but grief when Michelle lost their baby. I can't imagine the pain she went through burying that little life. Despite my own trauma, I know nothing of her suffering. I'll know nothing of that kind of loss.

"I don't expect you to stay with a son of a bitch like me. Go. Please, Posey, just go." His voice cracks.

His words finally penetrate the fog in my brain, and numbly, I turn and walk out of the room. Carefully, I go down the spiral stairs, step by step. I don't want to fall. Fox won't be there to catch me if I do. In the laundry room, I put my shoes on and reach for the doorknob without seeing it. The frigid wind slaps me in the face, stealing my breath.

Tears blind me, but the driver who brought me to the house is there at my shoulder, helping me get into the car and putting my luggage in the trunk.

I sit huddled against the door, praying I can hold it

together. This town car doesn't have a privacy screen, and I don't want the man who reminds me of my ex-stepfather to see me cry.

We retrace our path to the airport, Chaska's main street not so charming anymore.

Poor Fox, how torn he must have been. He never talked about Michelle, and I didn't know about her mood swings, her highs and lows, or what she'd been diagnosed with that she needed medication for it. All I know is when they met, she took everything he had, and rather than gradually fade out of my life, he disappeared almost overnight. Then he was at my door, ragged and raw, and though I knew there was more to it than just her breaking up with him, I was so happy to have him back, I didn't care. I was an insensitive bitch.

No wonder my news made him speechless. He had babies on the brain, and when I told him I couldn't . . . I'm so stupid. Had I given him just a second to think, but I was so certain he was going to tell me he didn't want me I never considered the alternative. That he would still love me.

He lost a little girl who would be an infant right now. I'll never hold a baby that my body makes, but Michelle will. She'll find another man who will love her, and she'll have other babies.

That won't be me, but I can have Fox, if I still want him.

He was so sure I wouldn't want to stay he never considered the alternative. That I would. That I would still love him.

Bad things happen, and it's not my place to judge. He didn't want to be with Michelle anymore. Her miscarriage gave him a way out, and if she hadn't lost the baby, she might never have gotten the help she needed.

I know better than anyone that bad things happen, and if I'm a terrible person for looking for the good in the bad, then I'm just as selfish as Fox is.

Fox is anything but selfish. His relief shredded him, and I won't punish him for it.

The car turns onto the long road that leads to the airport, and Fox's plane is waiting on the tarmac, ready to fly me back to Avondale.

The driver parks and moves to get out. It's now or never.

I grab his shoulder. "Please, take me back to the house."

"Are you sure, Miss Palmer?"

"I'm sure."

"I'll need a word with the pilot then."

"Thank you. I'm sorry I'm being so much trouble."

"I doubt Mr. Caldwell would think so."

Forcing a slight smile, I say, "I hope not."

While the driver speaks with the pilot, I text Fox and tell him that I'm on my way back to the house and to please wait for me. The message isn't marked as delivered, but that's not going to stop me. I understand Fox's metaphor now, why he said he couldn't be the glue that held us together. How can he be the glue when his baby's death shattered him so completely?

No matter how hard I stare at my screen or how much I wish he'd answer, he doesn't. We drive up to the house, but it's dark and a For Sale sign I didn't notice before—maybe because it wasn't there?—is stuck in a snowbank near the mailbox.

The car has barely stopped when I scramble out of the backseat and to the side door where Fox invited me in. It's locked, and I pound on it, the freezing steel burning my hands. Please, oh, please don't tell me I lost my chance. In a moment of weakness, in a moment of indecision, I lost the best thing that ever happened to me.

I pound until my hands ache but Fox isn't here.

He let me use his plane, so unless he's driving, he's not going back to Avondale. There's only one other place in Chaska he'd go.

Slipping on the snow and ice, I run back to the car. "Do you know where the Diamond Peaks Chateau is located?"

The driver meets my eyes in the rearview mirror. "Yes."

"Will you take me there?"

"Of course."

The right woman wouldn't want to leave him.

It took me a while to realize it, but I'm that woman and nothing he can say will change my mind.

CHAPTER FIFTEEN

Fox

Darcy only has to look at me for a second to know what the outcome was. "She didn't go for it."

"Nope."

I fall into an exhausted heap on Darcy's couch and loosen my tie. It feels like a noose around my neck, but that's only the secrets I've been keeping and the lies I've been telling trying to prevent all this from happening in the first place.

"Which part of it?" Darcy asks, opening the fridge and pulling out a bottle of beer. She pops the top off using the hem of her t-shirt, gives it to me, and drops to the floor at my feet.

"Thanks. Your choice. The part where I got Michelle pregnant, the part where I twisted her miscarriage to benefit me, the part where Michelle wanted to try again and I didn't want to. They're all horrific. Why would she want a man like that?"

"Things happen and you don't sound that bad. I'm sure a miscarriage has gotten more than one woman out of a predicament, but you don't hear about it because—"

"Because it sounds fucking cruel and heartless, that's why," I finish for her. I need the alcohol and guzzle half my beer, the fizz burning my throat. I wish she would have given me something stronger but she doesn't drink the hard stuff and doesn't haven't anything here.

She sighs. "Now what?"

I wipe my mouth with the back of my hand. "Posey's on the plane to Avondale. When it comes back to Chaska, I'll fly out and start the sale. I haven't talked to Paul about buying me out, but why wouldn't he? Keeping the company intact would be better for business and he can afford my price." He *will* give me what I want for my half. He might not have ruined what I had with Posey—no, I did that all on my own—but his jealousy didn't help and I'm not above being petty enough to make him pay for it.

"Are you sure you want to move here without Posey?"

"Yeah, I'm sure. You and Rodney will keep me out of trouble. I would've had an easier time after Michelle if I would have had my family close by. I wanted that to be Posey, too, but that's how it goes," I say, a weight settling in my chest I'm not going to be able to get rid of for a long time. "There's no other place I'd rather be."

"I'm glad," she says, squeezing my knee.

"Me too."

Darcy gets up off the floor. "Do you want anoth—" she starts to ask, but a knock on her door interrupts her. "I don't know who that could be. Rodney's schmoozing today, but we're meeting up for dinner later if you want to join us."

"Yeah, I guess."

I can't find the energy to feel anything other than wrung out. I'm never going to get over losing Posey. She's been an important part of my life for a long time, and losing her love meant losing her friendship.

Darcy opens the door and steps back, startled.

"Is Fox here?"

Posey's voice.

I sit up, my heart slamming. She came back.

"Yeah, he is. I'm going to . . . Let me just, ah . . ." Darcy mumbles, letting Posey inside. She grabs her purse off the kitchen table and hurries out the door leaving Posey and me alone.

Her bun is coming loose and tendrils frame her face. Her cheeks are pink and she's panting, her jacket hanging open. She must have run through the resort.

I can't look away. All the details, all the beautiful, lovely details, and I don't dare blink.

"Hey," she says, her voice husky.

"What are you doing here?" I ask, stunned. I should get up, take her coat. Offer her a drink or ask if she wants a cup of coffee, but I can't move.

She steps closer. "When we were at the airport, I couldn't, Fox. I couldn't get on that plane."

I set my beer aside, brace my elbows on my knees, and fork my fingers through my hair. "You should. I'm a mess."

"No more than I am."

"No, you don't understand. Michelle and I, we aren't over. I promised I'd go to therapy with her . . ." I fade off. I don't know how she'll react. I can't back out, but I don't want Michelle to be between Posey and me any more than she already is.

Clutching her purse strap, she says, "You told me you don't love her and that you don't want to be with her."

"I don't."

"Then why would I be upset if you want to help her? Fox, I've been going to therapy for years, trying to find peace. Why did I get cancer? Why did it happen to *me?* My therapist can't tell me that, of course she can't. Michelle's therapist won't ever be able to tell her why she lost her baby, but if it can help us take one step closer to, I don't know, closure, then we should go. You should go."

"You won't be angry?"

"No. Michelle will never get over what happened and I probably won't either, but I have one thing she doesn't."

"What?"

"You. She might have more babies someday—and that's something I can never give you—but I will always have you if you love me as much as you say you do."

"Yeah, I do. Come here, will you?"

She sits next to me, the cold air still clinging to her coat.

I can't be in the same room with her and not touch her. Skimming my fingers over her cheek, I say, "They're only words, but I love you, so much. I'll give you whatever you need to be happy with me."

"That's you. Plain and simple. That's you."

I crush my lips to hers, and she eagerly opens her mouth, letting me in. She tastes sweet, like hope and possibilities, and I lick at her as she drops her purse on the floor and wraps her arms around my neck.

A shiver runs through me. I never thought I'd have this again, and urgently, I kiss her, hoping she can feel how much I want this.

She whimpers, and I do nothing less than devour her.

Several minutes go by, and finally, she eases away, sucking in a breath. I could kiss her all night, but I know we have things to talk about and I help her take her coat off and nudge her into my lap. "Do you like the house? Would you be happy there?"

"I love the house, but . . ." She frowns and shakes her head.

"Fox, if you didn't want to be with Michelle, why did you get her pregnant?"

"Her therapist asked me the same question. All I can say is I was irresponsible, but I would have done what was right. I swear I would have." I'll regret the mistake I made for as long as I live, but I'll never forget the lessons it taught me or the pain Michelle and I had to go through to learn them.

"I believe you." She pauses. "I thought a lot about what you said. Fourteen weeks. You had prenatal visits, and I bet you two went shopping. Looked at baby clothes, bought a crib. You won't ever have that with me. Are you sure you're going to be okay with that? You won't grow to resent me?"

"Posey, I'll tell you the truth, and I'll tell you just this one time. Because if you're sad, or if we have a fight, or if you see a mother pushing a stroller, you're going to look at me with those big blue eyes and they're going to be full of tears, and I don't want to have to say this over and over again, so listen, please. I'm heartbroken—"

She tries to get up but I hold her still, wrapping my arms around her.

"Fox, let me go." She doesn't sound angry, only forlorn and resigned.

"No. I'm never letting you go again, so you'll just have to listen to me."

I see the shame in the seconds before she hides her face against my shoulder. I tighten my grip and whisper in her ear. "I'm heartbroken that you will never have that. I'm heartbroken that you and I will never have that because you want that for us. But I'm not heartbroken for myself. When I tell you you're all I need, I mean it with every cell in my body. Look at me, sweetheart. You'll know if I'm lying. *Look at me.*"

Her eyes meet mine, and I'm steady, unwavering. My best friend is here, in my arms, and she loves me. She had a chance to go back to Avondale, move on with Paul or alone with the millions I gave her, and yet she's here, in my lap, and there's nothing else in the world I need.

Tears drip down her cheeks and she starts to cry. Rubbing her back, I let her get it out. She's been so strong, never once in all the years we've been friends mentioning the pain she's lived with. I murmur, "You're enough," hoping she believes me.

Sniffling and huffing a laugh, she straightens. "God, I'm so sorry."

I take a handkerchief out of my pocket and dry her face. "Nothing to be sorry for. We both have a lot of emotions bottled up inside, but we're here for each other now. Cry on me all you need and maybe one day I'll cry all over you."

She gives me a tiny, watery smile. "Thanks."

"Anytime. And I mean that. Since you asked me a question, can I ask you one?"

"Nothing is off limits now, is it?"

"No, I guess not, but that's a good thing, isn't it?"

Dabbing the handkerchief under her nose, she says, "Yeah."

"What were you going to do with the money I gave you for helping me? Did you have plans for it?"

She tries to move off my lap again, but I don't let her. She's going to have to get used to that. Shrugging, she gives up. "I was going to use the money to pay adoption fees."

"It costs that much to adopt a child?" I ask, incredulous.

Fidgeting with the handkerchief, she says, "There are some agencies that work with the Chinese government, and they let single people adopt. I didn't let myself think I'd ever be with someone, so I decided to try to adopt on my own. The fees, the flights to and from China, staying there while the adoption goes through, and the house I'd need in a decent neighborhood, it adds up."

With a finger under her chin, I ask her to look at me. "Is that what you want?"

"It used to be, when I thought children were the only way I could have a family, but whenever we spent time together, I was happy. I was happy just being with you, and I could still be that happy if we decided not to have children. There are other ways to create a family, and I'll have one with you, Darcy, and Rodney. My mother and Nolan. I can reach out to Claudia, and I know Walter would love it if I called him and apologized. If I let the people who want to be there into my life, I'll find contentment without kids. I've been cutting people out for a long time."

"The house here in Chaska near Darcy and Rodney would be a start," I say, tentatively.

She wiggles to stand up, and this time I let her. It's been a long day, and her shoulders slump, fatigue weighing her down. Hugging herself, she shivers slightly. "I went back there, and a For Sale sign was out front."

"You went back to the house?"

"Yeah. I saw the plane, and it made me sick inside. I didn't want to go back to Avondale without you and I asked the driver to turn around, but you were already gone. I didn't know where else you'd go, so I came here." Her eyes widen. "I have no idea what he's doing. When the girl at the front desk told me you were at Darcy's, I ran here as fast as I could."

"Don't worry. I told him after he dropped you off at the airport to wait in the bar. If we live here, we're not going to need a driver. Our lives will be considerably . . . smaller." And I don't mind the sound of that at all.

Posey turns her mouth into a little moue that I want to kiss off her face. "What about Rusty?"

"He doesn't want to move his wife and baby. He was born in Avondale, and his entire family lives there. I'll cut him loose with a generous bonus and stellar references. He'll be okay. So, can I make a couple of calls, have a bed delivered?"

"I thought you didn't buy it. Because I left?" Posey stands uncertainly in the middle of Darcy's small living room.

I get off the couch and gently touch her lips with mine. "I wasn't going to buy it if you weren't going to live there with me, but I haven't asked for my deposit back. Janette's still holding it. I was hoping, Posey. You have no idea how much I was hoping that somehow we would work out."

"I shouldn't have left you there alone. You did to me what I did to you. We have to promise that we won't do that to each other anymore." She sighs. "I'm going to miss Rusty."

"*I* was going to miss *you.*"

She smiles at me, and I swear to God, I'm never going to get tired of seeing that beautiful smile light up that beautiful face.

"Fuck it. Why don't we fly back to Avondale tonight? We can nap on the plane. You look beat."

"I've had kind of an emotional day," she teases.

I cuddle her against my chest. "Then you can sleep. Don't worry, Posey, I'll always take care of you."

She mumbles, "I love you, Fox."

The words seem inadequate, but for now, they're the only words I can think of to say. "I love you, too."

After we tell Darcy and Rodney the good news, we find the driver in the bar sipping coffee and reading the newspaper. On the ride to the airport, I call Janette and finish the deal, Posey in my lap nibbling on my neck, her fingers skimming over my chest under my shirt. I have big plans for her on the flight to Avondale, but the second we're settled on the plane, she falls asleep in my arms. She's so angelic, I don't mind.

Rusty's waiting for us at the Avondale airport, leaning against the car in the cold. I wait until the last minute to rouse Posey, and by the time we step down the steps to the tarmac, the ground crew has already unloaded our bags and put them in the trunk.

"Hey, boss," he says, but his usual grin is gone. I'll miss this kid. Well, he's not a kid anymore, but when I met him through the Big Brothers, Big Sisters program, he was, and I got him off the streets and helped him figure out some family issues. I taught him to drive and put him through school. Posey doesn't know about any of that, but one day, now that the time for secrets is past, I'll tell her. Rusty's more than a driver to me, and he always has been. Even though I'll be living in Chaska, Rusty and his family will always have everything they need.

"Hey, Rus. A couple more trips, huh?"

"You know it. Miss Posey, he better treat you right."

"He always has, Rusty. Let's get out of the cold. Now isn't the time for goodbyes."

He nods and opens the back door for her. I pretend I don't see his wet eyes.

On the ride to our building, she snuggles into me and tips her head for a kiss. Friends to lovers wasn't as natural as I thought it'd be, or as easy as it could have been. I'll take the blame for that, but as I lower my head and nuzzle her mouth with mine, I swear things won't be that difficult again.

Rusty double parks and lets us out in front of our building, blocking the evening stream of traffic. I don't think I'll miss the constant glare of the city lights or the demanding, cranky people, or the energy that isn't always positive.

The elevator stops at the fifteenth floor, and I'm reluctant to let Posey go, even for a few minutes. "Let me check on Peaches and call the concierge's desk," she says, trying to untangle herself from my arms. "I don't need the pet sitter anymore, do I?"

"No. When we go back to Chaska, she'll come with us. I asked Darcy if she could stay in her apartment until the house is livable and she said she didn't mind."

"Thanks, that was sweet of you. See you in a few minutes." She kisses my cheek and steps out of the elevator just before the doors close.

My penthouse feels empty, strange. It's never been home, but it's different somehow, more permanent. Home has always been where Posey is, but it's more than that now. It's in Chaska where we're going to build a life in a house made of glass, where, if things get to be too much, we'll have family near who will remind us we're not alone.

My housekeeper's been in, and everything's clean. The bed has fresh sheets on it, but the fridge is empty as it always is. I eat at Posey's.

I shower quickly, change into lounging pants and a t-shirt, and choose a bottle of wine. It's second nature to do those things, but the elevator doors gliding open interrupt the routine.

Posey's standing inside barefoot and dressed in pajamas, Peaches struggling in her arms wanting to escape.

"What are you doing?"

Peaches jumps to the floor and runs off to explore, and Posey shrugs, a corner of her mouth lifting up. "We were friends downstairs."

"And up here we're . . .?"

She shows me her left hand, and the ring I bought her sparkles on her finger. "Engaged?"

I set the wine bottle on the table near the elevator. "I like it." I sweep her off her feet and carry her to bed.

For the first night in the seven years we've been friends, Posey sleeps upstairs with me.

"You didn't have to come with me," I say, holding her hand as we walk through the lobby of WellStone Interactive. I'm carrying my briefcase and dressed like I always am while I'm in the city. Posey clicks along next to me wearing a dress and stylish high-heeled boots. Her hair is pinned back like she's going to work, but after we talk to Paul, we're going out for lunch to celebrate putting all this behind us.

"I know, but Paul was your friend for years, and my boss. No matter how he feels about us or what your friendship has turned into, he was always kind to me and I think I should be there when you decide what's best for the company."

"I already know what's best."

She laughs. "Then what are you going to do?"

I kiss the back of her hand. "That will be up to us."

"If you're sure."

"I am. I like not knowing what's ahead. The infinite possibilities. I can handle anything that comes my way as long as you're with me."

We step into an elevator and she rests her head on my shoulder. "Okay, then I won't say anything."

"Do you have an opinion? You don't think I should sell my half of the company? Have you been thinking about what you want to do in Chaska? I want you to be happy there, and I know puttering around the house will keep you busy for only so long." The elevator bumps to a stop on our floor.

"No. I don't care what you do with your half. As long as you're happy, that's all that matters to me. This has gone so fast

I haven't been able to give much thought to anything except being in love with you and not losing you."

I scoff. "Christ. You really know how to bring a man to his knees, don't you? You'll tell me if what we're doing isn't enough, right? You'll tell me if you're not happy."

"Yeah, I will."

I block her from stepping out of the elevator. "Promise."

"I promise, Fox."

Searching her eyes, I look for a sign she's placating me, but there's nothing but calm reassurance. "Okay."

Lydia's sitting at her desk, though I don't know what she's been assigned to do. She waves and hands me a stack of messages like she always does, shooting Posey a curious glance as we pass by and head toward Paul's office.

A woman I've never seen before is sitting at Posey's desk, and we walk past her. She doesn't say a word, only watches me knock on Paul's door and open it before he has time to say anything.

He's standing near the window sipping coffee, the traffic below looking like a line of ants marching home.

"Fox, Posey." He quirks an eyebrow, his gaze darting between us. "Why do I get the feeling I'm being ambushed?"

"Because you made the dynamic feel that way," I say, not getting any pleasure out of the fact that he winces. He should know this is all his fault. He didn't need to be a sore loser. He called me a selfish prick, but he's worse.

I set my briefcase on his desk and he huffs, something between a laugh and a scoff. "Are you here to tell me you found office space? That you're starting the split? I get first choice of developers, Fox. This wouldn't be happening if it wasn't for you."

Popping the locks and pulling out a beige file, I say, "I decided I don't want half. I'm giving you the chance to buy me out. And I'm asking for what's fair, right down the middle. You can afford it. You can afford more than what I'm asking, and I should make you pay it just for being an asshole."

"Christ." He sets his mug on his desk and gives the papers a quick glance. "What the fuck am I going to do with the company?"

I narrow my eyes. "What do you mean? Run it. Develop the games, win the awards. Do what we've done for the past fifteen years. What the fuck do you think you're going to do with it?"

"Jesus Christ Almighty. You don't have a fucking clue, do you? Not one fucking clue. Of course you don't. Everything comes so easy for you. The grades, the girls. The business connections and the deals. Friends. What would I do with the fucking company? WellStone would be just fine if you ran it alone. If I take over, it'll dry up and blow away like a crusted turd. Give me a fucking break. 'Run it the way we always have,'" he mocks. "That's been you, Fox. It's always just been fucking you."

"I don't know what the hell you're talking about," I say, baffled. We've always been partners. I've never felt like I worked harder than he did.

"Remember the night we signed our first investor? Without him, we wouldn't be standing here. Who convinced him, huh? Who promised him that his money was safe with us and didn't break that promise? It sure as hell wasn't me. Who did the market research and came up with every single fucking concept that won every single fucking Starlight Award? The developers made the games, sure, but who brought the ideas to the table? You did. You had the ideas, the boys ran with them, and all I did was go to the goddamned dinners and help you collect. For fuck's sake. Don't be so stupid. I was always just along for the ride."

I look at Posey. Her lips are parted, her eyes wide. Like me, she had no idea this was coming.

"Is that really what you think?"

"It's what I know. I'm not buying you out. The second word got out I'm running this company alone, the stock would sink and there's no way in hell I'd be able to bring it back up. No one gives a shit about me. *You* buy *me* out."

I glance at Posey again. I could buy Paul out, keep the company, and she and I could work together, but I don't want to do that. I want to spend the rest of my life with her and our families, where they come first and the job comes second. She nods, letting me do what I need to do. For me. For us.

"No."

"Why? Got something better to do? It's not making babies." Paul sneers.

Posey sucks in a breath, and I have to summon every ounce of willpower I have not to punch him in the middle of his arrogant face. He's jealous and he's hurt and he's lashing out. I'm better than that.

"It's none of your business if we choose to have children or not. We're moving to Chaska to be closer to Darcy and Rodney. I can't run the company from there, and even if I could, I wouldn't want to. This part of my life is over. I was hoping we could still be friends, but that's not going to happen."

"No, it's not. I'm rich because of you and it's just another damned thing that's going to hang over my head. We've gotten a couple of offers. We'll sell to the highest bidder and that will be the end of it."

"Fine." I doubt that will be the end of anything, but I nod and close my briefcase. He can't accept an offer without my approval and he can run everything through my attorney.

Grasping Posey's hand, I say, "Let's get out of here."

We turn toward the door.

"I always knew it would happen," Paul says.

I stiffen. I don't want to keep dragging this on. "You knew what would happen?"

He waves his hand back and forth, gesturing between Posey and me. "You two. I saw it when I hired her, had to watch you two dance around each other for years. Seven years of fore-play. How was it?"

Posey tenses.

Wrapping my arm around her shoulders and holding her close, I tell Paul the truth, and I hope he carries it to his grave. "Indescribable."

She opens the door and we walk out of Paul's office for the last time.

In the elevator, she covers her mouth and muffles a moan. "God. I want to feel sorry for him, but I can't."

"We were good friends for so long," I say, shaking my head in disbelief. "I had no fucking clue that was under his skin. He never let it show until I told him I asked you to marry me. He knew the fake engagement wouldn't last."

"Because he knew it would turn real," she clarifies.

"There's no chance it wouldn't have." I play with the ring on her left hand. "Let's replace this with something more mean-ingful, okay?"

"No, I like it. It will be a fun story to tell our . . ." She fades off.

Kissing her forehead, I murmur, "We'll figure it out."

"I know."

She smiles, trust and her whole heart in her eyes, and I know she believes me.

Michelle's striding across the lobby when Posey and I step out of the elevator. Both women hesitate, but neither stops. Posey clutches at my hand, and I return her squeeze. There's nothing for her to be worried about.

"Michelle," I say when we meet. "What are you doing here?"

"I was going up to see you. You're not working today?"

"No. Actually, I won't be working here at all anymore. We're selling the company. Posey and I are moving to Colorado to be closer to my family."

Michelle frowns. "But I thought you said you'd go to therapy with me." Accusingly, she glares at Posey then back at me, the temper I used to dread simmering, her brown eyes sparkling with heat.

"I will. I'll fly to Avondale whenever you need me to. That won't be a problem."

"Tomorrow—"

I drag in a deep breath and hope Posey will understand. "I can go this time, but after that, you'll have to give me more notice."

"Yes, of course. I'm sorry," she says stiffly, her temper fading as quickly as it came, and she stares at the floor. I didn't mean to sound sharp, but it's a knee-jerk reaction whenever I'm around her. She's changed drastically in the past year, all for the better, but I'll never coddle her or put up with her tantrums ever again. She'll have to grow up, like I have. I'll never do anything to risk Posey's love.

"Rusty's waiting," I say, tugging on her hand. I want to get out of here. Away from Michelle and the way I feel around her, away from WellStone Interactive and the mess my friendship with Paul turned into. Posey's the only good thing to come out of the past year and I can't wait until we're alone. We'll have to spend the night because I don't want to break my promise to Michelle to help her whenever I can. Staying in Avondale isn't that big of a deal, but I'll breathe easier once we're in the air and on our way back to Chaska.

"Will you give us a second?" Posey asks, gently pulling her hand from mine.

Leaving Posey and Michelle alone together is a hellish idea, but there's nothing I can do that wouldn't make me look like an ass, and you know what? I'm tired of looking like that.

I kiss Posey's cheek. "Sure. I'll meet you outside. Michelle, text me the time."

"Yeah," she says, but her attention is on my fiancée.

I walk across the lobby pretending everything is just fine.

CHAPTER SIXTEEN

Posey

Michelle's gorgeous, and very much my opposite. I wouldn't be a woman, and an insecure one at that, if I didn't wonder what Fox sees in me after dating someone like Michelle. Her hair is long and healthy, not like mine that I have to condition within an inch of its life to make it shine, and the color's rich, I bet, without her having to dye it. She's curvy, ample breasts and lush hips, where I'm stick thin and the only way I can fill out a blouse like she can is if I wear a padded bra.

I force myself to speak before she gets tired of waiting. "Fox told me what happened. I'm sorry."

"Thank you. It's been difficult to get past it. When I see babies that could be the same age ours would have been, I have to try not to cry. I suppose I'll do that for the rest of my life. Fox took it hard too, but it gave him a way out. I want to blame him, but I can't."

"He didn't completely walk away, you know. There were plenty of nights after you broke up when he sat in my living room and cried. I thought he was crying over you, and I suppose he was, but he didn't tell me the whole story until recently. I don't want you to think that he's had an easy time of it, because he hasn't."

"I appreciate you saying that. He's a good man with such a kind heart. When he looked at me at that benefit, I couldn't believe it. And when he came over to talk, I was completely in love after only a half an hour of conversation."

I touch her shoulder. "I know exactly what you mean. When he looks at me, I feel like I'm the only woman on earth."

She lets out a shaky breath. "I messed up a really good thing. He begged me to get help and I should have listened. I could tell he was thinking about breaking up with me, and one night when he asked if he needed a condom, I said no even though I knew I could get pregnant. I never told him I lied. I'm too ashamed."

I stiffen and count to five, trying to control a burst of anger. Her attempt to trap Fox caused so much pain, and all for nothing. "You're right. He would have stayed with you. He would've given you and your baby everything he could."

"Yes, but after a while he would have hated me."

"Now he hates himself." No matter how many times I tell him, or how many therapists tell him he's entitled to how he feels, he'll always hate himself for being relieved when Michelle miscarried and told him she couldn't see him anymore.

She nods. "Once you and Fox have babies, he'll stop feeling like that."

I'm so tired of repeating this and I want to snap at her, but I say calmly, "I had cancer and can't have children. I don't know what we'll do, but when he says he loves me anyway, I have to trust him."

She smiles sympathetically. "I'm sorry. We both failed him then, haven't we?"

I bristle. "I can't think of it like that. I deserve to love and be loved, even if I can't get pregnant. There's more to me than my reproductive parts, as you know, because despite what was going on with your mental health, yours couldn't keep him."

As the words leave my mouth, I feel this heavy burden lift, and for the first time since I lost my ovaries, my heart feels light. I deserve to be loved the way I am. No matter how many times someone told me that, I never believed them, but defending myself against Michelle's slight, I do.

"That day in his office, I thought it'd be easy to convince him to give me another chance. I'd grown, gotten help. Changed into someone he'd want to be with. The last thing I thought he'd do was turn me down. He said he loved you, and I see it's true." She pauses. "Please don't tell him I tricked him."

"I won't. You need to be the one to tell him. It won't change anything—you both still lost a baby—but he never wanted to get you pregnant and he's blamed himself for being irresponsible. You need to be accountable, too."

"Tomorrow. Please let him go to sessions with me. I need him there." Her eyes fill with tears.

"I won't interfere, but you have to be honest and tell him the truth, because if you don't, it won't matter how many sessions you go to—they won't help. You need to share the blame. He trusted you, and you lied."

Wiping the tears off her face, she says, "I will. I promise."

"I need to go. I wish you the best. I really do. You'll find someone else and have another baby. Treasure that."

Tentatively, she hugs me, and I hug her back. "Take care of him," she murmurs.

I step out of her embrace. "We'll take care of each other."

"Of course. Goodbye, Posey."

"Good luck, Michelle."

I turn toward the lobby doors. Outside, Fox is leaning against the car, the breeze ruffling his hair, his hands shoved into the pockets of his coat, waiting for me. I hurry to the sidewalk and he sweeps me into his arms, covering my mouth with his in a passionate kiss. His scruff scrapes my cheeks, his breath hot against my skin, and I love every second of it.

"Everything okay?"

I brush my fingers over his jaw. "Everything's perfect."

"Good. Since we have to spend the night when I wasn't planning on it, we have more time than I thought. Let's grab that lunch and figure out moving arrangements."

I hesitate. I'm not sure of the kind of response I'm going to get asking him this, but I think it would be good for both of us. "First, let's go to the cemetery and visit your daughter's grave. We can say goodbye. Things may have turned out okay, but Fox, had she lived, she would have been a blessing. You don't have to deny it because you think I don't want to hear it. I would never take that away from you. I love you, and I would have loved her too."

His eyes darken and he rests his forehead against mine. Finally, just when I think he's going to ignore what I said or yell at me for suggesting it, he says, "I would like that. Thank you."

"You're welcome. Any child half of you would have been everything to me."

He searches my eyes, the car blocking the road, the weak sun trying to fight through the bleak cold. "I don't think I can tell you how much that means to me."

"You don't have to say anything, as long as you promise you'll always love me how I am?" I don't want to turn it into a question, but the uncertainty in my voice does it anyway.

"You have my solid promise."

With the way he kisses me, I believe him.

Moving's a lot of work. I didn't remember how time consuming it was when I moved into Fox's building seven years ago. Hiring movers and weeding things out we don't want to keep. Deciding what furniture to move to the house in Chaska—and deciding on none because despite my couch having sentimental value, we wanted to start a new life together in all ways.

We ended up staying in Avondale longer than we expected, but we were able to clean out both my apartment and his penthouse and Fox signed the papers at WellStone Interactive when Paul decided on a buyer. The sale went through in a matter of hours, and we celebrated that evening, going out to dinner and making love all night.

The time in Avondale also gave Fox the opportunity to go to several therapy sessions with Michelle, enough, in fact, she told him he didn't need to go to any more. Her lie kept her from making progress, and once she admitted what she did, everything clicked into place and she was able to tell Fox goodbye and mean it.

I wouldn't have resented her the time she needed from him, but I'm not above saying I'm glad he never has to see her again.

The house in Chaska is beautiful, but the extra bedrooms tug at my heart, just a little. This house was built for a family and one can argue that Fox and I are family enough, but one day, somehow, I think we'll add laughter to these hallways.

For now, the laughter that Darcy, Austin, Rodney, and Elaine add to our glass house is perfect, and I pour more wine to go with the dinner I made. We're sitting around the table, the lovely view of the mountains at our backs, the sun setting, casting a gorgeous glow into the dining area attached to the kitchen.

While we were in Avondale, Austin apologized to Darcy

and begged her to take him back, and she shines with him and Fox by her side. She missed her family, and I've never seen her so happy.

I feel the same, Fox's arm resting on the back of my chair, as I share silly smiles with Elaine. Rodney thanked me for putting that little bug in his ear, but I'm not going to take credit for something he should have done a long time ago.

Holding a glass of red wine and with a couple bites of lasagna left on my plate, I ask Fox, "We know if Darcy won the bet, you had to give her ten million dollars and your house in Florida, but if we had truly been engaged, what would you have won?"

He props his ankle on his knee, and swirling the last of his wine in his glass, he says, "If I really would have won the bet, Darcy said she'd come work with me, but I didn't mention it because she loves Chaska so much. I missed her too and it's nice we're closer now. She won't have so much trouble sticking her nose into my business."

Darcy sticks her tongue out at him and Rodney hoots. "You would've stolen my best manager?"

"Nah. Even if I would've tried to collect, she wouldn't have come."

"I'm glad. I got a taste of what it's like to be without her, and I don't recommend it," Austin says, nuzzling Darcy's cheek with his nose. She turns her head and their lips meet.

"I think this is a much better ending anyway," Elaine says, patting my arm.

"No, a much better ending is this," Rodney says, pushing away from the table and kneeling on the floor in front of her. "I should have done this thirty years ago, and I'm sorry, Lainey. If I'm not too late, will you give this old fool a second chance?"

He holds up a pretty platinum diamond ring, and I can't stop the tears that fill my eyes.

"Oh my gosh, yes!" Elaine exclaims, slapping her hands to her cheeks in sincere surprise.

I glance at my own engagement ring. Even though it was purchased under false pretenses, I didn't want to replace it. The circle symbolizes more than everlasting love. To me, it symbolizes a friendship that will never end. Besides, I love wearing the matching necklace Fox gave me the night I let him take me to bed. I never asked him when he bought it or why he brought it to Chaska, and I don't want to ruin the mystery of it all. I'm wearing the necklace now, and I skim my fingers over the stones. It's a reminder that even something as fragile as our friendship can be strong enough to weather any storm.

Rodney slips the ring on Elaine's finger and kisses her knuckles. He stands and raises his wineglass. "I'd like to make a toast. To family."

"To family," we all echo.

I sip my wine. "And to friends."

"To best friends," Fox says, skimming his finger over my cheek. "Always."

I hope you enjoyed *Faking Forever!* If you'd like to stay connected, sign up for my blog! You'll have front row seats to all my new releases, sales, and extra content. As a thank you, you'll also be able to download a free book—*My Biggest Mistake*, a billionaire, ugly duckling standalone novel. https://vmrheault.com/subscribe/

ACKNOWLEDGMENTS

Thank you to my family who give me the time and space I need to put the words down on paper. (Sometimes literally. Do you know how many notebooks I have?)

I'd also like to thank the writing community for all the support over the years. People come and go, so there aren't too many I can list by name, but if you've stuck by me this long, you know who you are.

ABOUT THE AUTHOR

VM Rheault writes billionaire romance and contemporary romance under Vania Rheault.

She lives in Minnesota with her two children and a newly adopted tuxedo cat named Pim. When she's not writing, she's working her day job, sleeping, or enjoying the four seasons with a hot cup of coffee in hand.

Find her at vmrheault.com.

Cruel Fate (King's Crossing Book One)

Cruel Hearts (King's Crossing Book Two)

Cruel Dreams (King's Crossing Book Three)

Shattered Fate (King's Crossing Book Four)

Shattered Hearts (King's Crossing Book Five)

Shattered Dreams (King's Crossing Book Six)

Loss and Damages

9 781956 431001